Beach Kill

by

Phyllis Smallman

PRAISE FOR THE SINGER BROWN SERIES

The first book of the Singer Brown series, *Long Gone Man,* won the Gold Medal in the Mystery/Thriller category of the Independent Publishers Book Awards in 2014.

"...a denouement worthy of Agatha Christie... a fascinating and engaging character..." - Crime Fiction Lover

"...this savvy author has delivered an original, compelling and, it must be said, altogether darker tale to kick off her exciting new series." - January Magazine

"I was really drawn into the story. It's no wonder. Smallman is an award-winning writer and one worth reading."- Mystery Maven Reviews

"The changeling, enigmatic central figure of Singer Brown is precisely characterized with murky strength and occasional clarity of purpose. She is a wonderfully sympathetic figure. I look forward to more from this excellent writer." - Carl Brookins

"Long Gone Man is one of those "you can't put down" novels." Mystery Reader

Also by Phyllis Smallman

Sherri Travis Mystery Series

Margarita Nights

Sex in a Sidecar

A Brewski for the Old man

Champagne for Buzzards

Highball Exit

Martini Regrets

Singer Brown Mystery Series

Long Gone Man

Novella

Saving Kali

Library and Archives Canada Cataloguing in Publication

Smallman, Phyllis, author
Beach kill / Phyllis Smallman.

(A Singer Brown mystery; 2)

Issued in print and electronic formats.
ISBN 978-0-9920536-7-3 (paperback).-
-ISBN 978-0-9920536-6-6 (pdf)

I.   Title. II. Series: Smallman, Phyllis. Singer Brown mystery; 2.

PS8637.M36B432016   C813'.6   C2016-902723-6
                                   C2016-902724-4

Chapter 1

Glenphiddie Island, Canada, 1995

In May, at the forty-eighth latitude on the eastern rim of the Pacific, at the very edge of a continent and straddling the border of two countries, morning comes early. By four-thirty the sky begins to brighten. The light can be blocked out but not the cacophony of birds greeting the dawn. Better than any alarm, they set the small world of Glenphiddie Island stirring long before anyone plans on rising.

While the inhabitants of the town of Kilborn snuffled and moaned, burrowing down beneath the covers to steal a few more minutes of sleep, a dinghy pulled away from a thirty-foot sloop anchored at the mouth of Kilborn Harbor. The yawning sailor steered toward Ghost Island while his trembling whippet stood with her front paws on the edge of the rubber vessel and whined in anticipation. Before the boat settled on the rocky beach, the dog leapt into the rolling surf and dashed on shore to relieve herself. She was still squatting when the wind changed. Her head went up and her ears went back. Keening with fear, and before she finished emptying her bladder, she was running away from the stench of death.

"Ginger, Ginger!" the man yelled. He turned off the engine and lifted it out of the water. He stepped out of the boat. Holding on to the encircling rope, he pulled the small craft up above the lapping waters. "Ginger," he called once more, with little hope that the excitable beast would return. He waited. Ten minutes passed and Ginger still hadn't come back. "Stupid dog." He sighed and began to walk carefully over the moss-covered rocks. It was his wife's dog but of course she was tucked up tight in bed. "You go, Howie," she always said, as if early morning dog walking was one more thing she deemed a man's work. "Stupid bitch." He'd be hard put to say whether it was his wife or the dog he was referring to. They were equally annoying.

He'd only climbed six feet toward the crest of the island when a rock rolled beneath his rubber boot, twisting him sideways. His gaze was caught by a flash of color below him. He froze in shock while his rebellious eyes took in what he didn't want to see. And then his brain tried to make sense of it. When it did, he spun away from the horror and vomited.

Chapter 2

Singer Brown woke at first light with the rest of the island and listened to the raucous birds. Beside her Louis Wilmot yawned and stretched before he rolled over to cuddle up against her back, nuzzling his face against her bare shoulder. His hand cupped her belly and his breath felt hot against her skin. A strange feeling of joy and security came over her. He was here with her, in this small cocoon of safety. No matter how long it lasted it was hers, one last chance to get it right, and she would hold on to it with her whole being. She reached out to cover his hand with her own. It had been a long time since she felt part of a couple.

A couple. The word brought back the intimate exchange she'd witnessed the day before. On the edge of sleep, she murmured, "What's Ghost Island?"

Wilmot kissed her shoulder, his whiskers harsh against her skin. "That small island at the mouth of Kilborn Harbor." He pulled her closer.

"Why do they call it Ghost Island?"

He yawned. "Because the winds out there do strange things to fog, dividing it, spinning it. Like gossamer ladies dancing across the water—ghosts dancing."

"That's beautiful." He never failed to surprise her. "Poetic even." Seeing gossamer ladies swirling across the water, she fell back into sleep.

The phone rang. Wilmot cursed softly and rolled over to pick it up before it could ring again and wake Singer. "Wilmot." He tucked the receiver under his chin, and rolled back to snuggle against her warmth.

"It's Duncan. We've got a body."

A jab of annoyance. Boating accidents were only one of the many forms of human stupidity the Royal Canadian Mounted

Police, the policing unit for the Gulf islands, dealt with during tourist season. Sure that some drunken fool had fallen overboard in the harbor, he said, "I start the midnight shift tonight and you know Fridays are always hell. Can't you handle it?"

"Sure, but I hate to have all the fun. It's a dead woman."

"So?"

"So-o-o, her head was battered in. It's unlikely to be natural causes."

He grabbed the phone off his shoulder and swung his feet out of bed. "Where?"

He was reaching for the trousers he'd thrown on the chair the night before when Duncan answered, "Ghost Island."

Wilmot turned back to face the bed.

After a long silence, Duncan asked, "Are you still there?"

"I'm here." He took a deep breath and asked, "How do I get out there?"

"The search and rescue launch is at the dock waiting for you."

He dropped the receiver back in its cradle. "Singer."

She turned over, nestled into his pillow, and mumbled something indistinct.

He zipped his trousers and reached for a clean shirt. "I've been called out."

Her eyelids fluttered but she didn't answer.

"Singer?"

He shrugged the shirt up onto his shoulders and then crossed to her side of the bed and leaned over her. Her wild hair spilled darkly across the pillow. Even in sleep her face was compelling. High cheekbones, a long thin scar on the right one that she would never explain, full lips that mocked the world and eyes that went from hazel to rich caramel. It was a face he never got tired of examining, and she often caught him staring. With her hand going up to her face, she'd ask, "What is it?"

"Nothing," he'd answer, when in truth it was everything. This woman took him out of his comfort zone, throwing him off balance while making him feel alive in a way he'd never experienced before. Louis Wilmot was no fool. He knew it couldn't last. Singer was a woman who was planning on leaving the moment she said hello. She'd warned him at the very beginning of their affair that she was only on the island until she could prove her residency and sell her house.

He shook her shoulder gently. "Why did you ask about Ghost Island?"

Her eyes stayed closed and her breath whispered softly between half opened lips. He reached out his finger and removed a strand of curls from the corner of her mouth, then he leaned over and kissed her forehead. There was time enough later to find out why she was asking about Ghost Island.

Chapter 3

As the boat approached the ragged little piece of land jutting up out of the Salish Sea, Wilmot studied it. It wasn't much of an island, maybe three acres, rising to a crown in the center, with gnarled and stunted fir trees growing out of the rocks. The shore was littered with logs that had broken loose from a boom and now waited to be shifted by the next king tide.

When the launch butted against the beach he stepped onto the shore and paused. He took his time, standing just above the tideline, and studied the whole scene. Sometimes impressions were worth as much as hard evidence. Satisfied, he took the dozen steps toward where Duncan waited beside the naked body.

Parts of her face had been eaten away and her right eye was missing. But it wasn't this horrific sight that sent a tremor through him. It was something much gentler, a memory he didn't want to associate with this scene. The dead woman's dark hair was fanned out in a halo around her head, just like Singer's had been when he left her. He wiped his hand across his mouth, trying to abolish that first impression, and said, "She's young, isn't she?"

Duncan took off her cap and rubbed vigorously at her short blond curls. "Still in her teens, I'd say. Early twenties at the most." Nearly as tall as Wilmot, and with a curvaceous body not even the severe uniform could hide, Duncan was the only woman on the island detachment of six Mounties that served a permanent population of ten thousand plus a further ten thousand in high season.

"Do we know who she is?"

"Nothing to identify her, only this." She bent over and pointed her forefinger at a butterfly tattoo on one ankle. "I've taken lots of photos."

"Is there anyone on Glenphiddie doing tattoos?" he asked.

"Nope."

He didn't question her pronouncement. Duncan had spent her early years on the island, still had relatives here, and there wasn't anyone or anything about Glenphiddie she didn't know.

"So she got it in Vancouver or Victoria." Wilmot squatted beside the body to look closer at the blue design. "How many ink parlors do you think there are in those two cities?"

"Hundreds, maybe even a thousand if you take in the amateurs."

"At least it tells us something about her. She's over eighteen. You have to be to get a tat."

Duncan snorted. "Like our legal drinking age, that law is easily bypassed. And even if you find someone willing to admit they recognize the design, they probably won't have a name. I'm sure they don't look too closely at ID and date of birth. Some artists follow the rules, but at over a hundred bucks an hour..." She shrugged. "Lots of guys are willing to break the law."

He grinned up at her. "Hey, Duncan, you have a tat, don't you?" His grin grew with her frown. "Let me see it."

"Screw you."

"In your dreams." It came out without thought, and he cursed himself, but Duncan wasn't paying attention to him.

"There's a scar on her arm." She pointed to the fine white line. "Maybe a break."

"That will help." Wilmot took in the area the fluttering yellow tape cordoned off. "This whole crime scene will be under water within the hour. We can't wait for the coroner." The incoming tide already lapped the dead girl's ankle and kelp washed back and forth between her feet. "We have to move her."

Duncan scowled at him. "I told the coroner that. Even if we ordered in a copter for her, Dr. Pearce couldn't get here from Victoria before high tide covers the body. She'd have to fly from Victoria to the helipad behind the hospital where a cruiser would pick her up and deliver her to the dock. And then the police launch would bring her out here. Not going to happen. Dr. Pearce is not happy, but there's no other choice. Dr. Glasson has done a preliminary examination and after we bag the body, a hearse will meet her at the dock and take her over to Victoria for the autopsy, which will be done tomorrow or the next day. It's the best we can do."

"Tell me what you've done so far."

She took a deep breath and let it out slowly. "I've photographed the scene, collected the dozen or so rocks that covered her to analyze them for finger prints, but there isn't a prayer, and I bagged what little evidence I could find. I've sent for divers to search the water within a ten-foot area offshore. Probably useless, but it was all I could think of."

"Seems like you've thought of everything," he said to reassure her.

She nodded. "I was just waiting for you before I sent her on her way."

"Did Glasson give an approximate time of death?"

"Liver temperature suggests it was around midnight but he says that could be out by an hour either way. He told me the liver temperature of a living person is about a hundred and two degrees and cools at the rate of one degree for each hour after death."

"We'll need to get the exact time of the last high tide. If she'd been here then, she would have been washed out to sea."

"Her killer started to hide her." She pointed to the rocks covering the mid-section of the body. "Something stopped him. The rocks might have held her in place when the tide came in."

He glared at the rising water. "We'll have to do a search fast."

"Well, it's a good thing I haven't been just standing here with my finger up my nose." When Wilmot jerked his head up to stare at her, she added, "Sergeant."

Duncan was the smartest member of the team, but she'd be done for noncompliance in any other detachment. He'd once asked her why she was so sure he wouldn't report her for insubordination and she'd pointed out that he'd been demoted for harassing a female officer. He explained that the corporal who had put in the complaint against him was lazy and incompetent. Her next superior officer made sure she left the force. He told Duncan not to fight a war that wasn't hers, but nothing he said or did had changed Corporal Duncan's attitude. Always irascible, her rudeness towards him seemed to grow with each passing day and Wilmot had given up trying to find a pleasant side to her. Strangely, she only acted this way towards him. It was beyond his understanding. He went back to studying the body. "No chance you found a bloody rock, is there?"

"Nope. My bet is he had enough sense to throw it into the ocean with the other fifty million just like it." A gull, hovering in the air above them, screamed. Duncan looked up. Watching the bird, she said, "He's waiting to see if we leave him a meal."

He stood. "Where are her clothes?"

Her brows contracted in a scowl. "That's what the divers will be looking for."

He could tell by her restless shifting from side to side that she had outlasted her patience and was eager to be doing something, anything but stand there waiting for him to catch up.

He fought down annoyance. Emotions only confused things. This was the crime that would get him away from Glenphiddie. He needed to be totally rational and clear-headed. "Collect everything else you can find on the island. It probably won't help either, but it still has to be done."

Wilmot pulled on disposable gloves and moved from the girl's ankles to her head. He examined her wounds. First man and then nature had brutalized the young woman. The left side of her face had been crushed by her attacker and then the open flesh had been eaten away. Her right eye, in an area undamaged by her killer's attack, had been pecked out. And her lips... Wilmot looked away, studying the horizon and regretting the coffee he drank on the ride over to Ghost Island.

"Crabs," Duncan said, answering his unasked question. "That's what was eating her when we got here."

He nodded and looked back at the body. Duncan had bagged the victim's hands in clear evidence pouches to protect any trace of evidence under her fingernails. Hopefully the victim had scratched her killer and they could get a DNA sample. Duncan had left the head uncovered until he had seen it, but they needed to bag it immediately or risk losing vital evidence.

When he had finished examining the face, he took the plastic evidence bag Duncan held out and gently pulled it over the victim's head. He sat back on his heels and breathed a sigh of relief. The bag put a barrier between him and the victim, turning her into an exhibit and less of a human being.

He slid one hand under the head and another under the lower shoulders. He looked up at Duncan and said, "Ready?"

Duncan nodded.

"Okay," Wilmot said, "To you on three." Duncan crouched down, slipping her hands under the hips and thighs.

When they turned the corpse over, crabs scurried out from beneath the body and water rushed into the depression where the victim had rested. "Shit," Wilmot said. "I hope we don't get any of the little buggers inside the body bag." The thought of crabs feasting away while trapped in with the body was something out of a horror film. He could imagine the coroner's rage. Dr. Pearce was always lecturing them on preserving evidence, and letting crustaceans feed on a corpse would have her screeching about their incompetence.

He examined the woman's back. Small creatures had eaten away the flesh in spots along the buttocks and legs. Lividity had turned the skin black where the blood had pooled, telling him the body hadn't been moved after death.

Together they lifted the remains into the heavy plastic body bag Duncan had laid out. They didn't close the zipper. The exhibit officer would do that, and then he would cover the zipper with a sticky exhibit tag and sign and date it so evidence inside couldn't be tampered with.

Wilmot pointed to the police launch. "We'll make Thoms the exhibit officer. He can ride with the body to Victoria for the forensic autopsy."

"So Thoms will be responsible for the collection and documentation of all exhibits?" Duncan's mouth narrowed in a grimace. "The detachment is already shorthanded. Losing an officer to forensic duty will leave even less staff for regular duties."

"Let's bring them in." He waved to Thoms and the two other constables on the police boat. "They can start the search."

The crime scene area Duncan had roped off included a bench made of driftwood and a charred circle of stones that contained the remains of years of fires. Anyone sitting on the bench could see Glenphiddie Island across the fire pit. Wilmot went to the pit and squatted down to study the ashes. "No telling when the last fire was, but we can ask any witnesses if they noticed one burning last night. It will help with the time of death."

Duncan said, "No one would even notice. Lovers come out to Ghost Island to watch the sun go down and everyone has a little fire to keep the chill off. It's supposed to be romantic."

"What happened to this girl wasn't about romance."

The motor on the police launch died. He turned to watch Thoms pull it up onto the rocky beach. "The first thing we need to do is identify the body. Go through the missing persons database to see if someone has reported her missing already. She could be a runaway. And get copies made of your pictures of that tattoo."

"We'll need help," she said.

"We'll get some auxiliary RCMP constables to help out."

"That's not what I meant. It's race weekend. A hundred boats are here from as far south as Seattle. With crews, there could be up to five hundred extra people in Kilborn, maybe a thousand, all in the mood to party. We can't manage all that and handle a murder."

The force was always stretched to capacity just with normal policing on weekends and this weekend would be worse, but he wasn't ready to call in Major Crimes and lose control of the case. In fact, Wilmot intended to do everything he could to hold them off. "Major Crimes will be just as pushed on a long weekend as we are and they're seriously understaffed at the moment." He knew because he'd tried to use that argument to get transferred back to the unit. "The boats here for the regatta won't leave until Monday. We'll all be working overtime but we can handle it."

Wilmot watched the last man climb out of the launch and stand by the others, waiting for instructions. "I'll get in touch with Major Crimes and fill them in as soon as I get back to the office, but I'll tell them we've got it under control. If we haven't got a solid line of inquiry by Monday, I'll be happy to have the Major Crimes unit take over. Three days, that's all I ask."

Duncan sighed. "I still think we should turn it over to them and go back to our own policing." She screwed up her face as if she'd tasted something bitter. "They might not even come on Monday. In the end it will be the unit commander who decides if the serious crime unit takes over. It will come out of his budget, and you know how he likes to keep that balanced. Money will be more important than some poor kid."

"Either way, they can't get here before the tide comes in. You and Thoms and I will work this, while the other three handle the day to day duties with the help of the auxiliaries." He could see she was about to argue. He raised both hands, palms out, as if to dampen down her impatience. "I said I'd call and explain the situation. If we mess up, it will be my responsibility, not yours."

"My name is on the case file. I was on duty when the call came in."

"Fine. Just blame it on me if it all goes wrong."

"Oh, I intend to."

While Duncan supervised the search, Wilmot boarded the police launch and headed back to Kilborn. The town was beautiful from the water. A flat green band of park hugged the shoreline above a small beach and multiple docks. A boardwalk stretched from one end of the park to the other. Fanned out above this green space, the streets rose in tiers like bleachers in a stadium. Overlooking the seafront, colorful patios, dotted with umbrellas and hanging baskets, made the community look like it was in permanent celebration. And it was just as interesting at night. From the water Kilborn looked like a giant ocean liner anchored in a sea of blackness. When the lights went out, one by one, the town disappeared.

He turned away from the view. Taking out a notebook, he began planning the operation to first identify the victim and then find her killer.

Chapter 4

When she woke, Singer vaguely remembered Wilmot saying he was leaving, but she couldn't remember if he said why. This was supposed to be his day off before he went on twelve-hour shifts for the next three nights of the long Victoria Day weekend. She sniffed the air. Normally he started the coffee before he left. Nothing. She smiled to herself. Maybe he had gone out to the bakery to pick up croissants for breakfast and he'd start the coffee when he got back. She lay there waiting to hear his key in the lock. When she decided it wasn't happening, she rose and pulled on his terrycloth robe, lifting the collar to her face to breathe in any trace of him. She loved wearing his clothes, delighted in running her hand along his perfectly ironed shirts, hanging at equal distance from each other in his highly organized closet.

She padded barefoot into the kitchen and started the coffee. While she waited for it to brew, she dug out the diary she'd found the day before and sat down at the table to read. To the soft beat of dripping coffee, she flipped the journal open to the middle. Using green ink, the handwriting was large and flowing.

Everyone wants to know what I want from the future.

I want a real life—to see the world and do exciting things.

But of course that's not what they want to hear.

What they want is for me to be sensible—to accept responsibility—to be like them—caught in the trivial day to day events of a small island.

Singer smiled. Normal wouldn't suit Trina Strickner, a girl more alive than regular people. She'd met Trina when she coached her for her starring role in *Grease*. The girl had been born for the spotlight. The drab reality of life for her elders wouldn't please Trina. But the young didn't know that no one wanted to grow up to be old, or hardworking, or boring. That's just what happened—if you were lucky. "So young..." She sighed. Trina was too young to know the opposite of conventional was often heartache. And while keeping life fresh and exciting was a noble goal, like turning straw into gold, no one Singer knew had ever managed it.

But Singer could identify with the sentiments in the diary. As a teenager, she'd been just as certain that her life would be exciting, sure that she would always land on her feet. She gave a huff of disgusted amusement. Not on her feet, but on the street and on her back was where she'd landed.

She skimmed through a few more pages, stopping here and there to read.

April 21, 1995

Glenphiddie Island

It's my seventeenth birthday and I long to be gone. There's a whole world out there waiting. What am I doing here?

Singer remembered that longing to be somewhere else, and the absolute unconditional self-confidence that she would succeed because she was somehow smarter and more adaptable than anyone else.

I talked to that guy in Vancouver and he said the job is mine starting June 27— and Cody can have a job too. Haven't told Mom—not going to—I'll call her from

Vancouver. Old shit face will throw a fit, thinks I should work all summer for no money changing sheets and ferrying tourists out to Cooper's Island. Mom may be his slave, but I'm not. God, how does she stand it? And doesn't she see him trying to feel me up every chance he gets? Maybe Mom knows all about him. She didn't squawk when I said I wanted to board in town, even took money out of my college fund for it and said she wanted me to have the full experience, extra-circular activities— drama, Olivia's creative writing course. Mom must know her husband wants to get it on with me. Maybe letting me board in town is her way of dealing with it but why can't she just stand up to him??????????

Singer looked up from the journal. "At least I wasn't being abused, just bored to death by routine and smothered by respectability." Fragmented memories of her own teen years welled up. Sixteen, that's how old she'd been when she left her home in Maine to sing in a rock band. She'd never gone back again except for a few days here and there. It wasn't just Singer who didn't want her to be in that pristine white dwelling. She was sure her mother heaved a sigh of relief when Alexandra, the person she'd once been, left town before totally disgracing the family. Nothing frightened the Warrens like inappropriate behavior and just about everything concerning their daughter was judged by them to be unsuitable for a Warren.

Her musical star had risen like a rocket and then faded just as fast, going downhill until she ended up singing on the streets of various big cities. Her homeless life was behind her now, thanks to Steven Davids and the legacy he'd left her up on Mount Skeena. But she hadn't yet decided if the inheritance was a curse or a blessing. To avoid paying a great whack of taxes she had to establish the home as her principal residence before she could sell the property. This meant living there for one full year.

One year. At first it had seemed like a prison sentence. But not now. Time was playing tricks on her. A remote island, with potluck dinners at the center of social life, wasn't a spot she would ever choose to live, but over the last few months the place had started to take hold of her. She now looked at it with eyes that recognized the rhythms of life, the ebb and flow of its inhabitants. More than that, island people were accepting. They smiled at her like she was someone they knew, not someone to be watched with wary distrust.

And then there was Louis Wilmot. She didn't know what that was yet. She just didn't fit with his image of himself. Although she made him laugh, she also knew that she sometimes embarrassed him. And while he gave her his key, and expected her to be there waiting for him, he reclaimed it and put it back in his pocket the moment he arrived. No use kidding herself that it was any more than sex for him. Still, they were good together and she'd figure out what came next when it ended.

Singer turned to the first page of the slim volume and began at the beginning.

Dec. 26, 1994

Journal #4 of Celastrina Strickner

So Trina had begun this journal the day after Christmas, Boxing Day, it was called in Canada.

Singer used her forefinger to mark the page and closed the book. She ran her hand over the smooth cool cover. The rich red leather was expensive so it was likely a Christmas gift. She noticed a white line of paper peeking out from the edge of the last page. She pulled out a professional-looking photograph of Trina staring straight at the camera and looking older and worldlier than seventeen. With strong features, wide eyes and a sensual mouth accented by a small mole to the right of her upper lip, she was handsome rather than pretty. Singer flipped the photograph over. On the back was written, "Author photo for my first book." Singer smiled at the absolute assurance of youth and opened the journal again.

> *This belongs to Celastrina Elizabeth Strickner and is for her eyes only. If you're reading it—<u>DON'T</u>! And that means you, Hannah Cutter. I'll punch your eyes out!*

Singer laughed. She felt no shame at looking into someone's private life. Guilt and shame were emotions she'd left behind in Maine.

> *What's the big deal about sex anyway? So teenagers sleep together—it's not like you're stealing or something—committing a crime. Why not just do what feels good and makes you happy? People should be allowed to be happy.*

She read it again and had the strange experience of peering into her own past, into the soul of the girl she'd once been. It was both shattering and wonderful to see that she hadn't been exceptional in her feelings and desires.

"Hostile glares of critical eyes."

Singer lowered the journal and stared at the sugar bowl without seeing it. *Yes*, she thought. *That's how I felt at sixteen, unique, the focus of criticism, and misunderstood*. Maybe the truth was that everyone understood Trina only too well, knew what she was experiencing because they'd been through it themselves.

She closed the red notebook, tucking it in her worn backpack. She'd take it back to the Cutter home on Arbutus Lane. But not today. Singer felt a strange protectiveness toward Trina and her journal. She didn't want to hand it over to anyone but its owner, and Singer knew Trina wouldn't be at the Cutter home this weekend. The Cutters thought she had left Thursday night and gone home to Cooper's Island on the Scholarship, the boat that took students to the outer islands. Her mother thought she was staying at the Cutters for the regatta weekend. Trina actually planned on spending her weekend with her boyfriend.

Singer had no intention of giving Trina's secret away. She threw the strap of her backpack over her shoulder and headed out to the post office to pick up her mail. Maybe today was the day the letter would come, the letter that would change her life yet again.

Chapter 5

The mid-morning temperature had climbed into the seventies, convincing Glenphiddie residents that the long wet spring was over. Singer walked over to Heath Street to where giggling girls from the graduating class flocked at the entrance to the community center, waiting for the opening of a traveling trunk show of prom dresses. She searched the pack for Trina, but didn't see her.

Down on Front Street a line of cherry trees grew between the sidewalk and the road. A rush of pink blossoms blew up the sidewalk toward her. She stopped as they swirled by her. She was still smiling when she climbed the four steps to the outdoor space of the Ferryman Inn, a long white structure overlooking Preservation Park. Beyond the park lay the harbor, with Mount Baker in Washington State jutting above the horizon. Already a string of boats was making its way up the inlet for the around-the-island race.

She paused on the top step, fascinated by the frenzied activity on the waterfront. It must be something to do with the regatta. The race was nothing to her, but hopefully it might generate more tips at her evening gig. She turned away and settled herself at a table on the far end of the patio, tossing her backpack on an empty chair. A seagull screeched and dived at the plates on the table next to her. Tom Woods, the owner of the Ferryman, came out onto the patio, flapped a cleaning cloth at the seagull, and started to load a tray with the dirty dishes. "So, where is she?" His normally mischievous eyes narrowed in annoyance. It was clear that Olivia had pushed his easygoing nature to the brink.

"Isn't Olivia in yet?"

Tom scowled. "You know she isn't."

"She'll be here."

"Yeah," he nodded in agreement. "She usually makes it in eventually. But how late will she be and who will show up? Little Bo Peep? A vampire? God, I hope it isn't the prom queen. When she turned up last Thursday night in that pink chiffon number I almost lost it." He piled up the dishes. "And every time she bent over she nearly lost both of them. Something about the fit wasn't quite right."

They smiled at each other and then a sudden worry swept over Singer. "You aren't going to fire her, are you?"

Tom took a swipe across the table and then tossed the towel over his shoulder. "Worst bartender we ever had, but she's worth the price in laughs and audience participation. I swear some people come in for a drink just to see how she's dressed. One time she actually came in wearing wings, like some kind of bloody Tinker Bell. Kept knocking things over every time she turned around."

Singer glanced beyond him and grinned. "Well, you'll be happy to know she isn't a fairy today."

He swung around to see who she was looking at and then quickly turned his back on the diminutive female biker approaching them. "Give me strength," he whispered and smiled.

Olivia Vincent stood before them and struck an aggressive pose, a biker babe barely five foot and unlikely to reach a hundred pounds despite the chains on her costume. With a jarring combination of features that didn't quite work, a triangular shaped pixie face with a round knob of a chin, her startling violet-blue eyes made the rest unimportant. Her hair, bright orange today, was spiked out six inches above her head. Her lipstick and her nails were black. She wore a very short black leatherish skirt and a matching jacket from the same shiny material, the entire outfit decorated with studs and multiple chains. To this she'd added black leotards and Doc Martins over gray work socks. Slung on her right shoulder was what looked like a pair of oversized saddlebags, stolen off a very large horse. "Like it?" she asked.

"Very original," Singer said. "Your own creation?"

"Of course." Olivia adjusted the dog collar she wore. "Rough chic."

Tom picked up the tray. "Things will be even rougher for you if you're not behind the bar in five minutes." To Singer he said, "Do you want something?"

"Just coffee."

"Wonderful. At this rate I'll be rich in no time." He pointed his forefinger at Olivia. "And you, no leaving early like you did last night." He left with his tray.

Olivia plopped down on a chair and picked up Singer's cigarettes, saying, "You aren't supposed to smoke out here on the balcony, you know. Tom says we can only smoke out back of the building." Olivia lit a cigarette and inhaled hungrily. "God, I wish he'd start smoking again. Soon, he'll have us going to the next block."

"How'd the writing go yesterday?"

Olivia took another long drag before she answered. "Oh, fine, I wrote six words and then I crossed out ten."

"Ah." Singer nodded in understanding. "Explains the new look."

"How attached are you to Wilmot?" Olivia asked.

"Why?"

Olivia worried a small section of her waxed hair between her fingers. "I think what I need to break out of this writer's block is mindless sex." She released her hair, which now stood out like a ragged corkscrew off the side of her head. "He'll do just fine."

"Only if you want to die."

Olivia exhaled twin lines of smoke through her nose. "Damn."

Singer reached for the cigarettes. "Do you know Trina Strickner?"

"Sure. She's in my creative writing course."

"Is she any good?"

"Damn good." Olivia wrinkled her nose. "I used to be that good." Pain flashed across her delicate features. "Or maybe I'm flattering myself."

"You've got an award-winning book behind you to prove you're good."

"But I've only written shit since."

Singer lit a cigarette and then asked, "How do you know it's shit?"

"I've got the rejections to prove it." Olivia stubbed angrily at the ashtray and then slumped back on the chair, angling her face up toward the sun.

Singer leaned forward. "What do you make of her? Trina, I mean."

Olivia didn't seem at all surprised by the question but it took her some minutes to answer. "In her writing, and that's the only way I know Trina, she's completely honest. Absolutely truthful, no matter how painful. Because she hasn't experienced the repercussions of honesty, she never sees the need to lie. I hope she can hold onto that truthful view of the world." She opened her eyes and stretched her neck from side to side. "She doesn't yet worry about how the world sees her. Maybe because she feels superior, but it makes her writing fresh and exciting." Olivia frowned at someone behind Singer.

Singer turned her head to follow Olivia's gaze. Peter Kuchert jogged up the steps and across the terrace toward them.

Wearing jeans and a gray hoodie he moved like a man on a mission. His brown eyes behind rimless glasses were intense and fixed on Olivia.

"Oh," thought Singer. "He wants her." But she quickly decided she was wrong about that. There was something else going on between these two.

He said, "I need my short story back, Olivia." Harsh and angry, it wasn't a request but a demand.

Emotions rippled across Olivia's face before she arched an eyebrow above a now blank facade. Her forehead wrinkled in the perfect approximation of confusion. "Why?"

"I did it really fast." In his late twenties, Peter radiated pent-up energy, as if he could barely stand still long enough to hear Olivia's response. "I've been working on it and I've made it much better." He shoved his hands into the pockets of his hoodie where they toiled like little animals trying to find a way out.

Olivia shrugged. "Don't worry. I'll look at it again before the end of the term." A small smile teased her mouth.

"I want to enter it in a literary contest next week so I need to get started."

Olivia gave an exaggerated shrug. "So work on it and print it out for me again. No problem."

Peter's lips thinned into a hard line. "Have you read it?"

"Nope. I've only read one paper."

The wind ruffled his rust-colored curls that were just long enough and wild enough to be interesting. Singer decided he would be handsome but for a forehead that was a little too high and a mouth a little too thin. He tilted his head to the side. "Out of curiosity, whose story did you read?"

Olivia lifted her left shoulder.

"I'm curious." He smiled without warmth and said, "It's Trina's, isn't it? You're doing the same old thing."

"And you're preaching the same old gospel according to Peter." The air crackled with the electricity of their antagonism.

"And how is Cody?" he asked.

"Goodbye, Peter." She closed her eyes again.

"Olivia..." He exhaled heavily. "Please, Olivia."

She waved a hand in his direction without opening her eyes. "I'll get to your story after the weekend. Don't worry about it. It will give you some perspective, to see if the things I comment on are the things you worked on." She tilted her face to the sun, ignoring him.

He grimaced. "It will be a waste of your time. And..." He was distracted from his new argument. He pulled his hand out of his pocket and pointed at the journal on the table. "Is that Trina's? She's always writing in a journal like that."

Olivia's eyes flew open and she followed his stare. Her hand reached out for the book.

Singer reacted without thought, grabbing at the diary and snatching it away from Olivia, away from the hungry look on her face and the fingers arched like claws. "She left it behind yesterday. I'm about to take it back to her," Singer explained.

Olivia twisted away from them, hiding her face.

"Have you read it?" Peter asked. "I bet she has some interesting things to say, being that she's the island hottie and the next great thing in Canadian literature."

"Is that how she seems to you?" Singer asked. "Talented, I mean."

With an ironic lift of an eyebrow he said, "Ask Olivia. She thinks Trina is going to make it all the way to the bestseller list." The bitterness in his voice wasn't lost on Singer.

Peter moved closer to the table to let a group of people edge by them. "Olivia's obsessed with Trina, but I don't get it."

"Obsessed?" Singer looked from Olivia to Peter. "What do you mean?"

But Peter was gazing out over the harbor and didn't answer.

Singer turned to see what had caught his attention. An emergency vessel was speeding toward the marina.

With his gaze fixed on the dock, Peter shifted restlessly and tried one last time. "Please, Olivia, I need my story."

She didn't open her eyes. "I have to go to work now. I'm no longer a writing teacher; I'm now a serving person."

A flash of anger crossed his face but he didn't argue. He took a deep breath and raised a hand. "Later," he said.

Singer watched him dodge through the traffic and jog toward the waterfront where a small crowd had gathered around a black hearse. "Something's happening down at the waterfront." She jiggled Olivia's arm and then pointed to the gathering. "What's going on?" People rushed forward to meet the vessel swinging into the dock. Was Louis one of those hunched figures? Singer strained to make him out.

Olivia's glance was the briefest possible. "Some exciting piece of marine life, no doubt. That's all it ever is."

"It's interesting enough for Peter."

"He's a reporter. That's what he does for a living and that's what kind of a writer he is. He'll hurry down there to be first with the news even though there isn't any other paper to steal the story."

Singer turned her head to study Olivia's face and asked, "What was that in aid of, giving Peter a hard time?"

Olivia gave an open-mouthed yawn. "I made a great mistake with him. We had this thing for about a second and a half and now he thinks it gives him rights."

"Always a problem. It doesn't seem it's quite over between you. Did he break it off or did you?"

Olivia eyes shot open and she frowned.

"Oh, I see. And now you're being as difficult as possible, enjoying not giving him what he wants, even something as simple as his story."

Olivia leaned her head back to catch a little slice of sun peeking around the roof. "No, I'm not. I'm just not going to jump when he rattles my chain."

"But is it wise to make him hate you?"

"There isn't enough passion in him for hate."

Singer wasn't sure Olivia's assessment was correct. "He feels strongly about something, and he seems to think you have a thing about Trina."

"Peter thinks I make too much of Trina and favor her above the rest of the class."

"And do you?"

"She has a fresh voice and an interesting perspective." Suddenly, Olivia was no longer indifferent. Her eyes popped open and she stared intently at Singer. "Trina has got something special. The short story she turned in is the beginning of a novel. She's not old enough to write it." She leaned forward, intense and concentrated, with her fingers curled into a fist. "But one day..." She turned away.

"Is it so rare, her talent?"

"Oh, hell, yeah." Olivia shoved back from the table. The legs of her chair made a harsh sound as they scraped along the deck. "She has what it takes. I hope it works out for her." Her words didn't quite translate into her body language. "We both know how rare success is."

Singer nodded in understanding. They shared the experience of being someone who almost made it, a shining light that burned out too quickly. "What about the rest of the stories people turned in?"

Olivia shrugged. "I have ten essays to read and every one of those writers thinks they've got the beginning of a great work of art."

"Including Peter?"

"Especially Peter." Her hands flew up. "How can he write when he can't feel? Always checking to see if he has the correct response. The guy is so uptight his middle name should be constipation."

"That sounds a bit harsh."

"Believe me, I'm no kinder to myself."

Singer knew what she said was true and wanted to smooth away the painful emotions. "Writers are everywhere on this island, aren't they?"

Olivia jumped to her feet. "Writers and seagulls, the island is full of them, and they all turn out a lot of shit." She flung the saddlebags over her shoulder.

Singer brushed back the hair blowing in her face and looked up at Olivia's asymmetrical face. With one eye tilted up more than the other, it was like looking at two people at once, one soft and elfin, and the other rather sinister. She had multiple piercings in her ears, a stud in her nose and one in her eyebrow. Her waiflike exterior suggested fragility, but there was something furious and hard underneath. "Can I read Trina's story?"

Olivia's eyes grew rounder. "Why?"

Singer spread her hands and tried to explain. "You made me curious, and..."

Before she could finish, Olivia planted her hands on the table and leaned over her. "Give me the journal and I'll let you read her story." She thrust out a predatory hand.

Singer drew the red leather protectively toward her. "Sorry." She turned aside, picking her backpack off the deck and tucking Trina's words carefully away. "I'm going to take it back to Trina. I only asked to see her story because I was interested in her writing."

Olivia straightened. "Well, guess you'll have to go on being interested."

Singer wanted to soften Olivia's annoyance, to patch over their disagreement with a new topic. "So, if you weren't with Peter last night, why did you slip away so early? Is there a new man in your life?"

"None of your business," Olivia spat out.

"Sorry. I was just trying to..." She couldn't think what she was trying to do. But it didn't matter anyway. Olivia was gone.

Singer murmured, "Shit," and watched the stiff back thread its way through the tables. Olivia looked more like a teenager than a woman in her early thirties. "There goes my free coffee." She sighed. Olivia could hold grudges for days.

Chapter 6

Singer sipped coffee and watched the comings and goings of the town. If she was ever going to belong anywhere it would be here on Glenphiddie, a place where old hippies grew pot and raised chickens, and where there were more artists than regular working people. Singing at the winery and various bistros felt like a standard occupation here. And if she told the residents about her years on the street, well, they would probably say, "Cool."

She took the journal out again and read on, finding a reference to herself.

> *—her past shows on her face but she sure can sing, a voice like sand in honey—raw and sensual—and when she sings a love song, it's like she knows there are no happy endings.*

Singer smiled, figuring it wasn't a bad description of her style. When Trina had come up to her and said, "I want to sing like you," Singer was about to brush her off but Trina quickly added, "I'll pay you to teach me."

> *The eagles were fishing for herring in the canal today. Counted eighteen eagles, screeching/talons out/wings spread/flying at another bird to take his place on a rock or dead branch, wanting to get the best spot, to get as much as they can...are we any different?*

> *Don't we cut and slash to get what we want? I do.*

She read on, unaware of her surroundings until a man asked to take the chairs from her table. Something was happening. A crush of people filled the deck, milling about and waiting for something. Like a herd of nervous sheep when the smell of a bear reached their noses, their restlessness was palpable. Even the islanders who normally didn't come into town except for supplies hung out on the edge of the crowd, arms crossed and eyes watching. Beyond the deck people filled Preservation Park, as busy now as it was when the Saturday market was on. Was it about the race? Had there been an accident? Well, whatever was going on, it had nothing to do with her. But Trina might be somewhere in the crowd.

She gathered up her belongings and worked her way through the packed patio and then dashed across the road to the park. A man wearing muddy Wellingtons and a straw hat nodded at her and made room for her to slip by.

Singer worked her way from one side of the park to the other before she gave up trying to find Trina. It was time she did what she had been putting off for days. She went to check her mailbox.

There was only one letter. She read the return address on the pristine white envelope and then stuffed it in her pocket and went to the boardwalk to read it.

Chapter 7

She stood at the railing with the letter in her hand. Below her a pair of yawning harbor seals stretched out in the sun. She watched a seaplane land on the water and taxi up to the dock. She studied all of the action along the waterside and then at last she opened the envelope.

It was exactly what she had expected, but she hadn't known she'd feel this badly about it. She leaned over the railing and told a seal, "It's too soon." He yawned.

Singer buried the letter deep inside her backpack and walked along the boardwalk. At the ramp going down to the marina, she ducked under the low limbs of an apple tree. From here she could watch people coming up from the dock. If Trina went by she'd see her. She sat down and leaned her back against the trunk of the tree alive with the buzz of bees. She pulled out the notebook to read the last few pages.

> *I hate living on these tiny little islands where people only think about their gardens, talk about having a simple life and living with nature. Why? What makes that so wonderful? Why would anyone want to be in the same place with the same people all the time?*

> *My mom is just like them. She sees the standoff in the Branch Davidian building outside Waco as evidence that the world isn't safe—thinks that's what will happen to me if I leave the islands. As though I'd get mixed up in some religious cult. Everything scares her, but not me.*

> *She'll die on her little island with her chickens.*

> *Not me.*

Singer's eyes closed. The journal slipped from her lap. She didn't see the hand come down to lift it from the grass.

She woke under a sky that was clear and benign above the branches of the flowering apple tree. It took her a minute to notice the man staring down at her. She smiled up at him.

"What's this? Sleeping in a public place? I could arrest you, you know."

She gave Wilmot a lazy smile and said, "Fun." She held out her wrists. "Handcuff me and keep me at your mercy."

"Tempting."

Gray was beginning to appear at his temples and new creases lined his handsome face, but they only added to his attractiveness. And then she noticed that he hadn't shaved. It was unlike him. No, it was more than that. It was something that had never happened in their time together. Concern rippled through her.

"I thought this was your day off." She picked up her backpack. "You had plans." *They had plans.* She was careful not to speak that thought out loud.

He frowned. "Plans changed."

Singer bent low and came out from beneath the tree.

A large woman, herself pushed from behind, jostled Singer back into the tree with a flutter of blossoms. The woman smiled and said, "Sorry."

Singer returned the smile and slipped past her to join Wilmot. She stood on her toes and spoke softly. "What's up? What did I miss?"

"Let's get out of the crush." He took her hand and led her to the edge of the square.

"So," she said, looking back at the people. "What's happening to make the natives so restless?"

"A body was found out on Ghost Island."

Singer's breath caught in her throat and in her heart a tiny prayer went up. "Who?"

"It was the body of a woman, a young woman."

She grabbed for his arm. "Who?"

"There was damage to her face. We couldn't identify her and we have no way of knowing if she was a local or a tourist. Maybe she belongs on one of the boats. Half the population in town this weekend is transitory. Someone on a boat may have killed her and left her behind before sailing back to Santa Cruz." Eight miles across open water from Vancouver Island and twenty minutes by seaplane from Seattle, the killer could be long gone. "Or maybe she was just hitching a ride on a boat. Happens all the time. They never expect to see her again so wouldn't know she's gone missing. If she's local..." He shrugged. "We're waiting for a mother to call and say her daughter didn't come home last night."

He was speaking his fears out loud, but she didn't need this long explanation. Her grip on his arm tightened. "Wasn't there anything to tell who it was?" Singer wanted to be told who it wasn't as much as she wanted to hear who it was.

"The only way she'll be identified is by the small butterfly on her ankle, a blue butterfly."

"Trina." The name came out on a breath of despair. "Oh, no, it's Trina." Damage to her face, he'd said, not only dead but beaten, tortured. She raised her face to the clear blue sky. "Trina's dead." She was absolutely certain of the truth of her words.

Wilmot reached out and took her in his arms. "Shush," he murmured into her hair. Around them people stirred restively and watched. Rocking her gently he whispered, "Who is Trina and how do you know it's her?"

She opened her mouth to explain, but only sobs came out.

"Okay, okay," Wilmot said. "Let's get you a coffee first."

She clutched at him. "Can we go to your place, somewhere private?"

"Sure." He looked from Singer to the crowd of people around them. "I should have thought of that myself."

He put an arm around her shoulders and pulled her up tight to him and led her toward the car with its red, yellow and blue stripes on its side.

"Wait." She pushed him away and frantically dug about in her backpack. "It isn't here."

"What isn't?"

But she was gone, back through the park, pushing and shoving people aside. She searched the ground beneath the apple tree, even raced around the tree and searched the lower branches in case someone had found it and put it there. There was no red journal.

"What are you looking for?" Wilmot asked.

"Trina's journal. I was reading it when I fell asleep and now it's gone."

She turned to the faces staring at her. "Has anyone seen a red book, a leather notebook? About this big." Her hands described the size.

Heads shook in denial and eyes watched her cautiously, one more crazy woman in the park.

Wilmot took her hand and drew her away.

Wilmot lived in the only apartment building on the island, a small concrete block of eight apartments, four up and four down with a staircase in the middle. Its very ugliness made the islanders swear it would be the only one of its kind.

He unlocked the door and stood aside for her to enter. Inside, every room was painted a pale gray, a color that turned to blue in the late afternoon. It was a space of neutrality, a place where nothing happened or anything could happen, a place in limbo. There were no personal items, no happy family in frames, not even a piece of colored glass from the beach. It looked like nothing more than a summer rental. When she'd asked him why he hadn't put his stamp on it, he'd said, "It's not worth it. I'm not staying."

"Right. Me neither," she'd said. "As soon as I prove I'm a resident, I'm out of here." That conversation had set the parameters of their relationship and she thought about it every time she entered the apartment. At forty-eight, two years older than Wilmot, she was past believing in forever, but still...

Wilmot pointed at a chair. "Sit." He dropped his keys on the table and went to the compact kitchen to start coffee. Then he opened the window over the sink and came back with a saucer, which he set on the table in front of her. He dug the package of cigarettes out of her backpack and placed them on the table. She looked up at him, questioning. "It's okay," he said. "You need it."

She reached greedily for the box as he sat down across from her and opened a blue notebook with lined yellow pages. "Tell me everything, but first, how do you know the body is Trina Strickner's?"

"I saw the tattoo yesterday. I don't remember ever seeing it before, but yesterday the rain was falling on it." She knew she wasn't making sense. Singer took a deep breath. "It was raining. I had the Martin and I didn't want it to get wet." The 1939 mahogany Martin guitar, with its ebony bridge and ivory inlay, was the only thing left from her golden days and more precious than life. "I ducked behind the bushes at the corner of the bank and took shelter under the overhang. Trina came by. She sat on the window ledge at the front of the bank with her feet sticking out in the rain. She took her diary out of her backpack."

She stopped to light the cigarette, but her shaking hands wouldn't cooperate. He took the lighter from her and flicked it into life, holding it up to her cigarette.

"I was going to call out to her but then the boy came... so handsome." She dragged deeply on the cigarette, letting the smoke dribble out slowly while Wilmot waited.

"I overheard their whole conversation. Trina told her mom she was staying at the Cutter's this weekend but that the Cutters had gone to the salmon fishing conference with the boy's parents. Cody, that was what she called him. She wanted to spend the weekend with Cody, but he didn't want to. He had other plans."

"Did he finally agree?"

"More or less. What teenage boy turns down a weekend of free sex? But..." Her voice trailed off.

"What?"

"She was bullying him, Louis." She leaned closer to him. "He had other plans. But she ignored his protests and dragged him off, leaving her journal behind. I picked it up and was going to take it back to her today, but I couldn't find her."

Wilmot changed course. "Why did you ask me about Ghost Island?"

"Because Trina wanted to get a bottle of wine and go out there with Cody. She was going away. She wanted to see the lights go out on the town and say goodbye. I wondered where it was and what made it so important to her."

"Apparently, it's something people do, almost a rite of passage for teenagers." He pushed back from the table and went to pour the coffee.

With the aroma of coffee filling the room, comforting and normal, the horror that had overwhelmed her took on an unreal quality, like there had been some huge mistake that would soon sort itself out. She watched him pour two mugs of coffee, watched as he brought them back to the table and set them down. He touched her shoulder gently and said, "I'll be right back." He went into the bedroom and closed the door. She reached for a mug and slid it carefully toward her, using both hands to pick it up.

When Corporal Duncan answered the phone he said, "I have a possible ID for our body. I believe her name is Trina Strickner."

"Oh, damn."

"You know her?"

"Yeah, I coached her soccer team. She's a kid we all thought would go far. Trina's mother is Pam Haver, a bit of a recluse. She's married to Frank Haver, Trina's stepdad. They live on Cooper's Island, been there for about six years."

"Where's the biological father?"

"No idea. He's never been around as far as I know."

"Take a picture of the tattoo over to Cooper's Island and see if Trina's mother can identify it. And if it turns out to be Trina, bring the mother and stepfather back with you. We'll track the father down after that."

"Right. It'll take over an hour to get there and back."

"Fine. I'll meet you at the office in an hour and a half. If it is Trina, we need to speak to all of her teachers and her classmates, and anyone else she came in contact with last night.

And we need to do it now. She was seen with Cody Frieberg about four-thirty. I'm going to pick him up."

"Even before we have a positive ID?"

"Time isn't on our side. We need to push hard."

When he came back to the kitchen Singer asked, "Did you find her backpack?"

"No." Wilmot sat down across from her.

"It was khaki-colored canvas and she'd written and drawn all over it." She swept the hair back from her face. "I remember there was a quote by Ernest Hemingway written on it, 'Never mistake motion for action.' Trina wrote underneath it, 'And never mistake talking for doing.'"

Wilmot reached across the table and took her hands in his. "Singer, I don't want you to tell anyone about any of this, okay? We have to notify her family first and we have to make sure the body is Trina's."

She looked up at him with a brief willingness to believe that Trina was alive, but she knew it was a false hope. "Promise," he said, gripping her hands tighter. "This is important. It can't get out."

"I promise." She looked into his shrewd eyes that saw through lies, eyes that uncovered mysteries. She lowered her head and withdrew her hands. She was already keeping too many secrets. "I won't tell anyone about the dead woman being Trina."

"Good. And don't tell anyone about the missing backpack or about reading the journal."

She nodded her head. "I won't tell anyone else about the journal."

He lowered the mug that was halfway to his lips. It struck the table sharply. "What do you mean, 'anyone else'?"

"Olivia knows I found it." After a pause she added, "And Peter Kuchert too."

"The reporter? You told him you found it?"

"Not exactly, but it was there on the table this morning when we were having coffee. We talked about it."

"He likely didn't know it was Trina's."

Singer shrugged, her ability to reason lost to shock and grief.

"Well, nothing we can do about that now, just don't tell anyone else. We have to make sure the body is Trina's." He pushed back from the table.

Wilmot brought a pad of paper and a pen and laid them on the table in front of her. "I want you to stay here and write down everything you remember about Trina's diary." He tapped the table in front of her with his forefinger. "And give me every name she mentions. Then bring it to the detachment office so we can record your statement about seeing her with Cody yesterday."

"Okay." The single word was barely audible.

"You can leave it for a little bit, until you get yourself together."

She didn't answer.

He picked his keys up off the table. "Are you going to be all right?"

Why did people always ask that stupid question? She nodded.

He bent down and kissed her. "I don't know when I'll be back."

When she heard the door close behind him, she folded her arms on the table, laid her head down on them, and cried.

Chapter 8

It didn't take Wilmot long to track down Günter and Loti Frieberg's son. The second person he called told Wilmot that Cody was out with the Lutheran youth group cleaning up a beach at the north end of the island.

Wilmot was uncomfortable about the coming interrogation. Günter Frieberg was part of the volunteer search and rescue group on the island, and the whole family was popular and involved in the community. Cody had been volunteering for the island search and rescue organization since he was sixteen, first on maintenance and now on a regular rescue team, and long-term plans were being made for him. He planned to join his father on his fishing boat when he finished high school in June. On an island where young people left for university or better jobs, never to return, he was the organization's hope for the future. They were paying to send him off on a special course in July. It was a small group of volunteers the Mounties depended upon, and Wilmot knew questioning any of them in a serious crime would be seen as a betrayal of the whole. More than that, even being asked questions during a murderer investigation would start rumors. It was one of the things he'd had to learn about small-town policing. Every act had repercussions. That knowledge had made him more cautious and secretive than he was normally inclined to be.

Wilmot drove out of Kilborn on a narrow twisting road along the edge of the North Channel, past towering firs and ditches filled with yellow broom. A war was being waged, and lost, against the invasive golden bushes a lonely Scot had introduced in the last century. Signs saying CUT BROOM IN BLOOM were everywhere. Their oily resin turned them into a fire hazard in the dry summer.

No more than a thousand yards across North Channel, almost close enough to swim to, he could see Cooper's Island. As near as the two islands were, the rocky cliffs would prevent boats from crossing the channel and docking along the rugged coastline. Duncan would be going around the tip of Cooper's Island to a sheltered cove on the far side.

Glenphiddie Island had similar hidden coves and beaches, accessed by random paths from the road. Most of these beaches offered no parking and no signage. After six years on the island, he was still finding new pathways to the ocean.

Twenty minutes out of Kilborn Wilmot slowed and turned into a narrow dirt track. At the end he found three vehicles parked haphazardly in a small turn-around. Wilmot recognized Cody's beat-up Ford pickup. The windows were down. He opened the door and had a quick look for the backpack Singer had described but found nothing. The bed of the pickup was empty.

Many feet had beaten a winding path through the weeds. It led past a peeling red arbutus tree to slippery moss-covered steps leading down to a rocky bow-shaped beach. The descent was on a point of land that jutted out to the right of the shoreline, so the beach could only be observed when you were actually on it. That fact, plus the steep climb, made it a favorite spot for teens. Not many adults were willing to risk their necks to get to it, but those who did complained about the litter. The youth group on the beach was doing something about the trash that midnight parties had left behind.

Wilmot could hear music as he started down. On the second step his foot slipped and he only saved himself by grabbing the handrail. Normally on such steep stairs open to the elements, roofing shingles were nailed to the treads, but not here. He swore expertly and proceeded to work his way more cautiously down twenty feet of slime-covered planks to a tiny lookout platform. Down below ravenous gulls fished in the shallow pools of trapped water along the shoreline. A shiver went through him. Trina's face had been eaten by crabs just like the ones the gulls were feeding on, crabs Cody's father sold to restaurants and the islanders. The unintended malice of nature, life feeding on life, would definitely take crab off the menu for him.

He shook off his dark thoughts and started down the last fifteen feet. Here a rubble trail replaced the steps, sending him skidding and sliding and grabbing at branches. Cursing, he slid to the bottom without falling. He stood at the edge of the beach, breathing heavily, and took in the spot where he'd landed. It was high tide so the beach was only about twenty-five feet wide and a hundred feet long, and cut off from access at the far end by giant boulders reaching out into the water. Waist-high logs, tossed there by storms or fallen from above, littered the beach.

Laughter drew his gaze midway down the beach to where three teenagers sat on a log. At their feet, two more kids were stretched out on a blanket. Further down the beach a boy and a girl stood with their heads together, unaware of his presence. The youth group seemed intent on making an all day job of the cleanup, a beach party as much as a work party. The girl on the blanket looked in his direction and spoke quietly to the others. They all turned and stared at Wilmot as if he'd just stepped off a spaceship in Roswell. His uniform told them he was a Mountie, but was there more to their reaction than that? Did they know about the body that had been found on Ghost Island?

A horseshoe crab scuttled sideways in front of him. Their shells littered all the beaches, a too persistent reminder of mortality. He stepped around it and picked his way over the wet stones, trying to avoid the slippery kelp and rocks that would tip and slide under his city shoes.

Someone lowered the volume of the music. A boy, his face pitted by acne, rose from the log and stepped forward saying, "Hi." He gave Wilmot a cautious little wave. Wilmot returned the greeting. The boy had guilt written all over him. Why? There were no signs of drinking. The faces watching him approach were all too panicky to be innocent. Probably some pot was involved. He couldn't detect anything over the stench of seaweed and dead crustaceans. Why did people go on about the aroma of the sea and the beaches? It smelled like crap to him. Better to have the smell of car exhaust and the cooking odors of city streets then the odor of death. As if echoing his thoughts, above them an eagle cried, a predator looking for prey. Wilmot was the only one to look up before he said, "I want to talk to Cody."

The boy turned and pointed down the beach. "There, with Alison." Was that bitterness in his voice? Wilmot looked to where the boy was pointing but he had already identified Cody by his height and the black and red baseball cap he habitually wore.

Wilmot nodded his thanks and started down the rocky shore. Curious eyes followed him. The whole island would explode with gossip when the teens got home.

Cody and his friend, a petite copper-headed girl with freckles across the bridge of her nose, weren't collecting much litter. Chatting and laughing, they were unaware that someone new was on the shore. Wilmot had almost reached them when the girl, coy and flirting, circled around in front of Cody and saw Wilmot approaching. She stopped and pointed at him. Cody swung around. The baggy paint-stained shorts and a ripped T-shirt didn't take anything away from his movie-star good looks and muscular build.

Cody recognized him. His smile was replaced by a quizzical frown.

"I'd like to talk to you, Cody."

The girl frowned and reached out for Cody's hand. He gave a soft shrug and said, "Sure," inquisitive more than concerned, and maybe a little self-important that the police had sought him out. And then his face clouded over. "My parents are all right, aren't they?"

"As far as I know, they're just fine. This isn't about them." Wilmot waved back to the coast path. "Let's have a chat. In private."

Cody's handsome face crumbled into confusion. He looked to Alison and then back to Wilmot. "What's the problem? What's this about?"

Wilmot pointed to the far end of the beach and the stairs. "Let's go back up top."

"I'm coming with him," Alison said and linked her hand with Cody's.

"I need to speak to Cody alone." Wilmot took a few steps toward Cody, grasped his arm above the elbow, and led him away. As soon as Cody was walking toward the steps Wilmot let go of his arm. They walked in silence with Alison following them. Cody glanced back at her several times.

The rest of the group had gathered in a clump in the middle of the beach. When he reached them, Cody stopped, undecided and uncertain, and then he turned away and picked up a red plaid shirt from the log and twisted it around and around between his hands before he walked toward the group without speaking. They parted for Cody and Wilmot, leaving Alison behind in their midst.

Cody made the twenty-foot climb up the embankment seem easy, standing erect and taking the hill in long strides, while Wilmot clutched at branches and struggled to keep from sliding down the path on his belly. He suddenly felt every one of his years. He puffed upward, promising himself he'd head to the gym as soon as this investigation was over. Cody was already at the top when Wilmot got to the stairs.

In the cruiser Wilmot said, "When did you last see Trina Strickner?"

Cody's eyes widened. "Yesterday."

"Tell me about it, starting with the time you met her."

"I met her downtown, about four-thirty, by the bank." He went silent, worrying his bottom lip with gleaming white teeth.

"And then what?"

He couldn't meet Wilmot's eyes.

"Where did you go?"

Diffident and a little ashamed. "We went back to my place." Cody's Adam's apple bobbed as he swallowed. "It was her idea."

"What happened when you got there?"

"Oh, no, I'm in trouble aren't I? What did she tell you?"

"You had sex with her, right?"

Cody's face reddened and then he nodded. "Don't tell my folks."

"Did she stay all night?"

Cody shook his head. "I wouldn't let her. I was afraid my folks would find out if she was there all night."

"Okay. What time did she leave?"

Cody picked at fir needles stuck on the sleeve of the flannel shirt he held, dropping them on the floor of the cruiser. "She left before nine."

"Did you have anything to eat?" Wilmot needed the information to help the coroner establish the time of death.

Cody looked up. His forehead wrinkled in confusion by the change of subject. "Yeah."

"Exactly what time did you eat?"

Wilmot watched Cody's brow furrow in concentration. "About six we had some cold chicken Mom left for me and then we made grilled cheese sandwiches about eight. Is she sick? I didn't get sick."

"What happened next?"

"After we ate I made Trina leave. I knew my aunt might come by. I'm not supposed to have anyone in when my folks aren't here. Besides..." He hesitated. "My mother met Trina once. My mom didn't like her... thought she was fast. Sometimes Trina says and does things that are embarrassing. She's... well, pushy, doesn't take no for an answer. Says what she thinks without thinking how others will take it. Mom would be piss... mad if she knew Trina was there so I didn't want her around if Aunt Nora came."

For all his long explanation, there was something Cody wasn't saying. "Did Trina leave alone?"

"Sure." He turned to look at Wilmot. "It was still daylight. It was perfectly safe to walk the three blocks to the Cutter's." Cody's face scrunched up as if he'd been struck by a sharp pain and then he said, "Was she attacked after she left my place?"

Wilmot went back to the one place he was sure Cody was lying. "Trina could have stayed over. No one would have known."

There was a flicker of fear in Cody's eyes before he looked down and watched his forefinger rub back and forth across the surface of the armrest.

"You're eighteen, all grown up. The story about your aunt checking on you is nonsense. What happened between you and Trina?"

His question was answered by silence.

"Sooner or later it will come out. The longer it takes, the worse it will be."

"We had a fight."

"Why?"

"I don't know." He looked out the side window, away from Wilmot. "She's always telling me what to do."

"What did she want from you?"

Cody continued to stare out the window, his face turned away from Wilmot. "My family is really religious."

Wilmot tried a new tactic, asking a harmless question that Cody wouldn't mind answering. "Where are your folks, Cody?"

"In Victoria at a meeting about the salmon stocks. My dad is a representative for the fishing union." Cody swung to face Wilmot. "Please don't call them."

"I'm just trying to get to the bottom of what happened last night."

"I didn't force her to have sex with me. I didn't rape her. In fact, it was her idea. I don't know what she told you, but it was her idea." Tears filled Cody's eyes and he turned away to hide them. "She thinks, because she has sex with me, she owns me and I have to do whatever she says. That's why she's saying I raped her."

Wilmot sighed and started the cruiser. "Let's just go to headquarters and get it all written down."

When Wilmot pulled back onto the gravel road Cody said, "Will Trina be there?" He was rubbing his palms up and down his jeans. "At the station, will she be there?"

"Why, are you afraid to face her?"

"She lies. Everyone will tell you that, and if she says I raped her, she's lying."

Wilmot waited for the island bus to pass before he could pull out onto the road. *The kid's good. He's prepared the perfect act to deflect suspicion. But what if he isn't lying?* The clock was ticking. The more time he spent on this suspect, the less time he had to find the real killer if Cody was innocent. Too bad he didn't possess those famous instincts that detectives were supposed to have.

Cody laid his head against the passenger window and didn't speak or look up until they reached the station.

When Wilmot parked outside the square block building of the detachment headquarters, Cody jolted upright. "If I raped her, I'd have scratches." He held out his arms, eager to prove his point. "Look, there's nothing." Pulling down the neck of his T-shirt he turned his head from side to side. "Nothing on my face or neck."

It was true. His skin was unblemished. "She's lying. You can see that for yourself." Cody pounded the dash. "I didn't hurt her."

"Why would she do that?" Wilmot said mildly. "Why would she say you raped her if you hadn't?"

"She just wants to make trouble for me. She wants me to go to Vancouver with her for the summer."

"And you think she's hollering rape to make you go?"

"To get even. I didn't rape her. I told you that."

"We're just trying to find out what happened, Cody, and you admit you had relations with her last night."

Cody's face crumbled into a mask of distress. "I wasn't the only one she had sex with."

A jolt of anticipation. "Who else?"

"Not sure." Cody's large hands gripped each other, the knuckles showing white beneath the skin. "There was an older guy she told me about. She said she felt sorry for him and thought that having sex with him would make him feel better but it made him feel worse. She said he felt guilty. She couldn't understand that." Cody looked alarmed at what he'd just said. "Maybe she was teasing. You can't tell with Trina. She likes to shock me and calls me a prude. And sometimes she tries to make me jealous."

He'd have to go back and ask Singer if there was anything in the diary about other men. "Tell me about this man when we get inside." They had to find that diary. Had Cody stolen it? Not likely. The minister at the church said the youth group had gone out before nine and had been together all morning. So who was the thief and why had he risked stealing Trina's book in the park? Wilmot opened the cruiser's door and said, "Come on. Let's get this over with."

Chapter 9

The story of an older man didn't sound like a lie to Wilmot. It was too detailed, while the other stories Cody told of Trina's sexual partners was vague and indistinct. The one thing Cody was perfectly clear on, the one thing he repeated again and again, was, "I didn't rape her."

After going over the details of Trina's movements on Friday night, Wilmot turned over the picture of the butterfly tattoo and slid it toward Cody. "Do you recognize this tattoo?"

"Sure, it's Trina's." He frowned. "Why are you showing me a picture of her tattoo?" His mouth opened and his face melted into horrified astonishment. He swung to face the door. "Where's Trina?"

"Did Trina mention Ghost Island?"

Cody turned back to face Wilmot. His answer took time. "Yeah." The one word was cautious and uncertain, like he had already figured out something more was coming. "She said she wanted to go out to Ghost Island to see the lights go out in Kilborn, to say goodbye. As soon as school is finished she's going to Vancouver to work and she's staying there until university starts in the fall." He took a deep breath and let it out slowly. "She has a job for me in the same restaurant as she's working in, but I told her I wasn't going over to the city and spending the summer with her." He slowly shook his head. "I'm not going to do that. I've got plans, but it doesn't matter what I want. She just ignores everything I say."

"And that's what you fought about?"

Cody nodded.

"Please say it out loud for the tape."

"Yes, that's why we fought. I'm glad she's going. I want her to go to Vancouver and leave me alone." He lowered his head, unable to meet Wilmot's stare. The picture lay on the table between them. He picked it up. "Why do you have a picture of her butterfly?" Cody understood now that he might have misread the whole situation. His eyes met Wilmot's. "Where's Trina?"

Wilmot told him. It took twenty minutes before Wilmot could get Cody calmed down enough to finish making his statement. When it was done the only worthwhile thing Wilmot had gotten from him was that he'd last seen Trina shortly after nine. She'd left through the backyard and gone down the short lane between the dwellings, taking a shortcut on her way to the Cutter home.

Wilmot sighed and rose from the table. "You'll have to give us a DNA sample."

Cody tried to answer but couldn't get the words out.

Wilmot said, "Cody, do you agree to volunteer a DNA sample?" Cody gulped out a muffled, "Okay."

At the door Wilmot said, "Your statement will be typed and then you can sign it. After that you're free to go, but I want you to come back later today." He had witness statements to check and see if they matched with what Cody had just told him and then he'd have Cody go over his statement again.

Cody put his head down on his folded arms. His shoulders shuddered.

Outside the tiny interview room Corporal Duncan leaned against the wall, waiting for Wilmot to finish the interview with Cody. Duncan pushed away from the wall as the door opened. Fit from taking martial arts classes three times a week, she moved with the grace of an athlete. "Singer's here. I put her in the staff room. There was nowhere else."

The unspoken text was that if Major Crime came they would bring their own incident trailer and there'd be room to move in the station. "Good idea," he said, ducking another confrontation.

She frowned. Her rosebud lips and a very pretty face belied her toughness. "She's been waiting for you a while." Noncommittal, just the facts, but she watched him intently. He was sure Duncan knew of his relationship with Singer but he couldn't decide why she cared.

"Did you take her statement?"

"Nope." Duncan's icy blue eyes gave away nothing but they also missed nothing.

"Did she give you her notes on the journal?"

"Yup." She held out a folder to him. Her eyes moved from his face to Cody, behind Wilmot. Wilmot reached out and closed the door. Had Cody heard that Singer was a witness to something? He cursed his mistake and motioned Duncan away.

Duncan said, "The Havers identified the tattoo from the picture. They're coming over on their own boat. They'll be here in half an hour."

"I'll read this and then go pick them up and take them to identify the body while you take Singer's statement. When Cody signs his statement, get a DNA sample and then he can go. But tell him I want him back here by four-thirty." He smiled but it wasn't with amusement. "It'll give him a little time to stew and help him to remember a little more. There's something he's not telling."

Wilmot gave the transcript of Cody's statement to the detachment clerk to type. The island policing couldn't happen without the two municipal employees who manned tip lines, typed up statements and handed out bulletins. Although they were sworn to secrecy, the office leaked information. Wilmot wasn't sure if it was the police officers or the civilian employees who were responsible, but it drove Wilmot to remind the clerk that she was working on a confidential document. In reply he got a stony stare and a brisk, "Of course."

On the porch of the funeral home, Frank Haver, Trina's stepfather, began to cry uncontrollably and refused to go past the front entrance, creating a scene of epic proportions. Pam Haver stood well away from her husband, with her arms crossed and her back to him, waiting.

They were a mismatched pair. Frank Haver had gray eyes that wouldn't settle, eyes that talked to a phantom to the right or left of the person in front of him. The mother had an angular face, with deep-set dark eyes, and long graying hair hanging in a single thick braid down her back. She was faded and sad, but strangely calm. But Wilmot knew her composed demeanor was likely shock protecting her from the full impact of the news. Perhaps she was even hoping this was all a mistake. Whatever was happening, Trina's death wasn't real yet, but when it actually became true for her, then she would break.

Wilmot left the husband with the victim services officer who had come over from Victoria, and took Pam into the viewing room where the body had been laid out. The remains were covered in a crisp white sheet with only the lower arms, legs and feet visible. Pam didn't question this arrangement.

Wilmot pointed at the butterfly and asked, so there would be no doubt, "Do you recognize this tattoo, Mrs. Haver?" She stepped closer. Wilmot braced himself and waited for the explosion of emotion the sight of the butterfly would bring. It didn't come. Still, expecting the worst, his hands hovered over her shoulders, prepared to keep her from tearing away the sheet. It didn't happen.

She reached out and traced the butterfly with her forefinger, saying, "Yes, this is my Trina." She laid her palm flat on her daughter's ankle, covering the design. "I asked her not to get a tattoo but Trina never listened." Her hand stroked the foot. "I'm glad she didn't pay attention to me."

Her calmness was freaking him out. "I am sorry for your loss." Wilmot wasn't sure that she heard.

Trina's mother gently took the exposed foot in both of her hands. "How cold she feels."

"Did your daughter have any scars, Mrs. Haver?"

"Yes." Her hands reached out for her daughter's left palm and turned it over. She traced along a jagged scar with her fingernail. "Trina ripped this on barbwire, trying to climb a fence into the pasture where she wasn't supposed to be. I was so afraid of tetanus." Her hand caressed this little bit of her dead daughter that was exposed to her. She turned her head to glance at him and added, "And she broke her arm when she was nine. The bone came right through the skin."

"Here?" He pointed at the pale left arm lying on the white sheet.

"Yes," she said and nodded.

There was no doubt now. Wilmot stood silently beside her for several minutes as she caressed the lifeless limb of her daughter. Then he asked, "May I please have Trina's dentist's name?"

Her eyes lifted to his. "Why...?" And then, "Oh, I see. Dr. Finlay, here on the island," she said and turned away from the body.

"This way." He led her from the room.

Wilmot took the husband's statement while Duncan took Pam Haver to a separate office. Slowly, gently, Duncan led the mother through the story of her child, trying to get a feel for the family and anyone who had a special interest in Trina. "Do you know anyone who might harm Trina, Mrs. Haver?"

A long silence while the woman thought about her reply. "No." She was composed and controlled except for her hands. With her answer they flew about as if they had a life of their own.

"What about your husband, what were his feelings for Trina?"

"He was always kind to her." A violent flurry of her hands accompanied this statement.

"He wasn't her father, was he?"

She clasped her hands, keeping them still. "No."

"And he always..." Duncan searched for words. "Always acted appropriately to Trina?"

"Yes." Her hands flew apart, telling their own true story.

The fact that Frank Haver left his wife alone to identify the body disgusted Wilmot. He wasn't as gentle with him as Duncan was being with Pam Haver. He expressed no sympathy for Frank's loss, even though the man appeared more devastated than the mother, but started brutally into the interrogation. "Where were you on Thursday night?"

Frank licked his lips. His eyes shifted first to the right of Wilmot and then to his left. "I was at home."

"Where is that exactly?"

"Cooper's Island."

"Were you there all day?"

"Yes." Frank's eyes still didn't meet Wilmot's.

"I know that's a lie." Wilmot knew no such thing.

Frank Haver grasped the sides of the wooden chair and squirmed sideways so he no longer faced Wilmot. "I was home."

"You were seen," Wilmot said. "Are you trying to get yourself charged with murder?" The astonishment in Wilmot's voice was almost real.

"No, no." Frank wiped his palms down his face. "I was only here for a little while."

"Another lie."

"I didn't even see Trina." The whine of his voice, the rounding of his shoulders, beaten and defensive, made him an easy target. "Why would I hurt Trina?"

Wilmot leaned in for the kill. "Because you were molesting her and she was going to have you charged." That Haver had touched his stepdaughter was the one clear thing Wilmot had understood from Singer's story. "That's why you killed her."

Chapter 10

"It's a lie. It's a lie." Frank Haver bolted out of the chair, sending it careening backward.

Wilmot sprang to his feet, blocking the exit. "Sit down, Mr. Haver."

"I didn't hurt her." His hands shot up to cover his head. "I loved her."

"Sit down."

Haver backed into the corner of the room. Wilmot circled the small table to pick up the chair and set it firmly in front of the table. "Sit."

Haver fell down onto the chair as if his bones had melted.

"You molested her."

"It's a lie," Haver whispered.

Wilmot crossed his arms and stood over him. "Are you saying Trina lied when she said you touched her?"

Haver wiped his hand across his mouth and spoke to the floor. "I didn't mean to. It was an accident."

Wilmot turned away. "Yesterday, what time did you arrive on Glenphiddie?"

It came out slowly, with many stops and starts and denials. Frank Haver was a diver who did small jobs on the undersides of boats, cleaning props and hulls and attaching new chains between the buoys and the blocks of concrete used for anchorage. He'd arrived in Kilborn Harbor after lunch and worked on the vessel, *Sweet Dream*, for three hours and forty-five minutes. He was very clear about the time because he billed by the hour and had wondered if he could bill for the full hour instead of a part hour. When he finished clearing the barnacles from the prop and stored all his equipment, he docked his boat and walked up to the liquor store and then to the grocery store for supplies. His chores had taken another three quarters of an hour and then he'd taken the provisions back to his boat and headed home.

The trip had taken a little longer than the normal half hour because his engine needed work and he hadn't wanted to push it. Telling this small fact had given him confidence, as if a failing engine was enough to prove he was being truthful. He was adamant that he hadn't seen Trina and that he had been on his way back to Cooper's Island before five o'clock.

Wilmot knew that Cody and Trina had been together until after nine but that didn't stop him from making Frank totally miserable, taking him around and around the story until the man finally dissolved and was unable to go on. Only then did Wilmot leave the room to see what Duncan had gotten from the mother.

"She says she was home with her husband all night and that neither of them left the island."

"And you believe her?"

"Nope."

"Why?"

"Listen to the tape and you'll understand. They ate dinner together around six-thirty, that's pretty sure, but after that I don't think she has any idea where her husband was or what he was up to. In fact, if I pressed hard enough, I think she might say she actually believes he did it."

"So why didn't you press hard?"

Her chin lifted. "I thought I'd leave that up to you. You're better at being a bastard than I am."

He bit back his sharp retort. He needed Duncan, but when this was over... "How could she not know where he was? It's a small island, right?"

"Yes, but there's the main building, an old two-story farmhouse with a couple of bedrooms, a barn and sheds and such, and then there are a half dozen small cabins, without electricity or running water, scattered around the island. Those are rented out during the summer, but at this time of the year they're probably empty. Mrs. Haver spends many of her nights in one of those cabins. I'm guessing the Havers barely live together."

Wilmot flung his hands in the air. "Jesus wept. At least the ID is positive. The body is Trina Strickner's. We'll get dental records to send to the coroner for confirmation. Get that picture of Trina that Pam Haver brought in and photocopy it with Trina's details. I want posters all over town asking people to call with any sightings of her on Thursday evening after nine o'clock. I want them on every ferry and every telephone post. Call in all our volunteers and get them on it. We'll need them to help man the tip lines. I'll go up to the radio station and record a request for information report that they can play."

"You're sure that Cody had nothing to do with her death?"

"No, but I'm sure they were together until at least nine. Let's see if anyone puts them together after that." He turned away and then swung back. "And see if anyone can put Frank Haver on the island during that time. Get a DNA sample from Haver."

Duncan nodded. She had come on duty at midnight and now she looked like she was barely functioning. "On second thought, I'll do it," Wilmot said. "You get yourself home."

"What about you? You're not even supposed to be on duty."

"Ah, but I'm a man. I can handle it." Her face grew red and she drew herself up. He grinned and walked away before she could spew out her indignation.

Wilmot returned from the radio station and glanced around the empty reception area, expecting to see Cody. He checked out the empty interview room and then stepped into the glassed in office where Duncan was still working. "Is Cody here?"

She looked up from the file she was reading. "No. He hasn't come back. I called his house, but there was no answer. I left a message that he was to come back in."

"Shit." Wilmot had wanted Cody to stew about the coming interview, but if his ploy had made Cody run it would waste a lot of time and manpower tracking Cody down. And if he had left the island it would be even worse. Wilmot was halfway to the door when Duncan called out, "Try his dad's boat, the *Oystercatcher*."

Chapter 11

In Preservation Park the Rotary Club was taking advantage of regatta weekend by having a lamb barbeque to raise funds for the new pool. It looked like half the island had turned out to support their efforts. A whisper went through the crowd and people turned to stare as Wilmot approached. He avoided eye contact, aware of the questions on the tip of their tongues. He was in no mood to answer questions. Running this gauntlet of the curious did nothing for his temper and the smell of sizzling meat set Wilmot's stomach rumbling. When had he eaten last? He worried this around as he started down the ramp to the boat slips. He decided it was when Duncan had shared half her sandwich on her return from Ghost Island. He tried to remember if he'd thanked her.

    The wharf where the working boats were tied up was off to the right, separated from the main harbor by a small spit of parkland. Wilmot was relieved to find the *Oystercatcher* still tied to the dock. At least his chief suspect hadn't fled. He walked down the undulating dock to the cobalt fishing boat and yelled, "Cody!"

    Cody started out of the tiny cabin but stopped at the entryway. He leaned against the door frame and crossed his arms, tucking his hands deep in his armpits, defiant but afraid.

    "You are supposed to be at the station."

    "I..." Cody's eyes rose to the onlookers staring down on them from the boardwalk above the harbor.

    "Never mind them. It's me you have to worry about."

    "You shouldn't have come here." The teenager stretched his arm up toward the people leaning on the railing and watching the scene unfolding below them. "Everyone knows I've already been taken in once. You coming here will only make them more sure that I had something to do with Trina's death. That I..." He couldn't say it. He swallowed hard.

"You brought it on yourself. If you'd come in like I told you, your friends and neighbors wouldn't be watching me take you away in handcuffs, wondering if you're a murderer."

With a sharp intake of breath and a stiffening of his body, Cody's attempt at casual indifference was gone. He blinked rapidly to drive back his tears.

"Why are you here and not at home?" Wilmot asked.

"My aunt... And then the phone kept ringing."

Wilmot turned away. "Come on."

But Cody didn't follow him.

Wilmot jerked his thumb over his shoulder at the onlookers. "Do you *want* me to handcuff you in front of everyone?"

Cody came slowly to the side of the boat. He stopped and stared hard at Wilmot before stepping up onto the rough planks.

They were back up on the boardwalk, halfway to the band shell, when Wilmot realized the impact of what he was doing. *Bugger it*, he thought. *He should have come in*, but his footsteps slowed and finally stopped.

"Cody, how do you feel about a lamb burger?" He turned back into the park and led the way to the line winding its way to the tables set up in front of the half dozen barbecues.

As they waited to be served, Cody stood awkwardly, his left arm across his chest, clutching his right arm that hung straight down. He was taking quick panting breaths like he was having a panic attack. Wilmot couldn't decide if the teenager was about to bolt or have a breakdown. "What's happening, Cody?"

"Trina." He took several deep breaths before he could go on. "Trina should be there. She volunteered to work, she was looking forward to it."

Wilmot could have told him that this was the part of death that was always hardest to accept—all the ordinary things that make up a life that has ended, and watching life go on as if the loved one had never existed.

Wilmot sighed. "Go back to the *Oystercatcher*. I'll bring the food." He didn't watch to see if Cody complied. While he didn't want to waste time looking for Cody, neither did he want the kid to fall apart in public. Or maybe he was too damn tired to care. He concentrated on the fragrance of grilled lamb, frying onions and peppers. Country music came from the band shell that hung out over the water. Like Cody, he couldn't help thinking of what should have been. He should have been here with Singer, enjoying a perfect day.

They sat on the deck of the *Oystercatcher*, using upturned plastic pails for seats, their sodas at their feet and the burgers, wrapped in red-and-white checkered paper, on their knees. Wilmot ignored Cody and bit into his burger. Juice squeezed out of the bun and ran down the side of his mouth. Nothing else mattered but the taste of the food.

He dabbed at the damp lines at the corner of his mouth and asked, "So, why didn't you walk her home?" It was something he'd been wondering about. A boy like Cody, raised to be polite and respectful, it would have been the normal thing to do.

Cody didn't touch his food, just sat staring down at it without seeing. "We had a fight, a bad one. Like I said, she wanted me to go to Vancouver and work in a restaurant for the summer. I want to take the search and rescue course. Her answer was that I could do that anytime, but we'd have only this one summer together. It was like what I wanted didn't matter at all."

He leaned forward, earnest and intense, as if he was about to voice an earth shattering truth. "Do you know what I think?"

Wilmot shook his head and waited.

"That argument is all I've been thinking about and I suddenly realized why she was insisting I go with her. She was afraid." Cody's voice was full of amazement. "I only realized it today. I never thought Trina would be afraid of anything, but she was scared to go to a big city alone. She'd always lived in the islands. It's different here, but Vancouver..." He shook his head at an idea he couldn't quite imagine. "She was frightened."

"Did the argument between you get physical?"

Cody denied it with a shake of his head. He wasn't angered by Wilmot's question, as people often were when asked if they'd acted violently. Instead, Cody was still caught up in amazement that the person he thought of as fearless had been afraid. "She was really scared. Maybe, in the end, she wouldn't have gone."

"Now that you've had time to think about it, do you know of anyone she might have gone to meet after she left you?"

Cody shook his head. "I just assumed she was going back to the Cutter's." He hunched his shoulders, drawing in on himself. "I was so mad at her, I let her go out alone. If I'd gone with her, this wouldn't have happened. How can I face people? How can I tell my parents?"

He lowered his head. His shoulders shook. In the few hours since Cody had climbed the embankment with Wilmot his whole world had changed.

"And you didn't go out again that night?"

"No."

It came out too quickly. Cody was lying. There was something else, some other story to be told, but did it have anything to do with Trina's death? Wilmot crumbled the greasy paper and drank the rest of his soda. Experience—not instinct, not gut feelings—told him to look beyond Cody. It was all about priorities. If he spent all his time working on Cody as the chief suspect, the real killer would get away. He could be wrong, had been before, but he felt he needed to start over, to go back and rework the files, look for anything they'd missed, cross-check all times and alibis and witness statements. Somewhere on the island was a murderer and Wilmot would find him. It might even be one of the people leaning on the railing above him, watching. Wilmot didn't look up.

He reached over and picked up Cody's burger off of the red-checkered paper. Planting his elbows on his knees, he ate the second burger and let the juices drip on the pristine deck between his feet.

Singer's interview with Duncan didn't go well. Prickly, that's what Mrs. Warren would call Duncan. Bitch would be the word Singer used. It was like Duncan thought Singer was the chief suspect in Trina's murder. More than that, Duncan seemed angry at her for reasons beyond the investigation. None of this was new. Duncan might be able to hide her feelings from Wilmot, but not from another woman. While Singer felt some sympathy for her, Duncan's attitude soon got under Singer's skin. When she'd had enough, she stood up, pushed in her chair and picked up her backpack off the floor.

Outraged, Duncan said, "We're not done here."

"I am," she said mildly, and headed for the door. She wanted fresh clothes and a rest before she started at the Ferryman at seven. She'd only let the interview go on as long as she did because she was hoping Louis would return from the radio station.

Singer was just outside of Kilborn, listening to the Glenphiddie radio station, when she heard Wilmot's community bulletin saying that the dead woman found on Ghost Island was Trina Strickner. Wilmot asked for anyone who saw Trina after nine o'clock on Thursday night to get in touch with the RCMP station. Volunteers would be manning a tip line. All calls would be answered and the information followed up on.

Singer had seen in Trina a younger version of herself, eager for life and all it offered. Overcome by sorrow and shock, she pulled into a farm entrance and put her head down on the steering wheel. It wasn't just Trina she cried for.

The sound of a horn made her lift her head. A pickup was trying to leave the farm. Without looking, she quickly backed out onto the pavement, forcing another car to swing around her to avoid a crash. Horns blared at her.

She took a deep breath and checked both ways before she backed the rest of the way onto the road. She had to be more careful or she'd be roadkill. This drive to her home wasn't one where her mind could wander. Singer swung between terror and awe each time she made the trip.

The road followed the ridge of low hills along the side of Mount Skeena, where it overlooked Garibaldi Channel, giving her one last idyllic view over the Pacific to other small islands before it left the coast. It twisted upward through giant trees, snaking inland through a dark forest where chartreuse moss clung to every surface, a place out of Grimms' fairy tales. The menacing atmosphere urged drivers to speed through the woods. Speed was a mistake. At the edge of the forest, on the rim of an abyss, was a sharp left turn that required almost a full stop to navigate. Now the pavement barely clung to the edge of the mountain. After that, the narrow road, without guardrails, rose three thousand feet. Snaking curves pointed drivers out into the sky, above a fatal drop to the ocean or down into forest below, before the potholed surface jolted them around a rock face to a one last bit of forest. A mile higher, on the left, was the narrow entrance to the mountain home she had inherited.

The crooked lane was rutted and nearly washed out in places. Plunging banks on either side were covered in bright yellow broom. Blackberry canes reached out to scratch her paintwork. At the bottom of a steep grade, a narrow wooden bridge spanned a deep chasm where a small creek ran. There were no guardrails on the sides of the bridge. Singer slowed to walking speed. Her heart beat madly as she rattled over the timbers, wondering how long it had been since anyone had checked the structure for safety. Never was her guess.

When she drove up the far side, she broke into the clearing where the sun shone on a meadow filled with wildflowers. In the distance the Cascade Mountains of Washington state jutted up above the trees. "Almost makes you want to yodel," Wilmot had said the first morning they woke up here.

Three structures nestled among the acres of wildflowers. All of the graying cedar buildings were shabby and dilapidated. She parked in front of a log house with soaring south-facing windows. Set back into the woods, and to one side of the main house, was a tiny A-frame cottage. The third structure was a rundown barn where Stevie Davids had made his beautiful guitars. It was Stevie who had left the property to Singer.

The telephone rang as she opened the door to the house. Years of living on the street without a phone had taken away the normalcy of a call so she was always surprised when it rang, amazed that the instrument actually worked, and that someone wanted to speak to her. She picked up the receiver and said, "Hello" in a cautious voice.

There was no answering greeting. Lauren just started right in with what she wanted to say. "I've been trying to reach you. I've got great news. I sold 'Heart of a Loser.'"

Singer had met Lauren when she came to Glenphiddie Island to kill Lauren's husband. But someone had shot Johnny before Singer could. Lauren and Singer had joined forces to stay out of jail and now Lauren, using Johnny's contacts, had become Singer's agent.

"I played your tape for David Wagner and he bought it for Justine. The best news of all is that they want to record it in July, and you're going to sing backup. They went crazy over the demo. So you just have to hang in there for another six weeks and then you come back to Van and a job. Does that work for you?"

Singer turned to look out the window. It was the break she had been waiting for, but things had changed. She didn't want to think too closely on what those things were, and she definitely didn't want to discuss them with Lauren.

Impatient now, Lauren said, "Singer, did you hear what I said?"

"It works. Just tell me when and where and I'll be there."

"Well, you may need to leave sooner than that. Have you got the letter yet?"

"No," she lied. And then, before Lauren could grill her, she added, "There's something else I want to talk about." She took the phone into the kitchen, hunting through the fridge for something edible while she told Lauren about Trina.

"I can't believe it," Lauren said. "I know Trina...knew Trina. Her mother raises organic chickens and vegetables. Twice a week in the summer Trina and her stepfather brought produce over from their farm by boat. I'd go down to the harbor to get it. She was always smiling."

"That's how I remember her too. Didn't Trina's mother come?"

"Not very often. I'd phone over and tell her how many chickens I wanted and find out what vegetables she had and that would be it. How can there be another murder on Glenphiddie?"

Singer had no answer, but Lauren really wasn't expecting one. Lauren asked, "Do you know why they call it Ghost Island?"

"Because of the swirling fogs."

"That, and because the natives buried their dead there. It's supposed to be haunted."

"Well, if it wasn't before it will be now," Singer said. "Every time we look at the island we'll think of Trina."

"Do you want to get out of there, Singer?"

"What? First you tell me I have to stay here or lose mega bucks in taxes, now you say I can leave?" She dropped some slightly dry cheese onto a plate and searched the cupboard for something else.

"It's not like you're in prison. You just have to declare it's your primary residence and spend some time there."

Singer slammed the cupboard door closed. "That's not what you told me before."

"Yeah, well... it's my job as your manager to look out for you. I didn't like that guy."

"You're my agent, not my mother." Her flash of anger quickly mellowed into amusement. "I should never have told you about my past. It's left you expecting the worst from me."

"Someone needs to keep you away from the wrong choices. And the wrong men. No more wasted days, and nights you can't remember."

"Which pretty much describes about fifteen years of my life. Lost memory and money... the high cost of low living." She closed the cutlery drawer. "Well, you can stop worrying. I've decided I don't like waking up with my eyes feeling like they're swimming in kitty litter and my tongue tasting like I've been licking the bottom of a dumpster."

"There you go," Lauren crowed, "the makings of another song."

"Yeah, I'll call it 'The High Cost of Low Living.'"

They laughed and then Lauren said, "Another murder must bring back bad memories."

"Yes, but this time no one is trying to kill me."

Chapter 12

Before Singer started her first set at the Ferryman, she and Olivia snuck out for a cigarette. Tom Woods had given up smoking and now chased everyone who kept the habit he longed for to the outer corners of the property. Most of the time Olivia and Singer ignored his rants about their filthy habit, but when the patio was full, as it was tonight, they went out through the kitchen to the alley for a smoke.

Olivia said, "It isn't right."

Singer threw her hands up in disgust. "What the hell has right got to do with anything? Lots of things aren't right, but they happen anyway."

"She was young." Olivia dug her hands into her waxed hair, driving the spikes skyward. "She had a future."

"And the rest of us don't?" Singer's voice was loud enough to startle a couple going by the mouth of the alley. They stopped and stared at Olivia and Singer. She waved a hand at them to let them know everything was all right and sucked in a big breath of garbage-scented air. "Sorry, Olivia. I'm upset with the whole world right now."

"Understandable. I can't believe this happened here." Olivia stuck out her palm to stop a further outburst. "You know what I mean."

"Well, things go wrong even in paradise." Singer viciously stubbed out her half-smoked cigarette. "Just ask Adam and Eve."

Olivia made a face. "I felt this was the safest place on earth. Not anymore. And it isn't just Trina." She looked around and then leaned closer to Singer. "Someone is following me. They were behind me last night when I went up the lane to my apartment. I heard something, someone stumbling over some trash. When I turned around to see who it was, I just saw this silhouette duck sideways into the shadows. He didn't want to be seen."

"He?"

"Of course, a woman wouldn't follow me." She frowned. "It was nearly two. No one should be in the alley at that hour." Then her eyes grew wide. "What if it's the murderer looking for another victim?"

Singer studied Olivia's face. How much credence did you give to a woman of high imagination who barely remembered what day it was and where she was supposed to be? "Why would anyone follow you?"

"I don't know." Olivia shivered dramatically and then she frowned. "And my bag was searched today." She leaned back against the wall, one leg bent up behind her with her foot flat against the wood siding. "But I can't figure out why, because they didn't take anything."

Singer laughed. "I've seen inside your bag. How could you tell if it's been searched?"

"I can tell." She nodded her head to confirm her words. "Things are getting creepy."

"Call the detachment and make a complaint."

"They won't come."

"Why do you say that?"

"They're too busy. Someone broke into three cars behind the library today. The Mounties didn't send anyone, said to come in and fill out a form. Everyone's pissed at them." Olivia's frown cut two grooves between her eyebrows. "I have an eerie feeling that things aren't going to turn out so good." She pushed away from the wall. "It isn't over."

"Psychic powers now?"

"Maybe."

Singer tucked her hair back behind her ear. "I feel so sorry for Trina's mother. 'If misery loves company, here I am'—that's what Trina said about her mother, an unhappy woman who only talks to her chickens."

Olivia was too caught up in her own worries to have time for anyone else's. "Well, all I know is I'm not going out anywhere alone." She headed for the kitchen entrance. "I've got two more hours and then someone's walking me home."

Singer grinned at the retreating back. Tom was going to love this new demand of Olivia's.

It was nearly dark when Singer took another break in the alley. The acrid pong of the dumpsters was the signature stench of all the alleys behind all the clubs and restaurants she'd ever played. Standing there, she decided she'd hung out in way too many alleys where human rubbish vied with the trash cans for the title of garbage. It was time for a change. She lit her cigarette and dragged in the smoke, leaning up against the wall and searching for stars overhead. Tonight her life seemed like a waste. She had nothing to show for her time on earth except a few songs, only one of which had ever been a success and that one was a hit for someone else. If she disappeared tomorrow, few would mourn or remember her.

The heat was disappearing with the last of the light. She shivered and dropped the cigarette butt on the ground, grinding it out under her toe as the sound of an angry voice came from the mouth of the alley. A couple entered the darkening lane. Instinctively, Singer moved into the shadow of a dumpster.

The man towered over the woman logging behind him. With shoulders hunched up to his ears and his hands stuffed in the pocket of his jeans, he puffed fiercely on a cigarette without removing it from his lips.

The woman stopped and said, "I don't want to stay here tonight."

"Don't be stupid." He took the cigarette out of his mouth and flicked it away from him. "You're crazy, Pam, you know that don't you?"

"I should know; you've told me often enough." Arms locked across her chest, she came slowly toward him but stopped well out of his reach. "Why can't we go home?"

The man took another cigarette from the pack in his shirt pocket and put it in his mouth before answering. "The cops want us to stay on Glenphiddie until tomorrow." His lighter flared. "Besides, we need to make arrangements."

"What arrangements? I'll have her body cremated and then I'll scatter the ashes on Cooper's Island. It will take five minutes to arrange. I want to go home."

"You're a cold bitch, Pam. You haven't shed a tear. I cared more about Trina than you did."

The woman came alive. "Oh, yes, you loved her." Fierce nodding of her head accompanied her bitter words. "But not in the way a father is supposed to love a daughter." She rushed toward him. "Why do you think I sent her away?"

He raised a fist to strike her but the woman ducked sideways from the blow. Spinning around him and out of his reach, she walked backward down the alley toward Singer. "You wanted her!" Her arms flew up. "Don't you think I knew that?"

"You bitch," he yelled, coming after her. "Don't you dare say that! Don't even think of telling the Mounties your crazy ideas." He caught up with her and shoved her hard, driving her down onto the gravel. Crab-like, the woman scuttled away from him as he kicked at her. She screamed as his foot connected with her ankle.

Singer stepped out from the shadows.

The man wheeled to face her. She recognized that look on his face, had seen it on a man who'd beaten her and controlled her until one night he'd knocked out a tooth and she decided that it was never going to happen again. She'd waited until her abuser was deep in a drunken stupor and then she'd stolen his gun, his money, and his old yellow camper van, but she left behind the drugs that had kept her tied to him. The next day she was in a different state with stolen license plates on the van. Now the tracks on her arms and the gun, wrapped in his old plaid shirt and tucked beneath the seat of the old van, were the only things that remained of her abuser.

But this man wasn't asleep and she didn't have the gun.

He took a step toward Singer, ready to explode into further violence. "We're busy here," he snarled. He hadn't lowered his fist.

"Fuck you," Singer said, and then she ignored him. Her eyes were on the woman getting slowly to her feet. She moved between the woman and the man. "Hello," she said. The woman nodded and wrapped her thin sweater tightly around her chest and crossed her arms over it. She was thin, too thin.

Singer said, "You're Trina's mother, aren't you? My name is Singer Brown." It was the name she'd given to the Mounties when she first came to Glenphiddie Island and she'd never felt the need to correct it. "I helped Trina with her singing."

The man grabbed her by the arm and shoved her aside. "I said we're busy. This is none of your business."

Driven by rage, Singer surged back toward him with her fist raised. "You touch me again and I'll have the cops so far up your ass you'll never shit them out."

He blinked.

She stepped in close and jabbed her finger at his face. "You're Trina's stepfather. I'm going to make sure the Mounties know all about you. Trina said you were a perv."

He opened his mouth to speak and then closed it.

"Called you an asshole. Seems she was right about that." Singer hissed, "Trina hated you."

The man jerked back like she'd slapped him.

Through all of this, Pam Haver neither moved nor reacted. Singer eased closer to her, as if approaching a frightened animal that might startle at any sudden move. She stretched out her hand. Seconds passed before Pam reached out to take it. Looking beyond Singer to her husband, she said, "Goodbye, Frank."

He gave a small grunt, but didn't move.

"I don't want to ever see you again."

"Don't be stupid."

Pam's voice rose. "Leave or you'll regret it."

He jammed his hands deep into the pockets of his jeans, and looked from his wife to Singer and back again, trying to decide how to react. When he saw there was no softening of their anger, he sloped off down the alley without looking back.

Singer said softly, "I'm so sorry about Trina. She was special."

"Her name was Celastrina." Her voice was faint and incredibly tender.

"It's a beautiful name."

"Yes," the woman agreed. "Celastrina, for the little blue butterfly in our garden. I used to like that butterfly." She tilted her head back as if searching for stars in the darkness, just as Singer had, or maybe it was to stop the tears from running down her face. "That's why Trina had the butterfly tattooed on her

84

ankle—it was her namesake." She lowered her head and looked at Singer. "I'm Pam."

"Trina told me about you. She said you talked to your chickens."

A small twitch of the lips. "My chickens understand me and need me. No one else seems to."

"Trina did. She was excited to leave home but hated to leave you—conflicted, you know. She loved you very much."

Trina's mother reached up and covered her mouth with her hand but it couldn't stop a deep well of sadness from cracking open with an animal cry of pain.

Singer took her in her arms and they held onto to each other, two strangers locked together in grief.

Finally, Pam pushed herself away. She glanced over her shoulder at the inn. "The Mounties got us a room for the night, but I don't want to go back in there, back to him."

"I've got a place where you can spend the night, if you don't mind waiting until I get off work, a couple of hours. It's up the mountain, away from town. It's quiet there. Will that be all right?"

Pam nodded.

"Good." She patted Pam's shoulder. "In the meantime, you can lie down in my SUV. Not the best place, but it has dark windows so no one will see you there. You can have some privacy, time to yourself."

Pam nodded again.

"Right, let's go."

Singer led the way to the parking lot. The Yukon that Lauren had liberated from Johnny Vibald's garage was equipped for leaving. Old habits die hard and safety had often meant being gone. For more years than she cared to remember her only home had been the old yellow van she called the Beast. While this new vehicle didn't have all the comforts of home the Beast offered, it was equipped to hit the road at any moment, ready to offer basic shelter. It was her giant security blanket, outfitted with a cooler that plugged into the lighter for power, bedding in a plastic bin, and first aid equipment. A second plastic box held extra clothes while another held canned goods and water.

    She gave Pam a pillow. Pam stretched out on the backseat, shaking uncontrollably even when she was covered by the blanket. Singer dug in a plastic garbage bag and brought out a tattered sleeping bag. She spread that over the blanket. Crouched in the open door, close to Pam, she said, "There's water in the cooler."

    Pam whispered, "He doesn't hit me often, only when I really make him angry." Tears seeped from her closed eyes. "You must think me a terrible mess."

    "Not me." Singer's finger went to the crescent scar on her cheek. "I was trapped in that kind of situation. Once I got out I promised myself never to let it happen again." She stood up. "Try and rest. I'll be back in a couple of hours."

    She locked the SUV and went back to the patio to sing, but her heart wasn't in it. The patio was still full when she finished her last set and hurried back to the parking lot. She unlocked her vehicle with some trepidation. The blacked out windows didn't let her see if Pam was still there, but she was sleeping right where Singer had left her. She put her guitar case in the back and then shook Pam gently.

    Pam pushed aside the bedding and sat up.

    "Are you still all right with going up the mountain with me?" Singer asked.

    "Yes." Her face crumpled into despair. "I fell asleep. How could I do that?"

"Sleep is a refuge, and lord knows you need it. You're exhausted. Don't worry about what your body does. Just let it do its thing. It knows best." She babbled on as she slipped behind the wheel, hoping to spit out some words that would ease the pain. She looked over her shoulder and asked, "Want to sit up here with me?"

When Pam was in the passenger seat and fastening her seat belt, Singer said, "There isn't much to eat at my place. Are you hungry?"

"God, no, I couldn't face food."

"See, told you your body knows best." She started the engine and eased out of the lot, already dreading the trip up Mount Skeena. Normally, she never attempted the steep climb after dark or if she'd been drinking. It was terrifying under the best circumstances, so if she didn't spend the night with Wilmot after a gig, she'd find a hidden place and sleep in her vehicle until dawn. At least then, with the sun coming up and feeling cramped and cold, she felt brave enough to take the switch-backing journey into the sky. She'd fall into bed for a few more hours of sleep, followed by a shower, before she attempted the trip down again. Tonight was different because she had company. But still, she was afraid. As she always did, she paused when the lights shone on the worn planks of the bridge, checking to see that it was still there. She held her breath as they clattered over the timbers.

Safely up the other side, the lights of the SUV swept across the meadow, past the barn and pointed to the timbered dwelling with the cottage off to one side. She turned off the engine, leaving the lights on, and considered what lay before her.

"It's beautiful," Trina's mother said.

Singer snorted. "It's a scary old dump." She reached into the glove compartment for a flashlight.

"It looks perfect to me." Pam's voice was full of a melancholic longing.

There was no real path to the front entrance, only the narrow ribbon Singer's feet had beaten into the knee high grass. "I guess I should really do something about this jungle." She swung the flashlight around them. "Sheep run all over this island. Do you think I can convince a farmer to bring some up here and let them eat this hayfield?"

Behind her Pam also stopped, considering the meadow. "You'd need to fence it."

"Then forget that idea." Singer crossed the porch and pushed open the unlocked door. "Welcome to Castle Brown." She switched on the light.

They stood at the entrance and surveyed the room. She'd never owned anything before, except a series of rattletrap vehicles, so this property was a step up, a new beginning for her. The thought brought a wry smile to her lips. Coming to Glenphiddie Island to kill a man had done wonders for improving her place in the world. "Crazy how things work out," she said as she looked around her home.

The dwelling was constructed of logs the color of honey. Large Navajo rugs hung on the walls, while more were scattered across the floors. Over the living area, the ceiling soared two stories to a gallery. "Stevie Davids made all the furniture from wood taken from this property. Amazing, isn't it?" She sniffed the air. "Can you smell mice? I think I can."

"Maybe."

"What in hell do I do about that?"

"Traps or a hungry cat." Pam moved past her. "Mice are nothing to worry about."

Not when you've just lost a child. The unspoken words hung in the air. Singer said, "I'm sorry. I..." She didn't know how to apologize.

Pam waved a hand. "Don't worry. I didn't mean anything by what I said. Mice are always around in the country. You just have to deal with them. That's all I meant."

"Well..." Singer blew air out through her lips. "Just tell me when I blunder. It's bound to happen. I've always had a mouth that worked faster than my brain."

Chapter 13

Singer stretched out on the couch, put her forearm over her closed eyes and tried to sort through her feelings. Things were beginning to happen in her professional life. Lauren was selling her songs and getting her backup gigs on recordings. It was what she'd been waiting for, but it didn't excite her the way the news would have even a month ago. And then there was the letter.

She heard the boards on the bridge rattle before she heard the car engine. With a panicky intake of breath, she rose and tiptoed to the window. There in the moonlight she watched the sedan, with the Mounties' emblem on it, turn around and rattle back over the wooden bridge, heading back on patrol.

She smiled. She'd seen him come into the inn, standing at the back of the room and watching her through several songs before he left. Now here he was again. Her heart swelled with the knowledge that he was checking that she was safe. When had she ever felt so valued? Never was the answer, and she wasn't about to give it up.

The aroma of coffee woke her. Hearing her stir, Pam turned from the window and said, "This is a beautiful property. Can we go out, maybe go for a walk in the forest?"

Normally Singer avoided the wilderness around the three acre clearing, clinging to the little circle of civilization where she felt moderately safe. The woods were thick and dangerous, full of deep crevices and the occasional bear that swam over from the big island. One wrong step could change a nice walk into a disaster. And then there was the lake, cold and deep.

"Okay," she said hesitantly. "Okay," she said again. "We'll go up the path to the lake. There's a bit of a track. We have to stick to it or we'll get lost." She pushed away the blanket and sat up. "First I need coffee."

Pam and Singer climbed the slope to the forest through cool, crystal-clear air. Among the tall trees the world was suddenly magical. Streams of light filtered down through the branches, as if conferring a blessing on them.

After a half mile, the woods gave way to the still waters of the lake. "Oh," Pam said. "How beautiful." They stood in silent admiration until the serenity was broken by the screech of an osprey. It swooped down, talons first, and dipped into the surface of the lake. It flew away with a dripping trout wriggling between its feet.

Singer set out two moldy old canvas chairs to overlook the meadow and the mountains beyond. They drank more coffee and breakfasted on soda crackers and the remainder of the dry cheese. There was even orange juice. Had Louis put the juice there? She never bought anything that needed refrigeration, expecting that the electricity would fail or that she may not come back for weeks. Eating unheated greasy food out of cans was another hangover from life on the road. Louis was always the one who produced fresh food to eat in front of the fire. Lately he'd started suggesting that she should consider this a permanent home, stock the shelves and bring in some things that would make it her own. She would have to tell him soon about the letter. But not yet.

Pam said, "You're lucky to have a place like this."

"It is peaceful, but I'm a downtown girl." She studied the snowcapped mountains and frowned. Was it true anymore? "All this nature. In the city I know how to survive but not out here. Here, I feel vulnerable and exposed. It's easier in the city, lots of places to hide."

"Yes, sometimes we want to hide."

They fell into an easy silence, each lost in her own thoughts, until Pam said, "I think Frank killed Celastrina."

"Oh shit." The words burst from Singer without thought.

"He left the island Thursday afternoon. He said he was going to work on a boat on Glenphiddie. He came home for dinner but then he left again. It was very late when he came home, I'm not exactly sure what time."

Singer didn't want to hear this confession, but it was too late to stop it. She stared at the mountain peaks and waited for it to be over.

"I don't know where he was, and that's what's so difficult. He told me to say he was there all night. I have no idea why I agreed."

A breeze swept through the tall grass around them, flowing like wind through fur, as if they sat on the back of a living animal.

Pam crossed her arms and rock forward and back in the wobbly chair while it creaked in protest. "That must seem strange to you, not knowing when my husband came home when it's only the two of us on the island. We don't sleep together anymore. I wander the island at night, until I'm exhausted, and then I slip into one of the cabins to sleep for a few hours. This time of year they're all empty. I like not sleeping in the same place two nights in a row, because he can't find me."

Singer twisted to face Pam. The canvas chair rocked dangerously under her. "You have to tell Sergeant Wilmot that your husband has no alibi."

Pam Haver nodded. "I don't want to protect him anymore." She sighed and swiped back the wisp of hair that had escaped her ragged braid. "Our life together is over but neither of us knows how to end it. I think the only thing we had left in common was Trina, and now she's gone."

"If you'd like to stay here..." Singer raised her shoulders, unable to finish. She didn't know what she was offering or if it was hers to give.

"I have to go back." Pam's voice was full of regret. "I realized that when I woke this morning. There's the chickens and the sheep."

"Well, this place is here if you ever want it." She pointed behind her to the A-frame cabin. The canvas chair wobbled beneath her. "You could move in there for a while if you want, until you can sort yourself out. Really, I wish you would. You could battle the mice for me."

Pam almost smiled. "I'll tell you something happy, shall I?"

"Please."

"Thursday morning, before school, Trina called. She sang to me as soon as I said hello. She sang that Stevie Wonder song. You know, '*I Just Called to Say I Love You*,' and we laughed." Her face was as soft as her words. "I'm glad I have that memory."

Singer turned away.

In the meadow, a doe, with a speckled fawn at her side, stepped out of the woods and raised her head. The doe stared at them for a moment and then walked gracefully to the gnarled plum tree and began foraging on its leaves while the fawn disappeared down into the long grass.

Chapter 14

When Singer and Pam went down into Kilborn, the Saturday market was in full swing. The sidewalks were jammed with pedestrians and buskers. Caribbean music mingled in the air with the perfume of fresh bread and popcorn. A stilt walker crossed the street in front of them. Singer watched him stroll through the shoppers at the edge of the park, seeming to have nothing more on his agenda than to convince the very young that giants still walked the earth.

On the surface the world hadn't changed, but the islanders knew differently. Visitors from off island, who came by ferry each week to shop for pottery and jewelry or to buy fresh produce, probably had no idea of the tragedy that had struck the island. But the islanders did.

As Singer waited for the last bustle of people to cross the road, she asked, "Are you sure you want me to go with you?"

"I don't want him there and there isn't anyone else," Pam replied. It was just a blank statement of fact and not a bid for sympathy.

They eased forward but a horse and buggy pulled out of the park with a load of happy tourists. The top-hatted driver gave her a wave, which Singer returned. They crept along behind the carriage for half a block until they could make the left turn onto Ramsey Street. Three driveways down, she pulled in front of the funeral home. She turned off the engine. Neither woman made a move to leave the car. After some moments of silence Pam said, "It has to be done," and opened the door.

Singer sucked in her lips, bit down on them and followed suit.

The stained glass windows of the sidelights threw lurid colors across the marble floor of the foyer. Ellis Wright, plump and jolly looking, more like a children's clown out of costume than a man who dealt with death, hurried down the dark hall to greet them. He ushered them into a gloomy little office where every surface was dark oak, a place where whispers seemed more natural than normal speech. Singer sat silently in a cold leather chair, her knees together and every muscle of her body clenched, while Pam made arrangements for when the coroner released Trina's body.

"I must tell you, it may be some time before the police return the remains," Ellis Wright said.

"That's fine." Pam leaned forward and signed the authorization paper in front of her. "Sergeant Wilmot already explained that."

Ellis Wright drew the signed paper near to him and placed his hand on top of it. "Well," he said happily, "I think that's everything."

Now that she had done this final thing for her daughter, Pam's strength seemed to seep away. She had to use the arms of the chair to push herself to her feet. Slowly and stiffly she shuffled into the hall toward the glowing red diamonds shining at the entry, a beacon of safety—or of hell. Ellis Wright hurried past them to open the door for their escape, offering condolences and reassurances that neither of them listened to.

They sat in the car for some time before Singer put the key in the ignition. She drove carefully down to the waterfront. There was no place to park, there never was on Saturdays, so she double-parked at the gateway to the marina. "Are you sure you want to go back?"

"No. But at the moment it's all I can think of."

They walked down to the dock to where Pam could get a water taxi to Cooper's Island. While they waited by the slip,

Singer tried one more time to talk her out of going. Pam said, "There's my chickens. He won't look after them."

Singer sighed. "Come any time you want. Bring your chickens." The strangeness of her words overcame her and she had to press her fingers to her lips to stop her giggles.

The taxi swung into the dock beside them. Pam said, "Thank you. I needed a friend." She hugged Singer briefly and then reached out for the hand the waiting boatman offered. She stepped on board and took a seat without looking back.

Going up the long ramp from the dock, Singer saw a picture of Trina tacked up on a piling, positioned to catch the eye of anyone arriving on the island by water. The flyer asked for information about Trina's whereabouts on Friday night. She reached out and laid her palm against the image, glad that Pam hadn't seen it.

On the deck outside of the Driftwood Café, Olivia looked up and said, "Hey," and then she went back to writing. The day before she'd been a creature that growled and scratched, but today her orange hair was covered by a boxy black velvet hat with a pearl brooch on the front. Her dress of cream lace was perfect for a delicate Edwardian lady.

Singer pointed at her outfit and said, "Love what you did with your curtains."

Olivia frowned. "Just for that, you can buy your own coffee."

"Oh, really? Like you were going to jump up and buy me a coffee?"

Olivia went back to her writing.

The fragrance of baking wafted from the screened door of the bakery, awakening a distant memory, remote as a dream, a memory of tree-lined streets and roses. The past washed over her, unexpected and unwelcome. She breathed deeply and pushed the door all the way open and went inside.

Singer watched the server make her latte and sprinkle cinnamon on top of the foam, but her mind was somewhere else. She had to call Wilmot and tell him that Frank Haver had no alibi. She didn't care about causing trouble for Frank, but it felt like a betrayal of Pam's confidence.

Doing the right thing, even deciding what the right thing might be, wasn't easy for her. Normally, she did what was best for her at the moment, but life had suddenly become more complicated. She wanted Wilmot's approval more than she wanted an easy life. She knew if he ever found out later that she'd held back information he'd be disappointed in her. She didn't want that.

Her mind scurried around the dilemma. Surely someone was checking Frank's alibi. Wouldn't they find the lie? Besides, the winery had called that morning, wanting her to fill in for their regular Saturday night performer. And really, she told herself, at the moment Louis would either be sleeping or working. It would be an intrusion either way if she called him right now. It would make him think she was going all clingy and calling him for the smallest excuse. Theirs was a relationship with clearly defined boundaries. No, she wouldn't call him just yet. The other option was to call Duncan. She decided she'd just wait until she saw Wilmot. That would be best. And doing nothing was always her first choice.

She took her coffee back outside and sat beside Olivia, who ignored her and wrote frantically on. Singer watched the comings and goings of people on the street, waiting for her drink to cool. Trina's death seemed to have changed nothing in the town, as if Trina had never been there. But then, weren't she and Olivia sitting here as if it was just another market day?

Olivia picked up her mug, saw the last of the caramel foam settled at the bottom of the mug, and said, "Shit." She set it down, reached for Singer's mug, blew across the foam, and took a sip.

Singer pointed at her mug. "I'll get another, shall I?"

Olivia was already writing.

When Singer returned Olivia looked up and said, "What's happening in your world?"

Singer told her about her guest of the night before. "I wish Pam would come to Glenphiddie."

"You can't make other people happy. No matter how much you care. We're each responsible for our own bliss."

"Bliss, interesting word."

Olivia tilted the cup at Singer. "Live long enough and you learn a few things."

"Yeah, like don't give an idiot a second chance. A mistake you and I have both made and now Pam is doing the same thing." Singer jolted upright.

"What's the matter?"

"Nothing." It wasn't quite true. The thought that nearly brought her to her feet was a sudden fear of what Pam might be capable of. She had been so concerned with Pam's safety she hadn't worried about Frank's. She looked across the harbor to open water. What was happening on Cooper's Island?

She understood only too well the emotions loss generated. It was losing Michael that had started her own slide into hard living, and it was finding out how he had died that had brought her to Glenphiddie Island to execute Johnny Vibes. That's how she thought of it, an execution. If someone else hadn't already killed Johnny, would she have gone through with it? It was a question she had diverse answers to depending on the day.

She was hit by a sudden longing to see Wilmot. "What time is it?"

"Not sure," Olivia said. "Nearly noon, I think."

He'd worked all day and then all night, going off duty at seven that morning, so he'd likely be sleeping. She took a deep breath and told herself to be patient. "What's that?" she asked, pointing at the pages in front of Olivia.

"I think I'm writing again." Olivia ran her hand across the pages, caressing them lovingly. "I stayed up until three this morning, and then got up at eight to write."

Singer smiled. "Five hours sleep, that's not at all like you."

"No." There was wonder in her voice. She reached around behind her for the jean jacket on the back of the chair. Her face beamed with delight. "I think I'm better."

"I didn't know you were sick."

"In a way." Olivia shoved her arms into the coat and shrugged it up onto her shoulders. "Are you staying with Wilmot tonight?"

Singer shook her head. "He's on the night shift."

"Will you go up the mountain?"

"Nope."

"You'll sleep in your car, won't you?"

"Maybe." The truth was, a terrifying drive to a lonely house was harder than camping in her van.

"Come on, this is me, the one you have no secrets from."

"I only stay up there if someone is with me. I hate it up there alone at night."

"Stay with me then. Don't go up the mountain."

Singer tucked her hair behind her ear. "Are you sure?"

"Sure. You bring the wine and the cigarettes."

"Thanks, Olivia. I won't be too late, before midnight. I'm singing at the Vineyard. Helen got an offer in Victoria and left Elaine flat."

"Okay, see you then."

"Wait, aren't you working tonight?"

Olivia tilted her head to the side, considering it. "I think I may be coming down with something."

"The writing plague? Tom is going to freak."

"I can't help that." She patted the pages she cradled against her chest like a baby. "I'm going to ride this wave to the end." Her pixie face screwed into a grimace for a second. "Don't be shocked."

Singer laughed. "Honey, it would take a tango with an orangutan to shock me."

"I want to write about Trina, need to write about her. It's important to me. It's the only time I've felt this way since my first book."

Despite her vow to be unshakeable, Singer was stunned.

Olivia grinned. "Looking at you, I think I've just had that dance."

"You may have taken a little twirl around the floor."

"The story is there, wispy and fleeting. And the voice..." Her face was filled with fierce intensity, an excitement that had never been there before. "It's a great book, and I need to write it."

"Will you use Trina's short story?"

Olivia started to walk away without answering.

Singer grabbed her arm as she went by her chair. "Pam might like to have that story and the police need Trina's diary to help find her killer."

Olivia shook off Singer's hand and asked, "Why are you telling me this?"

"Only you and Peter knew I had it. The answer to who killed Trina may be in that book."

A jumble of emotions scurried across Olivia's face. "Do you think I killed Trina? Killed her for a plot?"

"Michael was killed for a song."

"Well, I didn't murder her." She swung violently away, hesitated and turned back. "She may have been killed by a stranger, in which case that diary would have nothing to do with her death."

"You can't decide that, Olivia." Some uneasy feeling stopped Singer from saying more. She couldn't have defined what it was. She just knew that at that moment, even here in the sunshine, she was suddenly chilled. "Fine," she said. "Do what you want."

Her final words were wasted because Olivia was already hurrying away with her pages clutched to her chest.

Chapter 15

Singer started for Wilmot's apartment, needing to see him, but she saw Hannah Cutter first. Hannah was one of Singer's guitar students. Normally introverted, Hannah came alive when she played, changing into a confident, almost elegant person. Unlike Trina, who told Singer everything about herself, Hannah only shared music with Singer. There was never a word about school, friends or plans. And even though Trina had boarded in the Cutter home, Singer didn't know if the two teenagers had been friends. But they had shared a part of their lives, and surely that had meant something.

She felt a stab of sympathy for the girl trudging along the street with her head down. *Leave it to the parents*, she told herself, even as she was pulling over to the curb. Hannah took no notice of the vehicle stopping beside her.

She leaned across and opened the door. "Hey, Hannah."

Hannah lifted her head. Her ashen pudding face remained blank.

"How are you doing?"

Nearly six feet tall, Hannah hid inside her clothes, a shapeless taupe sweater over a long heavy skirt, presenting a rectangle for a body with no suggestion of what might be underneath. Her long hair was an undistinguished mousy brown, hanging in unwashed strings. Her eyes were pale blue, almost gray. She had beautiful alabaster skin that always flushed pink when she bent over her guitar.

Behind Singer a horn blared. She grinned and tilted her head at the car. "Mainlanders." A red hatchback pulled around the Yukon with another sharp blare of the horn.

Hannah watched the red vehicle until it reached the end of the block and then turned back to stare at Singer.

"Hop in," Singer said and straightened.

Hannah slumped onto the seat, slammed the door shut, and leaned her head against the window.

Singer said, "Let's go for a drive, okay?"

There was no response.

"Want to go out to the Houseboat?"

Wrapped in a blanket of despair, Hannah's response was barely audible. "Guess so."

Singer pointed to the bandage around Hannah's left wrist. "What happened?"

Hannah gave her a sharp glance and then covered the wrapping with the bottom of her sweater. "Sprained it."

"Not a cut? Because if it is a cut, you should have it looked at."

Silence. Hannah's hair formed a barrier between them.

A flash of brightly outfitted bikers charged down the hill and pedaled energetically past them. Singer pulled away from the curb and searched for words of comfort or distraction. She was way out of her depth and worried about saying the wrong thing.

A mile out of town, they passed a low stone wall along the edge of an apple orchard where sheep grazed. She read out loud from the weathered board hanging from a tilting post. "ORCHARD COTTAGE. I'm thinking of naming my house. Stevie might have had a name for it, but no one knows what it was." She glanced at the silent teen. "Got any ideas?"

No answer. "I wanted to call it '*Still Meadows*.' It's always so still and peaceful. You should come up."

Hannah glanced over at her. "Did you ever take Trina to your place?"

"Nope."

Hannah turned away, no longer interested.

The Houseboat, a place of sunlight on water, rented out a few rooms and served breakfast and light lunches. When they pulled into the graveled parking area, a flock of newly sheared sheep ran to the white rail fence to greet them. Singer turned off the engine and watched them jostle each other for a place in front of the Yukon. "They must be cold." Nudged tightly together, as they were now, the sheep would stay warm. Or they could take shelter in an old lean-to, with deep straw for bedding. But still, Singer felt sorry for them.

Singer got out and waited by the fence for Hannah. She was about to get back in the vehicle when Hannah finally joined her and stuck her hands through the fence, reaching out to the sheep. "Did Trina ever come here with you?" Hannah asked.

"No. I never saw her except when we were working on the musical. I didn't really know her that well."

"But you're alike."

Singer gave a small grunt of astonishment at this echo of her own feelings. "Let's get something warm to drink and sit outside in the sun."

After Ron poured their mochas and urged fresh banana bread on them, they sat on the broad porch that ran the length of the dwelling overlooking the ocean. Singer said, "You know what happened to Trina?"

Hannah nodded.

"Who told you?"

Hannah pulled a hank of hair free from the rest of her mop. "Dr. Glasson. And then Corporal Duncan came."

"Tell me about Trina."

Hannah shrugged, twirling the strand of hair. "She was like some kind of a star. Everyone noticed her." She abandoned her hair and began to pick at the quick of her thumb with its nail eaten down to nothing. "Always the center of attention, even for my parents."

"That must have hurt."

Her eyes were fixed on her finger, pulling at the skin and pressing at the blood that sprang up around her nail. "They were always wishing I was more like her. Telling me to try and be like her, but they didn't really know Trina." She lifted her head and gave Singer a strangely calculating look. "I bet you didn't know her either." Secrets were hidden behind that sly expression.

"I'm sorry you feel that your parents might have favored Trina over you."

Another shrug. "Everybody did. They couldn't help it."

"Did your parents know how you felt about Trina getting all the attention?"

Hannah went back to worrying her thumb.

Singer lifted the blue mug. "I'll tell you how I felt about her."

Hannah's pale eyes rose to watch her, cautious and waiting.

"Trina was what I used to be and still would like to be. I was jealous." Seeing the disbelief on Hannah's face she nodded. "It's true. She had a future and talent. And she had sex appeal."

"Yes," Hannah agreed, "Yes, she did have sex appeal, and everyone reacted to it. All the boys wanted her." She lowered her head. Her hair fell around her face like a veil. "Even people who shouldn't have, wanted her."

Who was Hannah talking about? Did Hannah know that Frank Haver lusted for his stepdaughter? Perhaps Hannah's father had as well. Singer wrapped her hands tightly around her mug, needing the warmth. Such a strange day, the heat from the sun disappearing with every passing cloud. "Trina was well aware of how people reacted to her. It wasn't that she tried to draw them in, it was just a part of her, like her skin. That's an intoxicating power to have and it can go to your head. Perhaps she wasn't always wise or nice about it."

"She got off on guys wanting her." Hannah returned to twirling a coil of her hair into a tight ringlet. "The more attention she got the more conceited she became. There was no living with her." She stuck the end of her hair into her mouth.

Singer said, "Being admired is a heady experience."

"Sometimes..." Hannah pulled the piece of hair she was worrying across her face like a mutated moustache and whispered, "Sometimes she made Cody have sex with her."

What she was saying? Had she spied on Cody and Trina? Singer watched the clouds drift overhead, picking out shapes, unsure if she wanted to know, but even before she'd decided she was asking, "She made Cody have sex with her? He didn't want to?"

Hannah pushed her hair behind her ear. "His family is pretty religious. He was supposed to be saving himself for marriage, signed a pledge and everything. Trina laughed at him, teased him, and bullied him into being with her." Her voice was full of anger. "He couldn't help himself. He had to get away from her." Hannah gazed over the trees at the distant mountains. "Well, he's free of her now." She smiled, pleased and satisfied.

"Will you miss her, Hannah?"

"She felt so superior to everyone."

"Did she feel superior to you?"

"Sometimes. And she could be mean. Once she called me an ox when she was showing me a dance step. Other times..." She swallowed hard. "We could laugh and laugh at nothing. She liked to sing while I played. We did that a lot. She'd act all sexy, like she was on a stage."

Singer looked away from Hannah's raw emotion and watched an eagle land on the tallest fir tree across from them. Was he hunting some small creature in the sheep meadow? Hunting and killing, animals and people—it never ended.

"I don't have anyone now, no one to do things with." Hannah's voice was barely a murmur. "That makes me sad. But once in a while... just for a second..." Hannah picked away at a new finger.

When it was clear she wasn't going to continue, Singer sighed and said, "When people die we have all sorts of emotions that worry us. We don't have control over those feelings. They're just there. It will get better. Give it time." She sipped the last of her coffee, but it had grown cold. She pushed it away. "Did you and Trina ever go out on a boat together?"

Hannah shrugged. "Sure, sometimes. Trina loved the ocean. She really liked being on the water and went out every chance she got."

A cloud partially covered the sun, sending a shadow across the small lawn and the three yellow kayaks tipped upside down on the grassy shore. "Did Trina ever talk about her other boyfriends?"

Hannah went back to digging at her nail. "Bragged, more like."

"Did she ever tell you the name of the guy she called the creep?"

Hannah's head came up, wary and surprised. "How'd you know about him?"

"Trina mentioned him once, said the creep followed her home. Who was he?"

Hannah dismissed the question with a lift of her shoulder. Singer persisted. "She never told you?"

"Can't remember."

She was lying. "It could be important, Hannah."

"Why?"

"Don't you want the police to find her killer?"

"It won't bring her back, will it?"

"No, but it will help the people who are still living. Imagine her mother never knowing." Knowing anything about the stalker might put Hannah at risk. "Secrets are dangerous and they won't help Trina. If you know who was following her, know anything that might point out her killer, you have to tell Sergeant Wilmot." She didn't want to scare Hannah, but neither did she want her to keep this secret. "If you know anything, you have to tell."

Hannah looked directly at Singer. "Sometimes she told me things."

"Like what?"

A sly sideways look. "About Cody, about other men. She liked sex, a lot."

"Were there many? Men, I mean."

"In her mind, every guy wanted her. She'd tell me how they'd look at her. She liked doing that, got off on bragging, thought it made me envious." She tilted her head to the right, considering what she'd just said. "But she wasn't just bragging. It was true. It was like she had some kind of power over them."

"So how many men were there?"

Hannah frowned. "Mostly Trina wanted Cody."

"Why?"

Hannah's eyes opened wide in astonishment. "Have you seen him? He's so handsome. And he's nice. Most of the boys aren't, but Cody is."

"Maybe now..." Singer left the thought unfinished. Even with Trina gone, Cody was out of Hannah's reach. No use holding out false hope, but she couldn't help adding, "Cody is free now."

Hannah lowered her head and let her hair fall forward, obscuring her face. "She didn't have to die for it to end with Cody."

"You think it was over?"

"He's going to be a fisherman like his father. Trina would hate being married to a fisherman and living on Glenphiddie."

"No," she agreed, "Trina wouldn't want that. She had bigger dreams."

"She was going away. She wanted to see the world and do great things."

"Do you have dreams like that, Hannah, or do you want to marry and stay on the island?"

"I want to be myself. It's all I want, doesn't matter where I am."

The words were spoken with an intense passion that Singer didn't understand.

"Trina was going away when school ended. She wanted to take Cody with her, not for keeps, you know, just to have fun for a while, just for the summer. She didn't want to be alone. I would have gone with her, but she didn't ask me." Hannah's lips hardened into a bloodless line. "Vancouver would be bad for him. He needs to stay here, but Trina didn't care about Cody enough to see that."

"But you did. Did you tell Trina she should go without Cody?"

"She was selfish." Angry now, her fist pounded the table and her voice grew louder. "She didn't care about anyone else, didn't care about what was best for Cody or what I wanted, a selfish bitch."

Singer stood up. "Why don't you go see the sheep? I have a call to make and then I'll take you home."

Hannah glared at her, almost as if she wanted to strike out at Singer, but then she rose resignedly from the iron bistro chair, shoving it carelessly aside before walking heavily down the porch.

Singer sighed in relief and sorted through the violent emotions that emanated from Hannah. Then she picked up the mugs and went inside to borrow Ron's phone.

She didn't waste time apologizing for waking Wilmot. "If Cody threw Trina out, wouldn't she go back to the Cutter's?"

"It seems likely, but their daughter says Trina didn't come back there."

"Have you talked to the parents?"

"They're in Victoria until today."

"I know, that fishing thing. Hannah told me. This morning's ferry was already full when they went to catch it so Hannah is going through this on her own. She doesn't have anyone else on the island, at least anyone she wants to spend time with. People were calling and coming by, so she's been out walking to get away from them. When I first saw her, well, I thought she was sick, really sick. She's a strange girl, Louis."

"And?"

She opened the door a little but Hannah still leaned up against the fence, staring at the sheep. "Have you met Hannah?"

"Duncan interviewed her."

"Hannah is big and strong, strong enough to overpower Trina if she took her by surprise."

"What are you saying?"

She sighed. "I don't know, except someone must have a lot of hate and anger to do that to Trina. If Trina went back to the Cutter's after being with Cody, that's what she may have faced.

And there's another thing I have to tell you. Frank Haver hasn't got an alibi after about seven Thursday night. Pam doesn't know where he was."

He groaned loudly. "God, why do I bother? I could just lie here in bed and wait for you to figure out who murdered Trina."

She looked out the door again and saw Hannah turn her head to look back at the house, then she pushed away from the fence. "Gotta go," she said and hung up with no goodbye.

When she pulled up in front of the Cutter home to drop Hannah off there was still no vehicle in the driveway. Should she leave the girl there alone? "Do you want me to stay until your parents come home?"

"Why would I want you to do that?"

Why indeed? "I just thought...is there someone else I could call for you?"

Hannah smiled but it didn't warm her face. "No matter how nice you are to me, I'm not going to fall apart and tell you anything." She jumped out of the Yukon, slammed the door and walked away without a backward glance.

"Nice to know you do have things to tell." She watched Hannah's lumbering figure plod to the front steps. When Hannah was safely inside, she backed out onto the street.

Was Hannah a second victim of this crime, a young woman just beginning her life whose future would be forever marred by this event? Or was she a killer? Either way, one thing Singer knew, Hannah was suffering.

Chapter 16

Singer planned on running a few errands before she headed for the vineyard, but Hannah was impossible to get out of her thoughts. Victim or perpetrator, the argument raged in her head. But one thing stood out. It was a bad time for Hannah to be alone. The bandaged wrist worried her. A sprain or an attempted suicide? Strange that she would sprain her wrist the night Trina died. She sat the red basket of personal products on the floor and left the drugstore.

Back at the Cutter home, she parked on the street and studied the house. No car in the driveway but it might be in the garage. Her plan was to make sure Hannah was still there and still all right.

Ward Cutter opened the door about a foot and jammed his body into the opening. Unusually tall, he was broad shouldered and fit, a mountain of a man who would intimidate anyone. He owned the local fish store, and several fishing boats, and was a political force on the island, a man accustomed to getting his own way. "We don't have time for visitors today."

Singer raised a placating hand. "I understand. I saw Hannah earlier. I just wanted to check that you were home and she was okay."

From behind him a voice said, "Let her in, Ward." Diane Cutter slid past her frowning husband and opened the door wide. "Hi, Singer." Unlike her husband and daughter, Diane was petite, barely over five foot. They had first met when Singer came to the house to give Hannah guitar lessons. "Thank you for taking care of Hannah." Diane reached out with two fingers and shoved her husband back into the hall. "Come in."

Singer stepped into a foyer crammed with rain gear and a jumble of shoes, uncertain of what to say or do now that she was inside. Diane swung away, saying over her shoulder, "Come to the kitchen."

Ward Cutter backed into the arch of the cluttered living room, scowling at Singer. She gave him a brief nod and followed Diane down the dark hall to the kitchen at the back of the house. Large and sunny, and decades out of date, it was clearly the center of their home. On the counter, along with a jumble of household clutter, were three plates of cookies and a cake under a clear plastic cover.

Diane followed her glance. "People have been bringing food like it was our child who died."

Singer pulled out a chair and sat down. "It's not just her death. It's the way it happened. Bringing food is all they can do."

Diane sank onto a chair across from her. "In a way it's true. Trina's been here since September, a part of the family." Her red rimmed eyes welled with tears. She choked out, "She was like our daughter." Her face wrinkled up in distress and she swallowed several times before she could go on. "We made too much of Trina. Poor Hannah had to take second place because Trina's personality just demanded attention. You couldn't ignore her. She was always full of life and excited just to get up in the morning. Hannah, well, she's more difficult, surly and never telling us anything. Trina you couldn't stop from talking. Even things you might not want to hear." She laughed and then her hand went to her mouth to block out the sound.

"I know," Singer said. "That's what's so hard to grasp. All that energy..."

Diane hugged herself. "I feel so bad that Hannah was here alone all Friday night. It seemed safe and Grant Glasson said he'd keep an eye on her."

"Dr. Glasson?"

"Yes. He lives right next to us. He was awfully good to the girls." Her mind was elsewhere. "There's going to be a memorial at the high school. The principal came and talked to Hannah. That made it worse. And then the police came and went through Trina's room. I have no idea what they wanted. We weren't here, but Hannah..." She swallowed. "That Corporal Duncan, well, she came back and interviewed us as soon as we got in, before we'd even had a chance to talk to Hannah. She seemed to be accusing all of us of something, but mainly Hannah. Hannah was in trouble in public school. She was being bullied. She hit a girl. It was pretty serious. Duncan knew about that and she asked if Hannah was ever violent with Trina."

"I don't think you should read too much into it. They'll question everyone."

From overhead came the sound of a guitar.

Diane massaged her forehead. "Oh, god, how can she be playing that thing now?"

"Maybe she needs to."

"If the police came in now, they'd think she had no feelings at all."

"Well, they'd be wrong. And they aren't going to come."

Diane gave a snort of amusement and said, "Not with Ward on the door. He won't let anyone in." The smile left her face. "I've never seen him so angry. Not sad yet, just angry. He's ready to kill someone. I hope he's never alone with the person who did this."

"Does he have anyone in mind?" Singer reached out for the sugar bowl with its hard crusty lumps and turned it around and around while she waited for Diane to answer.

It took some time. At last she nodded and then said, so faintly that Singer could barely hear, "He thinks Hannah had something to do with Trina's death." Her eyes were wide in disbelief. "How can he think that of his own daughter?"

Chapter 17

Singer was about to step into the Yukon when a hand slid past her, barring her way. She turned to face Peter Kuchert. He smiled and said, "Hey, Singer, I'm glad I bumped into you. I'm doing an article on Trina Strickner for next week's paper. Can you spare me a few minutes?"

"Not really." There was no way she wanted to be quoted in the paper. "I'm in a hurry."

"It won't take long," he coaxed. "Let me buy you a coffee."

"No." It came out sharp and too strong, but the days when her time could be purchased for the price of a drink were long gone. She tried to soften her words. "Sorry, Peter, but I've had my fill of coffee for one day, and I really have to go. I've errands to run and then I'm working at the vineyard."

"Sure, I understand." His smile was disarming. "How about later?"

"I'll call," she said and slid behind the wheel, eager to get away.

He placed his body in the opening to prevent her from closing the door. "Better still, I'll meet you at the vineyard."

She gave a quick smile that promised nothing and said, "See you," as she turned the key.

The vineyard, on the southern slope of Mount Skeena, overlooked Seaward Landing, where the flotilla of sailboats waited for the morning and the final run into Kilborn Harbor for the end of the Island Cup race. The late afternoon sun streamed down on the scene below. There was no evil out there, just gently bobbing little vessels on a tranquil sea.

Tables sat at the upper edge of acres of grapevines running down the hill to the road and the ocean beyond. Huge rose bushes grew at the beginning of each row, their oranges, yellows and reds echoing the evening sky and filling the soft air with their scent.

All the tables were filled, tips were good, and the music was coming easily. The western sun, ragged with blood in its dying, had almost set when she began an old Beatles song that Trina had loved. Sadness opened a well of emotion that flowed into her music. Her eyes filled and she raised her head to blink away the tears. At the edge of the diners a middle-aged man stared at her. The grief on his face gripped her and she lost her place in the song. She had to resort to humming along until she found the chorus again.

She'd seen him before. She came to the end of the song and paused to sip some water, while she tried to place him. Dr. Glasson, that was his name, he'd treated her bronchitis. In his late forties, he had thinning hair combed straight back from a long lean face that was rather like a Bassett hound. That face was now swamped with heartbreak. How had Trina described the man she called her sad friend, the older man she'd had a sexual relationship with? The man turned away. His shoulders were rounded as if they carried more weight than they could bear. She watched him walk to the small cottage opposite the sales and wine-tasting shop.

It was some time before she saw the solitary man walk slowly back down the path through the apple trees and out to an ancient Audi parked in front of a shed.

As the man reached his car, another car pulled in beside him. She recognized Peter's battered sedan. She picked up the tip jar and emptied it into the bottom of her bag and then darted into the storage barn. Huge barrels lined one side of the central passage while racked bottles of wine filled the opposite. A sliding door was open at each end of the building. A long trestle table in the middle was lined with bottles.

"Going so soon?" Elaine pulled the cork on the bottle of red wine in her hand. Three more, that she had already opened, stood waiting.

"Someone I don't want to see."

"Aah, want me to run interference?"

"No, I'll just go out the back and it'll all be good."

"Fine," Elaine said. "See you next Sunday."

Night was coming on quickly as Singer followed the lights of the doctor's car along the coastal highway that climbed halfway up Mount Skeena, skirting the edge of the Salish Sea, before it dipped down the north side of the mountain on the way back to Kilborn. At the high point of the road Singer saw the brake lights come on. The car made an abrupt right turn and then the lights of the Audi went out. The car had gone off the mountain.

She hit the brakes and sucked in air, staring at the spot where the lights had disappeared. There was no crash. Nothing. Maybe the mountain had muffled the sound. And then a glimmer of light appeared, but only for the second it would take for him to leave the car.

She took her foot off the brake and let the Yukon roll forward. She saw the widening in the road, a lookout. She'd forgotten about that. She steered into the tiny parking space behind the Audi. Her lights shone into the empty interior. She felt a bit foolish. Why was it any of her business if he stopped at this isolated piece of the mountain? Beyond the Audi she saw a figure silhouetted against the sky, a man standing at the edge of the void. Perhaps he wanted to watch the lights of the town go out down below. *Sure, and I want to learn to levitate*, she thought. It was the utter sadness of the man that convinced her that the doctor was in trouble. She turned off the engine and got out of the Yukon. She walked around the car. "Good evening," she said. He didn't acknowledge her presence in any way, just stared out into the dark void.

She moved closer. Her foot slid on loose gravel over rock. She went down on her ass. A stone, dislodged by her foot, continued to tumble along the sloping rocks in front of her, gathering speed and debris before it spun off into space. She sat there in startled terror until she heard the mini landslide hit the rock face far below and then she scuttled backward away from the precipice. When she bumped into a boulder, she turned to it, wrapping her arms around it, holding on as if she might slip away like the pebbles. "Shit."

"Are you all right ?"

She didn't answer until her breathing calmed, and she decided she wasn't going to slide over the verge. Then she said, "Dr. Glasson?"

She pushed herself upright, keeping a hand on the boulder. It felt solid and permanent. Was it? Best not to think of that. Instead, sliding around behind it, she asked, "What are you doing?"

"I thought that would be obvious. I'm enjoying the view."

"What if you don't die?"

"What?"

"I fell off the mountain once and I didn't die." She stretched out her neck, trying to see over the edge. "What if you just break your back and lie there? You could be paralyzed for life and unable to do anything about it."

"If you're trying to talk me out of jumping, you aren't doing a very good job."

"It's all the same to me whether you live or die, but there has to be a better way. This scares me shitless." Singer leaned forward far enough to see the sparkling lights of Kilborn below, but she didn't leave the safety of the boulder. "God that's scary." She moved further back and settled down on an outcropping of rock. "What's with this island? Not even a bloody barrier."

"Go home and leave me in peace if you're so afraid."

Singer made one of those wild leaps of logic that had kept her alive on the streets. "You were Trina's sad friend, weren't you?"

A sharp intake of breath. "She told you?"

"No, I read her journal. Oh, don't worry. She didn't mention you by name, so you're perfectly safe."

"Except from you." He turned on the ledge to face her.

Now she remembered Diane saying he lived next to the Cutters. She reached down and picked up a large rock. Clouds drifted across the moon. She could barely make out his outline against the sky. "I'm no threat to you."

Minutes of silence passed before she said, "I know your wife died just before Christmas."

He turned away and eased closer to the drop. "And I know you're the songstress." His head swiveled to look at her, but he stayed where he was. "She liked your voice. We listened to you at the Ferryman last summer, dined there whenever you sang, even when she was too sick to eat."

"You must miss her a lot."

A derisive snort, and he raised his hands to heaven. "You see? There are no secrets in this place."

"You were called out to see Trina's body when they found it, weren't you?"

"Yes." The word was so faint she could barely hear it.

"You knew it was Trina."

Dr. Glasson inched forward.

"You knew it was Trina Strickner and yet you said nothing. Why was that? You could have said you recognized her body without incriminating yourself. But then, maybe a butterfly on a patient might not be noticed by every doctor." She was talking only to delay him, not because she thought it would help. "You could have made up a story about it, could have said Trina was proud of it and pointed it out to you. That wouldn't have raised an eyebrow."

"I'm a coward. That's why I said nothing. Her face was battered to a pulp and crabs had eaten it, gulls had pecked at her flesh, and still I did nothing." He lowered his face into his hands.

"You were sensible, unlike now. Besides, it wouldn't have done Trina any good."

"I denied her by not identifying her."

She shrugged. "I would have done the same if I was the one sexually involved with her. But what good is killing yourself? You did what you did, and now it's over. We have to live with our choices—good and bad. Guilt is a stupid thing."

"How? How do I live with what I did to her?"

A brief spurt of anger made her growl, "What makes you think you're the only one who carries around hurt and regrets?" She tossed the rock into the bushes.

"I don't want to carry mine anymore."

"You should stay alive and punish yourself properly. If we all jumped off a cliff out of shame and remorse the ground would be littered with bodies. There'd be no one left to bury us."

He gave a bark of laughter.

"Trina wanted to help you. Isn't that strange? She thought sex with her would make you feel better, but it made you feel worse, didn't it?"

He mumbled, "She was too young to understand that. It wasn't her fault. None of it was her fault."

"Did you kill her?"

"God, no."

"Then why kill yourself?"

"It will all come out, all the sordid details, and I'll lose my license."

"Not necessarily, and if it does, well, you can kill yourself then."

"Death has become preferable to life."

"Tough shit!"

And now he laughed with genuine amusement. "You really aren't very good at this, at saving people."

"Well, I can't say I've had a lot of practice." She dug her cigarettes out of her skirt pocket. "But it seems I'm all you've got."

"You shouldn't smoke. Those things will kill you," he said as her lighter flashed.

She blew out a stream of smoke. "Says the man on the edge of a cliff."

"Good point. Don't listen to me. No one should."

"What were you doing at the winery?"

He rubbed his forehead before saying, "Dylan came back from the hospital in Victoria today. I wanted to check on how he was doing."

She didn't ask who Dylan was, just nodded into the dark and waited. When he remained silent she said, "You stayed a long time."

"He was worried. It took a while to reassure him." They both became lost in their own thoughts. Finally, he said, "It's the guilt that's impossible to live with."

"We all have to live with that, for big things and small." Now that his death seemed less immediate, she began to feel the results of her fall. She rubbed at her hip. "I ended up in this bucolic hell because I came here to kill a man. Mind you, I don't think I'd have felt much guilt if I'd managed it. He deserved to die." She reached down and dabbed at a scrape on her ankle with her sleeve. How had she got that? She straightened. "It's the people I've hurt without meaning to that's the most difficult to live with."

"Well, I'd rather not live with my regrets. Besides, that corporal, Corporal Duncan, she asked if I'd seen Trina Thursday night. She looked right at me. She knows something. She was accusing me and watching to see how I reacted."

"No, she wasn't." She inhaled smoke deep into her lungs and then added, "That's one thing I'm sure of. Duncan just comes across as suspicious and accusatory. She always seems about to charge me with something—breathing, mainly. Trust me, if she had an inkling of your involvement with Trina you wouldn't be standing here, that bitch would have you behind bars."

"It doesn't matter. If it's today or tomorrow, it will come out."

"I don't see how."

"Charlie Como, from the club, saw my Zodiac on Thursday night. He was out on his boat late, getting ready for the race this morning when he saw it go by on the way to Ghost Island. You can't miss my Zodiac. It's covered in flags."

"Were you in the boat?"

"No, I was on call at the hospital. Remember, there was that accident."

"That's right. I heard the copter pick someone up late that night."

"The driver. I thought he was stable but he took a turn for the worse."

"So you have an alibi."

"Yes. It was a busy night. Toward morning there was a stroke in the Continuing Care wing."

"Wilmot will check on your alibi to see if you were in your boat and will find out you were at the hospital all night. You haven't any reason to be concerned. Trina, or the person who killed her, stole the boat."

He swung quickly to face her. "You don't understand. It isn't just being charged with Trina's death that bothers me. It's what I did. I took advantage of her."

She fluttered her hand at him. "Could you step back from the brink a little? It makes me nervous, and I can't think. Heights give me vertigo and frankly this is closer than I like to be to the edge of anything."

"You think you can save me, reach out and grab me?"

"Hell no," she protested. "Not me. If you jump, or fall, you are on your own."

"Just out of curiosity," Dr. Glasson asked, "What will you do if I jump?"

"Go to bed and catch up on some sleep."

"You won't report it?"

"Why in hell would I do that? Trouble I don't need. I've spent my life running from it." She sucked in more smoke. "You go off that rock, I was never here. You go home, I don't know you." The end of the cigarette burned her fingers. She rubbed the butt out on a rock. "This has nothing to do with me."

With a small gurgle of mirth, he eased back and sat down on a rock projection. "God, my legs are all cramping," he said, rubbing his calves.

"Tell me about Trina."

He sighed and arched his back. "What do you want to know?"

"How did your involvement with her begin?"

"Trina lived next to me, at the Cutters. I have a sailboat called the *Wind Catcher*. Trina was always at the yacht club, just hanging around. She loved the water. One day I was getting ready to go out for a sail and she asked if she could go. Like a fool I let her. After that every time I took the boat out, she was there. I enjoyed her company and she enjoyed the water. You can guess what happened next, only the once, but it was enough."

"Did she mention any other men in her life?"

"My god, she was only a kid."

"She was nearly done school. And you weren't the first guy she had sex with."

He waved her words away. "It doesn't matter. I broke all the rules. I was the responsible adult. I should have prevented it."

"Well, yes, that's true. But Trina didn't take sex too seriously. I understand that. Back in the sixties we thought we invented sex. Remember, *make love and not war*?" She chuckled, a deep throaty sound in the night. "Make love not war, I took that as my motto and damn near saved the world. Truth is, I was in love with being desired. Trina wasn't any different than I was back then. I could have ended up dead in a ditch, just as my mother predicted, hitchhiking around the country and taking rides with strangers. It might have been me murdered if I'd met the wrong person. It was just a matter of luck. I had good luck, Trina had bad luck."

"Is it as simple as that?"

"Pretty much. No matter how careful we are, shit happens." She shifted her weight on the hard surface. Her hip screamed in protest. "Did she mention anyone else she was involved with?"

"No."

"I know it was a very violent attack. That seems to say there was passion behind it, so not a stranger."

He rubbed his forehead. "He destroyed her face. No one could identify her from what was left."

"Why do you say he?"

"You think a woman would do that?"

"In a brutal rage? Yes. It would explain why her face was destroyed." The image of a pale pudding face slid into her mind. She pushed it down and rose from the stone. "It's late." She took a few steps. Her right side had stiffened, and her ankle would barely bend. She leaned on an arbutus tree and made a few circles with her foot and then gingerly limped toward her car.

"Where are you going?" The doctor's voice was filled with surprise and more than a little indignation.

She kept on walking and didn't look back. "Like I said before, I'm going for a good night's sleep."

"Of all the good Samaritans in the world, I got the one who needs to sleep."

She stopped and looked back at the doctor. "Kill yourself or don't, it's your decision. I'm not taking responsibility for it either way. I have enough trouble saving myself."

"Sensible," he said and then waved her to him and added, "Don't go. Come back and talk to me."

It took her a minute to decide and then she limped back to the boulder, pulled out her cigarettes, prepared to listen some more.

Chapter 18

Wilmot should have gone off duty at seven on Saturday morning. Instead, he'd worked through the day with only a two-hour nap in the staff room. Besides the regular duties for the day shift, he'd sketched out tasks for the officers that related to the investigation. Now, with his night shift about to start, he was having trouble concentrating. His hands were shaking from the coffee he'd been drinking all day. He laid the fluttering paper on the desktop. There was a stack of pages like this, tips from islanders. He was trying to discover if there were any new possible avenues of inquiry that needed immediate attention. The volunteers had written down all the information, even from calls that had nothing to do with Trina's death. Some were just a way for islanders to settle scores or to vent. One of the tipsters mentioned Singer and said, "Watch her."

Wilmot smiled and said, "I am." He dropped the paper in the trash can and went on to the next, a man ranting on about how this death was going to hurt tourism. The Mounties better get the lead out and find the killer before the tourists stopped coming to the island.

"My number one concern, sir, is tourism and not the victim," Wilmot said, and added that one to the trash. There was a man who felt sure the murder was committed by an American, "because you know how they are. It happens all the time down there." There were several vague reports about strangers. Three callers had seen a Zodiac going out to Ghost Island but none of them could identify the occupants. When he got to the man advocating ethanol from kelp, Wilmot gave up and left the rest for Duncan. He got up and poured himself another coffee before he started rereading the witness statements, looking for any inconsistency, the one small thing that shouldn't be there or didn't agree with what others had said.

Thoms stuck his head in. "There's a woman here to see you."

Wilmot smiled as he got to his feet and went to meet the woman he thought was Singer. The woman waiting for him at reception was in her early fifties. He identified the family resemblance even before she held out her hand and said, "I'm Nora Frieberg, Cody's aunt."

When Wilmot showed Nora Frieberg out, Duncan followed him back to his office. She closed the door behind her and said, "We have to talk." She slumped onto the chair by Wilmot's desk. The dark circles under her eyes, and skin that had lost its normal bloom, spoke of the toll the investigation was having on her. Wilmot figured he was probably showing the same signs of strain.

Duncan said, "I think we need help with this."

He closed the file in front of him and added it to the wire basket on his left. "Not yet."

"You leave it any longer and there will be nothing left to turn over. All the leads will be cold and the suspects will be gone."

"I know. I had a call this morning, one of those 'just checking in to see how it's going' calls that really mean, when do you want us? I'm just not ready to give up yet."

Duncan thought about it for a second and then gave a nod of agreement. "Okay, but I just want to remind you that this is your call. When it all goes in the toilet, I'll claim not calling in Major Crimes was all your idea and since you're the superior officer, I had to go along with you."

"You really want me to call them in?"

She hesitated, thinking about his question and then she said, "Nope, but neither do I want to go down with you."

"Well, thanks for being a team player."

"You're welcome." Duncan pushed herself to her feet and, like a dog shedding water, shook herself. She squared the chair with the desk and said, "So what's next?"

It was close to midnight and Wilmot had already dealt with a domestic and two minor accidents. He called Singer on Mount Skeena and listened to the ringing. "Pick up," he said, but the ringing went on. The answering machine cut in. "Just me. I'll call later," he said, telling himself there was no reason for alarm. But he couldn't shake his need to know she was safe.

And there was something else eating away at him, the missing journal. Was it the killer who had taken it? The thought of a murderer being that close to Singer sent a shiver of horror down his spine. Was she in danger because she'd read Trina's diary? She said she hadn't read anything that identified the murderer, but would Singer know she had an important piece of evidence? She may have read something that would identify the killer without attaching any importance to it.

His anxiety grew with each passing hour. Why didn't he know where she was? This was ridiculous. He told himself reassuring things he couldn't quite believe. As the night wore on he became more and more convinced that she was in danger. He started searching in earnest, telling himself that his burning need to find her was no more than his concern for any citizen under his care.

He drove slowly through town, pausing to examine every deep shadow. Everything was long closed and even if she had a gig she'd have left for home by now. Lots of tourists were in town. Maybe she'd been invited onto one of the boats for a party. He checked out the harbor but it was quiet. As he pulled out of the marina parking, he saw someone on the sidewalk, walking toward him. He rolled down his window and yelled, "Singer." The figure on the sidewalk walked on. He rolled up the window against the damp night air and drove the length of the main street again, turned around at the bakery, and drove back.

No town he'd ever patrolled was as dark as this one. Without street lighting or neon, the only illumination came from the faint glow of lights left burning in the stores. There wasn't even a single stop light. He coasted through parking lots and walked the boardwalk along the waterfront. The only person he met was a dog walker off a boat.

He was searching the alley behind the Ferryman when a call came about a party getting out of hand. A fight had already broken out and the homeowners wanted help immediately. He turned on the siren. She wouldn't be there, but he couldn't beat down hope.

The party goers were shocked at the anger of a normally easygoing Sergeant Wilmot. He'd barely stepped into the living room, had only glanced around, before he was threatening everyone in sight with arrest.

"It's okay, man," Dave Wilson said, getting between Wilmot and an inebriated man who cursed him. "I'll take him home," Dave said. He put his hands on Wilmot's chest. "Relax. I got it." Dave, the owner of the local liquor store and the host of the party, was regretting calling the Mounties.

Wilmot stepped back. "I'll be back in half hour. I want this all shut down." Heads nodded and someone shut the music off. "Anyone still here when I get back will be arrested."

Empty glasses were gathered up and purses found before the lights of the cruiser swung onto the road.

Wilmot started up Mount Skeena, still searching for Singer.

It was a full moon. The dark house stood in the field of silver grass. His headlights swept the length of the log building. Nothing moved. There was no sign of a vehicle. He left the engine running and the lights on to guide his path to the porch.

He pounded on the door. There was no answer. He tried the doorknob, but it was locked. A sliver of unease. Despite his nagging, Singer generally left it unlocked. He reached up and felt along the sill for the key and unlocked the door. "It's me, Louis." He stepped inside. "Singer?" Silence. He went further into the room, half expecting to be attacked. She wasn't the passive type and he was ready with a joke for when she swung at him. There wasn't a sound. "Singer." He switched on the light.

Downstairs the living room was empty and looked just the way it always did. He searched the kitchen, the den and the powder room. There was no sign of a disturbance or any sign that she'd been there. He called out again. Nothing and no one answered so he climbed the stairs calling her name. In the main bedroom the closet was open. It was still full of her clothes. If she'd left the island she would have taken her clothes. Was there anything missing? He didn't know. He closed the sliding closet door.

Neither of the other two bedrooms were furnished so it took no more than a brief glance to know she wasn't there. He stood at the railing of the walkway and looked down at the living room. At last he acknowledged another dread that was driving him. A new and unfamiliar emotion was working on Wilmot. He'd never worried before about where she spent her nights, assumed she'd been here. Now the fear she might be with someone else wounded more than his pride. "Idiot," he said and stomped down the stairs.

He slowed when he drove past the party house. It was quiet, the drive empty of cars. No use stopping. Besides, central dispatch was calling him to a break-in at the liquor store in Kilborn.

Dave Wilson stood glaring at the broken window.

"Think the party I broke up moved somewhere else, Dave?"

"If I knew, I'd go with you and this time I wouldn't stop you from taking them apart."

"Anything on the cameras?"

"They took those too."

"You need one where no one can see it."

"Or better policing," Dave snapped. And then he added, "Sorry, long night."

"For both of us." It was a familiar complaint. "Let's get this done," Wilmot said and grabbed the plywood panel Dave had brought with him. He held it over the window while Dave nailed it in place.

When Dave pulled out of the parking lot Wilmot sat in the squad car and tried not to think where Singer might be. A call came to go to the hospital emergency ward where an abusive drunk had shown up with a bad cut on his hand.

Howie Bell had passed out by the time Wilmot arrived at the hospital. "He said he cut it on the liquor store window," Dave's sister, the emergency room nurse, told Wilmot. "Swore the place down and threatened us when we took away his bottle of vodka." She grinned. "Just another fun Saturday night on the island."

There would be time enough to charge Howie for breaking into the liquor store in the morning. Dave would probably just make him fix the window and that would be the end of it, except everyone would know about his drunken escapade and for the rest of his life they'd remind him of it. No getting away from your sins here.

The sun was rising and Wilmot was hunting for Singer again. Checking out the parking lots in town one more time, he found her Yukon behind the health food store. He rattled the front and back doors and then pressed his face up against the unlit glass even though he was willing to bet that she'd never been in a health food store in her life. So why was her vehicle here? And where was Singer?

He shone his flashlight around the lot. It told him nothing. He checked under the bushes to one side, holding his breath until he was sure they didn't hide a body. He worked his way along the back of the row of buildings, searching the area inch by careful inch. There was no sign of her. Relief mixed with more concern. He returned to the Yukon. What had brought her here? He could hardly stop himself from yelling her name at the top of his lungs.

"Shit." He yanked open his cruiser door and slammed it behind him. "Shit, shit, shit." He slammed his fist on the steering wheel. "Where are you?" The only thing he could think of was to go to his apartment and see if she'd left a message on his answering machine. He yanked the transmission into drive.

Chapter 19

It was after one when Singer arrived back in Kilborn and found Olivia sitting on the steps leading to her apartment above the organic food store. Light spilled out from the kitchen behind her, turning her into a dark silhouette at the center of the brightness.

"I think I got fired," Olivia said.

Singer held up a bottle. "I brought the wine."

"Perfect." Olivia picked up the ashtray and the pack of cigarettes beside her. "Welcome home."

Singer pulled herself tiredly up the stairs and went past Olivia, standing by the open door. Barely inside the apartment, she stopped in awe.

Chaos was a kind word for what she saw. The room looked like a household in the process of moving after the best bits had been taken away, with piles left here and there, waiting for the homeowner to decide whether it needed to be sorted through or just sent to the dump. Art projects, worked on and then abandoned, occupied every surface. Garments still pinned together, along with outfits looking complete, hung from curtain rods and the ledges of doors. Paintings in violent colors covered the walls and leaned against the baseboards. Overflowing ashtrays and unwashed dishes littered the furniture. The stale air smelled of cooking and dust, with an undertone of flowery perfume.

Singer turned in a tight circle, taking it all in. "Impressive." Singer had never obsessed about tidiness but this went way beyond even what her laisse faire attitude could accept. "Did they get the guy who set off the bomb in here?"

Olivia pushed the door closed with her hip. "Watch it. I'm the sensitive type." She took the bottle of wine out of

Singer's hand. "I know it isn't much, but it will be better than sleeping in a car."

"Oh, don't get me wrong, I like it, like the... organic feeling. Very homey." She pointed to a desk shoved under the high window. "Is that where you write?"

Olivia followed her to the desk. As she ground a corkscrew into the bottle of wine, something she saw on the desk made her yelp in shock. "Oh, no, someone's been messing with my stuff." The bottle of wine plonked down on the desk.

"How can you tell?"

"This, for one thing." She reached out for a file folder in the middle of the desk. She tidied the material inside and set the folder delicately down, squaring it to the edge of the table. "Someone has been looking inside this folder at my notes for my new novel." Her voice trembled.

"Ahhh... You think they broke in to steal your ideas?"

Olivia picked up a pencil off the floor and laid it reverently next to the file. She studied it for a second and then adjusted it. She gazed up at Singer. "Maybe. Someone's been in here."

"When do you think it could have happened?"

She tilted her head to the side, considering Singer's question. "I've been here, working at the kitchen table, since I saw you this morning so they either broke in when I was at work yesterday or this morning when I was having coffee with you."

"Let me get this straight." Singer picked up the bottle of wine and finished opening it. "You've been here all day. You didn't go to work?"

"Well, for a couple of hours. But it wasn't busy so I left."

"Was it Tom's idea for you to leave or did you just do it?"

"I couldn't waste time behind a bar. I needed to write."

"Of course. Did Tom call after you left?"

Olivia nodded. "He fired me."

"Fancy that. And now the papers are disturbed? Is that it? Is that why you think someone has been in here, because the pages don't line up?"

Olivia looked around. "There might be more things."

Singer pointed at the manual typewriter on the table. "Did they take your computer?"

"No computer. Computers stifle creativity and make writing too clinical and detached."

Singer nodded as if she actually understood what the hell the crazy woman was talking about.

Olivia wrung her hands. "Should I call someone, report it?"

"Why don't you see if anything is really missing first?"

"Okay." She sounded as uncertain as she looked. "Okay." She gamely headed down the hall but stopped at the first door, looking back beseechingly at Singer. "What if he's still in there?" she whispered, jabbing a finger at the wood panel.

Singer coughed to cover her laughter and said, "Shall I come with you?"

Olivia smiled broadly. "Yes, please." She waited until Singer was at her side and then, with a brief nod of determination, she pushed the bathroom door open with her fingertips.

When they'd searched the small space and decided nothing was missing, they drank the bottle of wine and mourned Trina. Olivia insisted that Singer take the bedroom while she slept on the couch. Singer suspected she wanted to go on writing.

Singer fell asleep instantly, but was awakened by the sound of a siren. Her first thought was for Wilmot. He would be the officer with the siren on, flying to some disaster. "Keep him safe," she whispered into the night, an instinctive prayer rising in an uncertain universe. Her whole life seemed suddenly balanced on that narrow ribbon of sound, ready to fall toward happiness or sorrow, and she had no control over the outcome. She pulled the sheets up to her neck and listened as it faded.

Her thoughts drifted to Trina and her wish for a life filled with excitement and accomplishment. Hadn't she been just the same at seventeen? She'd wanted so much from life back then. What did she want now? The answer came quickly. Most of all she wanted to be safe, and to be loved.

It was near dawn. Pale light slipped in through the gaps in the curtain as she fell asleep again.

The local radio station was playing softly in the kitchen when Singer woke. She stretched and got out of bed and followed the bar of light across the floor. The window was open about six inches. She pushed aside the curtain to see what kind of a day it was, even though she wouldn't be setting up on a street corner with her empty guitar case open for donations. Hopefully those days were behind her, but old habits were hard to escape. Upon rising she always thought first of the weather. The difference between sunshine and rain was the difference between eating and going hungry. The day was fine, a day to eat.

A rug covered the metal landing of the fire escape outside. There were three pots of yellow pansies on the windowsill. One lay on its side. The dirt spilled on the rug held the imprint of a large foot in a honeycomb pattern. It was far too large to be Olivia's. Singer looked down at the floor inside the window. More soil littered the painted wood floor of the bedroom, carrying a partial footprint in the same honeycomb pattern.

They hadn't turned on the bedroom light the night before, checking the room only in the light from the hall. And they hadn't even discussed how someone could have gotten in. Later, after the wine, she had pulled off her clothes and fallen on the bed without paying any attention to the room. She hadn't been concerned. Trina's death had everyone uneasy and Olivia definitely had an excess of imagination. What was a crooked file to worry about, especially in a place as messy as Olivia's? But this? This footprint wasn't paranoia but a dangerous reality. She pushed the window closed and locked the sash. She shouldn't have dismissed Olivia's claims so quickly.

Chapter 20

Olivia was already writing and barely looked up when Singer came into the kitchen. Seeing Olivia turning dreams into stories, Singer smiled. It was the same thing that happened when she had a new idea for a song. "Something new to astound us with?"

"I think so."

Singer lifted a partially finished painting off the second kitchen chair. "I have something to tell you, but I don't want you to freak out."

Olivia slowly raised her head, waiting for what came next.

"Have you, or anyone else, been outside your bedroom window where you have that little rug?"

"Not lately, not since I broke up with Peter. We used to sit out there and smoke a joint. Now I just water the plants. Why?"

"And you leave that window open when you're out, or maybe just don't always lock it?"

"Never lock it."

"Maybe you're not crazy." She reached out and patted Olivia's hand. "Come with me."

In the bedroom Olivia stared down at the footprint. "Oh, my god, was it last night, while you were sleeping, did someone come in then?"

"I doubt it. I'm a light sleeper."

"I can't stay here." Olivia darted to the bed, got down on her knees, and pulled a battered pink suitcase out from beneath the bed.

"Where will you go?"

"I don't know, but I can't stay here." She looked up at Singer. "Change places with me."

"What?"

She stood and put the suitcase onto the bed. "You stay here and I'll go up Mount Skeena."

"Are you crazy? You want to stay up on that mountain alone?"

Olivia threw open the case, letting the lid flop against the bed. "Being alone doesn't bother me. Just don't tell anyone where I am and I'll be safe. You can stay here." Her forehead wrinkled into a frown. "Would you be afraid to stay here after a break-in?"

Singer smiled. "I don't think burglars return to the scene of the crime, especially if they've been disappointed. Besides, this apartment is no way as scary as my place."

Olivia went to the battered oak bureau, pulled out the top drawer and gathered up an armload of clothes. "Does Wilmot know you're afraid to be up on the mountain alone?"

"No. Why would I tell him?"

"He might be interested in how you feel about it. Might ask you to move in." She dumped her clothes into the suitcase.

"Not going to happen." Singer sat on the bed. "This is a momentary thing between us. He doesn't need me getting domestic. Speaking of Louis, are you going to call the Mounties about this?"

Olivia picked a limp yellowed bra out of the case. She held it up to the light, then threw it back in the drawer and shoved the drawer halfway closed. She looked over her shoulder at Singer and asked, "Should I?"

Singer shrugged.

Olivia's jaw hardened. "They aren't interested in anything but Trina's death right now."

"Aw, you already called them about being followed."

While Olivia packed like a mad woman, Singer shut the bedroom door and went into the kitchen to make a call. After the tenth ring, she was about to hang up when Pam Haver answered. Singer said, "I want to give you another number where you can reach me."

"You said I could stay at your place..." She heard Pam sniff. "I can't be here anymore. Can I still come?"

"Sure." Singer glanced at the bedroom door. "You can stay in the cabin. I'll pick you up at the dock."

"What about my chickens?"

Singer gave a small hic of amusement. "Oh, hell, bring them."

When Olivia came out of the bedroom with a load of clothes in her arms, Singer said, "You won't be alone at my place. Pam Haver is going to be staying in the cabin."

Olivia dumped the garments on the table. "Look," Singer said, grabbing at the clothes sliding off the table. "She needs a little help."

Olivia pulled a garbage bag out from under the sink, slamming the door shut. It bounced open again. She ignored it and furiously stuffed clothes into the bag. As many fell out as stayed in. "It's turning into a bloody commune. In no time, you'll be taking up knitting."

"I just didn't want you to be lonely up there."

"Horseshit."

Singer planted her hands on her hips, grinning at Oliva. "You look exactly like a kid." It was true. Olivia wore ripped jeans and the washed-out T-shirt she'd slept in. Her hair was exactly as it had been when she crawled off the couch. And she was pouting. Olivia glared at her and marched off to the bedroom.

Singer followed and watched her gather a pile of stuff off the bureau and dump it on the bed. "You're taking this moving business seriously, aren't you?"

"Damn right. I'm not coming back here until Trina's killer is caught." She went to the closet and pulled out a box of books and dumped them onto the floor.

"Fair enough. But Pam needs to get away from her husband. She needs to be safe too."

Olivia quickly sorted through the books, dropping some back on the floor and putting others in the box. "I'm easily distracted. I need to be alone. I need to be somewhere quiet." In one fluid motion she rose from her knees and went to the bed. "I want to see if I can really write." She picked up a jewelry box and considered it before dropping it back on the bed.

"What about getting your job back?"

Olivia started with the bottom drawer of the desk, opening it and taking out papers and then, leaving the drawer open, went on to the next. "Not going to happen." Olivia stacked some of the files on top of the books. "I'll teach my night class but that's it. I want time for... well, to see if I can actually produce something worth reading. Whatever that happens to be."

Chapter 21

Nearly falling off the chair with tiredness, Wilmot tugged his tie down and undid the top button of his shirt. Across from him, Duncan wasn't looking any better. She sat slumped in the chair with a steno pad open on her lap and said, "Major Crimes called again."

"I know. I've taken a couple of those calls too." Wilmot closed the dossier he'd been working on, laid it aside, and then picked up the next buff-colored file. His desk had a row of lined yellow sticky-notes running down the edge, reminders of calls to make, questions to ask, facts to recheck. "Bush asked me if I was waiting for another death before I did what I should have done on Saturday and called them in."

"Shit," Duncan said. "He's an ass but he may be right."

"We'll give it to the end of the weekend and then we'll call them. There's a final wrap-up event for the regatta today. I'm going to make a pitch asking for information regarding the Zodiac or Trina's whereabouts. We should both be there to take statements."

Duncan yawned and stretched. "The flyers are up everywhere."

"Still, I'll do another radio ask. Someone has to have seen something."

Duncan got up slowly. "Waste of time," she said and left the room.

Wilmot understood her frustration. So much of what they did turned out to be a waste of time. Patience was needed to find that one tiny thing that would lead them in the right direction. Getting focused on the wrong person was always a risk. For now, they were building a case against both Frank Haver and Cody. They seemed the most likely suspects, but that wasn't to say that either of them had actually killed Trina. New information could come in that would send them in a totally different direction, but time was running out. With every hour that passed the chances of finding the culprit lessened.

And there was another thing to consider. The deaths had affected everyone on the island. Residents were all turning over stones in their minds, hunting for answers they couldn't find, and blaming others on the strength of a glance or some small misstep. Calls came in every hour from angry and suspicious citizens, tying up the phones and adding to the workload. Nastiness was breaking out in all kinds of ways, and the detachment was coming in for more than their share of criticism. People were in no mood to be understanding and supportive. They wanted answers. The fallout from this would take years to heal.

And then there was the other thing driving him crazy. He still had no idea where Singer had spent her night. He'd checked out the parking lot behind the health food store on his way home for a shower and on his way back to the office. Her SUV was still there, but there was no sign of her. He was making a list in his head of all the things he could try next when Olivia called. She said Singer was with her and had told her to call about the break-in.

"I'll come right over, Olivia." But it wasn't Olivia he wanted to see.

Olivia had gone to the Whole Food store for more boxes so Singer was alone when she heard heavy footsteps on the stairs and a knocking on the unlocked door. Anxious and uncertain, she went to the door as silently as possible, turned the deadbolt, and then pushed aside the flimsy curtain to see who was there.

She felt her face light up. Wilmot grinned in reply. She unlocked the door, threw it open, and held out her arms. "You can't stay away from me, can you?"

After a long embrace, he pushed her away to look at her. The concern he experienced when he hadn't been able to find her hadn't left him, but he had no intention of showing it. At that moment he realized that not having her in his life would be unbearable. "You look like some kind of exotic gypsy in that outfit."

"I picked it up at the market last week." The dress was a peasant concoction that seemed to be made of flowing scarves, in colors of jewel green and electric blues. A matching scarf swept her hair up on her head. Small escaping tendrils caressed her face and drifted across her cheeks as she twirled for his approval.

"Olivia called – again, so I'm here on official police business. Don't try to distract me."

She moved in close. "Am I distracting you? Sorry." Her hands stroked his chest. "Let me help you investigate."

Wilmot slipped away from her hands and looked around the room for the first time. "Good god, you don't need the police. You need emergency services, there's been a disaster."

"No kidding." Olivia undertook packing with the same lack of planning and order as she displayed in the rest of her life. The table was covered in food she'd pulled from the fridge and from cabinets, leaving drawers and cabinet doors open behind her. Boxes littered the floor and a pile of shoes had been dropped on a corner of the table with the food.

Olivia's footsteps tapped up the wooden stairs. She came into the room and dropped her load of cardboard boxes, ran her hands through her already disheveled hair and said, "Moving is hell."

Wilmot laughed and asked, "Where are you going?"

"Olivia's moving up to my place, only she wants to keep it a secret."

"Why are you moving?"

Olivia said, "Are you kidding? What if he comes back?"

Wilmot eyes shifted from one woman to the other.

Olivia said. "I'm not going to sit here and wait for the killer to get me."

"This burglary is unlikely to be connected to Trina's death."

If he'd meant to reassure Olivia, he'd failed. "How do you know?" In a voice pitched high and shrill, she said, "You have no idea who killed Trina and no reason to think he isn't coming after me."

"Well, show me what frightened you."

Olivia's jaw hardened in anger. "Are you sure it won't be too much trouble?" She pivoted away from him and marched down the hall.

When he started to follow, Singer reached out and took his arm. "You look kind of dazed. Are you tired?"

He nodded. "Asleep on my feet."

"You should go home to bed," she said, and then held up a finger, "but not until you buy me brunch at the Ferryman." She smiled at him. "I have some things I have to tell you."

"Okay." The single word sounded uncertain and tentative, like he might not like to hear what she was going to say.

She shoved him away. "Go do your detecting thing."

"Honestly, we haven't got time for petty crime; we're run off our feet. I should have told her to come in and put in a report."

"Don't you want to dust for prints or something?"

"You watch too much TV," he said and went off after Olivia.

After the waitress had taken their order, Singer said, "Lauren sold one of my songs. It's going to be recorded and I'm to sing backup."

He picked up his glass of water, took a sip, then set it down carefully. "So you're leaving." His face was unreadable.

"Only for a couple of weeks."

"And then what?"

"Why, I'll come back here, of course."

He smiled. "Good."

She wrinkled her nose, a sign he recognized. It was as close as she got to coquettish. "It may feel like a long time." She reached out for his hand. "Have you got any holiday time coming?"

"I just might have, and Vancouver would be exactly the place I'd want to spend it."

She laced her fingers in his. "There are some other things I have to tell you, Louis. I know how Trina got out to Ghost Island. She stole Dr. Glasson's Zodiac."

"How do you know that?"

"Can't tell you."

"That doesn't work."

She picked up the coffee carafe and poured coffee into her cup. "Then arrest me." She didn't look up from stirring in cream.

He considered her for a moment. "I would if I had to get the answer out of you, but we already know about the Zodiac. More than one person saw it but none of them knew who was in it."

"Maybe Dr. Glasson went out with Trina."

"Nope. He has an alibi for the time of Trina's death." He studied her. "So what's Dr. Glasson to you?"

She smiled. "Nothing. Here's the food."

He couldn't leave it alone. When the waitress was gone he said, "I had no idea that you knew him."

"Knew?" She picked up the salt. "As in the biblical way?" She raised her eyes to his and smiled.

They didn't talk of death while they ate, but after the waitress had cleared the plates Wilmot asked, "Does Trina mention any other men besides her stepfather and Cody in her diary?"

"Didn't you read my notes?"

"I read them. Cody, the sad man, her stepfather and the creep, but no names. Who's the creep?"

"No idea. That's all Trina called him, the creep." Hannah came to her mind. Her brow furrowed. "I'm not even sure it was a man."

He frowned. "If she was being stalked it was likely a man. Was there anything that could identify him?"

"No name and no description, but there was something in her writing that made the creep seem familiar, like someone I recognized, but I can't remember what it was."

He sighed. "Alright, let it go for a while. Maybe it will come back to you."

"Trina said he followed her home one night, and Olivia said someone followed her too. I wonder if he's been stalking other women."

"We haven't had any complaints like that." He reached for a packet of sugar and said, "I wouldn't take too much notice of what Olivia says. She's a half bubble off level."

"Perhaps, but sometimes she comes out with really insightful things. And there's that footprint."

But Wilmot had spent enough time on other people's problems. He reached out and took her hand. "I might not be as exhausted as I thought."

On the way to his car, Singer stopped so suddenly he bumped into her. She turned to him, wanting to see his reaction. "I forgot to tell you that I met the Havers. Pam spent the night at my place Friday night. She knew about her husband pestering Trina."

Wilmot frowned. "Was he the creep?"

"No. He was the asshole."

Wilmot folded his arms and leaned back against his bright blue Mustang, a car for a man who, unlike Wilmot, hadn't reached forty. "Start at the beginning and tell me how you met the Havers."

When she'd told him everything, he asked, "Where's Pam now?"

"Back on Cooper's Island, but she's moving up to my place on Mount Skeena. Olivia says I'm starting a commune."

"So they'll both be there?"

"Seems like it, at least for now. Pam is broken inside, may never be whole again. There's really nowhere else."

"Not Cooper's Island?"

"Not unless you want another murder to investigate."

"Right," he nodded. "But I'll miss the fireplace. We did have some fun in front of it."

She smiled. "You might not have a fireplace, but I bet we can make some heat."

Wilmot grinned and unlocked the passenger door. Leaning on top of the open door with both forearms, the key hanging from his right hand, he asked, "Why did you stay with Olivia last night?"

"It was late. I hate that drive up the mountain in the dark."

He turned his head to study the boats out in the harbor. "You could have stayed at my place."

"You weren't there."

He met her eyes. "Does it make a difference?"

"I don't have a key."

"Oh," he said. "I..." Whatever he might have said didn't materialize. A woman, tall and Nordic-looking, gave him a warm smile and said, "Good morning, Sergeant Wilmot."

"Hi," Wilmot said, and nodded.

The woman headed for the restaurant entrance.

"Who was that?" Singer asked, sliding into the passenger seat.

"That was Nora Frieberg." When he was behind the wheel he added, "She's Cody's aunt and his alibi."

"She says she saw Cody on Thursday night?"

"Yup." He shoved the key in the ignition.

"I don't think so."

His hand released the key and he turned his head to her. He knew there was more to come. He waited.

"Louis, what time did she say she was with Cody?"

"From nine until eleven."

She shook her head. "No, she wasn't." She left no room for argument. "One of the things that happens when you're singing is you watch people, at least I do, and she's a woman that people watch." She jerked her thumb toward the restaurant. "That woman was still in there with a man when I left. It was well after ten-thirty then."

"Maybe she left right after. She still works as an alibi."

"No way. They were just being served dessert and they were far too friendly to rush. Tom will remember because I bet they closed the place. And I bet she didn't run right over to tuck her nephew in."

He sighed. "Do you mind going back to Olivia's on your own?" He took the key out of the ignition. "I have to go talk to Tom."

She groaned. "Me and my big mouth."

Chapter 22

Singer pulled out of the alley and turned left on Harbor Road, following Olivia's white Volkswagen bug. The first of the sailboats had entered the harbor and spectators were jammed up against the railing above the marina to try and identify the first boat. A shout went up when the sailboat in the lead was one from the Glenphiddie Yacht Club. No one saw the rusted beetle, covered in flowers, leave town.

After they'd carried Olivia's boxes into the main house, they checked out the A-frame where Pam would be staying, opening the windows to air it out. Singer was surprised at how practical Olivia suddenly was. She knew how to turn on the water and the electricity. She even plugged in the appliances and checked the smoke alarm.

"How do you know all this stuff?"

"I'm not the dummy people think I am." There was something about her sly grin that made Singer suddenly aware that Olivia was capable of actively deceiving people by creating an image that was far from reality, a woman who was always putting on a performance. But who was the audience?

Back at the main house, Olivia turned at the door to block Singer's entrance. "Thank you."

A thin thread of annoyance wound through Singer. "I thought I might come in for a minute."

"There's no need."

"I hate to leave you here. Are you sure you want to be alone?"

"That's exactly what I want."

"Okay. I'll be back in a couple of hours with Pam."

"Fine." Olivia shut the door.

Once Singer was back in town, she settled into Olivia's apartment. She was removing a stack of books from the night table when a magazine slid off the top and onto the floor. A sport-fishing magazine was a strange publication for Olivia to be reading. Curious, Singer picked it up and read the name on the address label. "Wow."

Not all of Olivia's secrets had flowed out with the wine the night before.

A few minutes later, while trying to create some room in the closet, Singer discovered the painting. Olivia's talent was enough to make the two nude figures perfectly recognizable.

"Oh, Olivia, you definitely took that dance with an orangutan."

When she'd done enough to satisfy her minimal sense of order, Singer went off to the Driftwood Café. She met Peter Kuchert at the entrance. He waved her in past him with a disarming smile. Singer remembered how Olivia had described him: "Clean cut and tidy-looking in a Beaver Cleaver sort of way. His good looks and boyish eagerness beguile people into sharing their secrets. I've watched him do it." Singer warned herself to be careful. She had no desire to see herself in the paper as, *'a source close to the investigation.'*

"Where's Olivia? I've been trying to call her."

"Not sure. She's gone off island. Something to do with her writing." She studied the bakery items under glass domes.

"When's she coming back?"

"No idea."

"Damn. She's upset with me. I need to make it up to her."

She lifted her head to study his face as she said, "I saw you the other night."

A fleeting emotion that Singer couldn't decipher flickered across his face. "Oh, yeah? Where?"

"It was late and I was on my way home. I saw you on the boardwalk." Singer put in her order and then stepped aside to wait for her Danish and latte as Peter took his turn.

He ordered his coffee, laid a bill down and sorted through his change, counting it out onto the counter, taking his time. "I like to be out at night. Things happen at night when the town is full of tourists. And I get ideas for short stories." He put his hand out for his change, dropped it in the tip jar, and then smiled at Singer. "Walking helps me work through storylines."

"Too bad you weren't out Thursday night. You might have seen Trina."

"I would have been, but there was that accident, remember? I was working."

She took her food outside and sat at a table near the steps. Peter followed her and, without asking permission, pulled out a chair and sat down across from her. She said, "The night I saw you, someone was with you."

His hand jerked, splashing coffee onto the table. He set it down again and then he looked around him before he quietly said, "Please, don't tell anyone about that."

"Beth Thoms, is she where you get your information?"

"It's not like that. We never talk about the RCMP. Besides, I doubt her husband ever shares anything with her." His hands cradled his mug. He leaned toward her, intense and sincere. "She's very fragile. She needs a friend and that's where I come in. That's all it is."

She blew on the coffee before taking a cautious sip. "A friend to go for a walk with at night?"

"It's nothing more. Neither of us sleeps much so we walk. She hates being home alone at night and has panic attacks.

Walking helps. If you think you have to tell Wilmot, let me know first, okay? I'll try and cushion the news for Beth. She's very fragile and confrontation isn't something she handles well."

"You seem to really care for her."

"She reminds me of my sister. Trauma weakens some of us and, like heat on metal, makes the rest of us strong."

They drank their coffee in silence until Peter said, "Do you think Olivia's obsession with Trina is strange?"

"What do you mean, obsession?"

He grimaced. "Don't know exactly, but her interest isn't normal."

"Maybe she saw her younger self in Trina. You knew Trina well, didn't you?"

"Not that well. She's a good ten years younger than me. It's a big difference to a teenager. But we did talk about writing during breaks. I told Trina she should study journalism as a backup for novel writing."

"How did that go? From what I knew of her I don't think she'd appreciate anyone offering advice."

He grinned. "You're right about that. She said that sort of writing would destroy her creativeness, although it didn't seem to hurt Hemingway, George Orwell, Gabriel Garcia Marquez, Hunter Thompson." He ticked them off on his fingers. "Mark Twain, Daniel Defoe, Ian Fleming, Stephen Fry…"

Singer held up her hands in surrender. "Okay, okay, I get it."

He smiled. "Olivia gave her false confidence about her writing, made Trina think she was special. She had that kind of attitude, thought she could just write a book without any experience of life."

"What did Trina write about?"

"Her life... being Trina." His words were accompanied by a flash of annoyance. "Very *Catcher in the Rye* sort of stuff. Olivia loved it, but I didn't get it. I could never figure out why Olivia was so fixated on her."

Singer brushed crumbs off the table and onto her plate. "I'm beginning to understand that no one was indifferent to Trina. Strong sentiments bring powerful reactions. It might have something to do with her death." Dr. Glasson came to mind. He certainly had strong feelings, but he had been at the hospital. Was she sure of that? And how strong was his alibi? The Mounties might look closer at him if they knew he'd had relations with Trina.

She realized that Peter was silently studying her. "Sorry, wool-gathering, thinking what it would take to make a person kill someone." But she knew exactly what it would take.

"Maybe the reason is in the journal. Did you read anything like that in her diary?"

"Nope." She picked up her mug, planted her elbows on the table and looked out at the water. "Shouldn't you be out there getting pictures and writing down details of the winning boat?"

"I don't take the pictures, and the yacht club will give me a fact sheet. So I guess Wilmot has read Trina's innermost thoughts by now?"

Singer didn't rise to the bait.

"Did Trina ever tell you about..." He waggled his hand back and forth.

"What?" she asked. "I have no idea what you're talking about."

"I know you helped her with her singing. Did she ever confide in you, tell you about her boyfriends?"

"Never! I hope you aren't going to speculate about Trina when you write your piece for the *Barnacle*."

"Don't worry." He grinned. "That kind of an article won't fly here, so I'm saying all the right things. She'll be next to a saint when I'm finished."

"And the big city papers, will sex and murder work for them?"

"What do you know about Trina and sex?"

"Like I said, nothing. But I'm sure there will be lots of it when you sell your story to the city papers. You're the one out there in the dark, watching. I bet you know a whole lot more than you put in the paper. I'm sure you know all about Trina."

"Maybe."

She could see he was waiting for her to ask, wanting to tell her more, but some perverse reaction kept her silent. Did Peter know about Dr. Glasson involvement with Trina? She wasn't likely to have told Peter. Still, maybe he'd seen them together. If challenged by Peter, Dr. Glasson would quickly collapse and confess. "I hope you aren't intending to write about Trina's personal life."

"Not in this little paper." A muscle jumped in his jaw.

"But you will write about it. You're planning on writing an expose, aren't you?"

"I don't intend to stay here forever. The Vancouver papers will lap up this kind of story. I need that one big headline to get the attention of a major newspaper, or maybe I'll even write a book about it, and then I'll be gone."

She wrapped her hands around her coffee mug. "So Trina is your ticket out of here?"

A soft shrug for an answer.

Even in death, Trina was being used. "Alright," she said. "Tell me about Trina. How did you see her?"

"Trina used her sex appeal. She wanted attention, wanted to have control. A tease. Not the innocent she pretended to be."

"Harsh, but I don't remember her ever pretending to be the Virgin Mary. In fact, I think she worked pretty hard to seem sophisticated. She probably came across as more adult than she was."

"Sexy, you mean." He sipped his coffee.

"Young. Without understanding what she was doing, she awoke strong emotions."

He pushed his mug away. "Perhaps she was just in the wrong place at the wrong time and met the wrong person."

"Person? You said person and not man. Do you think it might have been a woman?"

"Olivia..." He leaned back in the chair and looked out over the bay.

"What about Olivia?"

"The fireworks have been cancelled because of Trina's death." He brushed his curls back from his forehead.

What did he know about Olivia he wasn't telling? And did she really want to know? "I suppose we'll survive without fireworks."

"Yes, but it makes..." He couldn't find the words. "Her murder likely has nothing to do with the island. There are lots of people here from away." Peter took a deep breath and said, "Suspicion is toxic and spreads its poison everywhere. You start distrusting everyone, don't you? I went to the hospital Friday night. I wanted to interview Dr. Glasson about the accident. The nurse couldn't find him." Now they were getting to the secret he wanted so much to tell. "He wasn't anywhere in the hospital."

"And?"

His chair scraped along the deck as he moved closer to her. He looked around them to make sure no one was listening. "The nurse made an excuse, tried to cover up for him." The words were spoken so quietly she had to move forward to hear. "He never did come out to talk to me, although he was listed as being on duty."

"I'm sure there's a simple explanation."

"Maybe. But I thought you should know."

She didn't ask why, although she could see he wanted to tell her.

"Everyone has secrets, even Olivia and the good doctor." He relaxed back on his chair. "Before this is over, lots of secrets are going to come out."

"Even yours, Peter?"

"Walking around town at night with an emotionally ill woman who needs a friend isn't much of a secret."

She drew her hands through her hair. "The sad part is the truth doesn't matter. People see what they want to see and innocent people will be destroyed."

"You're right. And the guilty party may never be found. If that happens Cody Frieberg will be screwed. Everyone knows the Mounties are looking at him. The graduation prom is next week. He was supposed to go with Trina. I've heard that the principal has asked him not to attend."

"He probably wouldn't have gone anyway."

"Still, there's a stigma. People will look at him differently. And then there are the Cutters."

"Why them?"

"They were supposed to be looking after her. Substitute parents. They'll be blamed. It's always the ones closest to the victim who get battered. Whispers are already starting about Ward Cutter."

She started to protest, to say that the Cutters didn't even know that Trina was going to be on Glenphiddie. But that piece of news wasn't public knowledge yet. The Cutter's thought Trina was going home to Cooper's Island. That's what she'd told them. And she'd told her mother that she was staying at the Cutters. All this so she could spend the weekend with Cody. Singer had heard her explain all of this to Cody. It had come as a complete surprise to him. Singer had seen his distress, maybe even anger, when he heard that Trina was making plans without consulting him. Singer shifted uneasily. "Let's just hope they catch the killer soon." Remembering what to keep secret was becoming more and more difficult. "What do the winners of the race actually get for being first?"

Peter wouldn't be distracted. "Ripples will go out from this murder. We depend on tourists. Are they still going to come if there is an unsolved murder? And with a crime like that unexplained, people here will never feel safe again." He frowned. "I've told Beth not to go out alone at night." He stretched out his long legs. "It's the not knowing. Trina's murder will taint innocent people, reveal things that have nothing to do with her killing and turn everyone against their neighbor."

"And if Cody is innocent, but the guilty party is never found, it could ruin his life."

"It will on this island," Peter said. "He won't be able to stay. Everyone's got their favorite horse in the race." He pushed away from the table and bent over to tie his shoe. "In a small place like this we all know too much about our neighbors. And everyone has secrets, even you."

So now they were getting to what he'd wanted to tell her earlier. "What surprises have I been hiding?"

"You and Dr. Glasson, parked up at the outlook. No affairs go unnoticed on an island." He raised a hand. "Don't worry. I'm not about to tell anyone."

"Oh, go ahead. I like the thought that people will think I'm still a hot babe." She picked up her mug and took a look at the dregs. "At least if they're talking about me it will give others a rest." She set the mug back on the table. "So what are your secrets, Peter?"

He leaned his chair back on the post behind him. "I wish I had some. Since it ended with Olivia, I'm probably the most boring person on the whole damn island."

"Somehow I doubt that."

Singer left Peter sitting at the table and went off to the bookstore to buy a paper. When she walked back along the deck, past the coffee drinkers and the girl with the watering can, she saw a damp footprint, fading even as she watched.

She'd seen that tread before. The person who'd come through Olivia's bedroom window had left that same print behind. But perhaps the honeycomb was a common pattern, one that lots of people had on the bottom of their shoes.

On the sidewalk Cody stood with a muffin in his hand. He must have come and gone from the cafe while she was buying the paper. Peter was talking to him earnestly, but Cody was shaking his head and backing away. Peter followed, his arms wide and his palms up, trying to convince Cody.

Obsessed, that was what Peter had said about Olivia and her interest in Trina. But it wasn't just Trina who Olivi

a was interested in. The nude painting made it pretty clear why the magazine was in Olivia's bedroom. Did Peter know about Olivia and Cody?

Was this another thing she should tell Wilmot? The things she was keeping from him were piling up and she didn't like it.

Chapter 23

Before she picked up Pam Haver from the dock, Singer had a stop to make. On the street where the Cutters lived she studied the residences on either side. The green raised-ranch to the right of the Cutter's house had bicycles and a basketball hoop over the garage door. Did the doctor have children? Somehow she didn't think so. The driveway to the left of the Cutter's curled away from the road, heading up to a sixties bungalow on a small rise. She walked a few feet up the paved drive. Past a clump of overgrown bushes, she saw the Audi.

The home had been loved once, but now the grass was uncut and large rhododendron bushes, with brilliant fuchsia blooms, grew taller than the roof and covered half of the front window. She followed a path worn in the grass, catching a glimpse of the original concrete walk now hidden by the overgrown bushes. She rang the bell and waited. The alcove of the front door was littered with dead blossoms and flyers which had overflowed the rusted letter box.

Through the rippled glass insert she saw a figure shuffle toward her. Dr. Glasson opened the door. He looked weary beyond bearing, his eyes smudged black and sunken in his gaunt face. It took a minute for him to place her. When recognition came, his head jerked back as if he'd been struck.

"May I come in?"

He grimaced.

"I have something to tell you. It's important and I don't want to say it out here."

He closed his eyes. Then he drew himself up, gave a small tilt of his head, and stepped aside for her.

The foyer opened onto a living room that stank of a fireplace where ashes had been left for a long time. "Are you alone?" she asked.

"Yes." Beaten, dejected, and waiting for the final blow, he shuffled away. "Come to the den."

She followed him down the hall to a small room filled with bookshelves and a desk that was littered with food-encrusted plates, dirty coffee mugs, newspapers and stacks of files.

He pointed at a wingback chair in front of the desk. She slumped down on the flowered damask and waited while he went around the desk. When he'd collapsed into the leather chair she said, "Peter Kuchert knows you weren't at the hospital for all of Friday night. He tried to find you to get information on the accident victim."

This clearly wasn't what he'd expected to hear. A spark of life showed on his face. "But I was there."

"Except when you went to the Cutter home."

A nerve twitched in his right eye and his jaw worked, chewing on words of denial. When he finally spoke his voice was quite calm. "Did you come here to accuse me of something?"

"Nope. I just wanted to make sure that you didn't go jumping off any more cliffs. Hannah may need you alive to give her an alibi."

His eyes widened, but he didn't respond.

"The Cutters live one block up from the hospital. You could be up here before anyone knew you were gone." She crossed her legs and smoothed her skirt over her knees. "Home all alone, the perfect chance to experiment with what she found in the medicine chest or in the liquor cabinet. Did she hurt herself? Had she been drinking and taken a fall? Or maybe that bandage hides a slash on her wrist."

He stayed silent but his expressive face gave him away.

"Right, she was in trouble and called you."

"I'm not telling you anything about a patient."

"You don't have to. That neatly wrapped arm, with its little metal clips, did that. If she had gone to the hospital she would have said so, but she didn't. She called you and you came and bandaged her arm."

"And that's why you're here, just to confirm your guess?"

"I'm just saying Hannah needs you. Even her father thinks she killed Trina."

The lurch of his body sent his chair backward. "That's ridiculous."

"Is it? I'm not sure." She raised her hand to stop his defense of Hannah. "I'm also worried that if the police come around to talk to you, you'll assume they are here because they know about your relationship with Trina. It's Hannah they'll be interested in. You and Hannah can alibi each other, so don't go spilling your guts about something they know nothing about."

He wiped his mouth with the back of his hand and took a deep breath. "Thank you, Singer. You're right, as soon as they came through the door I'd have told them everything. It's on the tip of my tongue to tell someone."

She stood. "You already have. You told me."

"But is it enough?"

"What good would it do to tell the Mounties? They'd just waste time on you and your alibi."

"Aren't you worried you're aiding and abetting a criminal? Do you want my sins on your conscience?"

"Let me worry about my conscience." She grinned. "I'm not sure I even have one. Besides, sinners like us have to stick together. I read Trina's diary. You didn't hurt her. Trina was a girl who made her own choices, and if she hadn't wanted to have sex with you…" A flash of insight. "Maybe that's it, someone wanted sex and Trina rejected him, laughed at him, maybe that's why she died."

He came around the desk and stood beside her. "There could be reasons we can't even imagine."

"Yes, that's true. Best to think of the living. Glenphiddie is already short of doctors, so stay healthy." She headed down the hall. "I'm really worried about Hannah. She had strong feelings for Trina. Do you think there's any chance she's suicidal?"

"Oh, god, I've been so worried about myself that I never thought of that." His exhaustion seemed to lift. "I'll see if I can talk to her."

"She isn't likely to tell you anything, but at least she'll know she can if she wants to."

Dr. Glasson walked down the drive with her. They were almost to the street when a vehicle with the RCMP logo on its side pulled into the Cutter driveway. Duncan and Wilmot got out.

Singer raised a hand in greeting, but Wilmot turned his back on her and strode purposefully to the Cutter home.

"Oh, crap."

"Problem?"

"I'll have to explain what I'm doing here. Louis will think I'm interfering or that you and I are getting it on."

"Which would you prefer?"

"The truth, interfering. I'll tell him I was here asking about Hannah."

"Works for me."

"Well, let's hope it works for Wilmot. He's not a trusting man."

"Few of us are when it comes to women."

Chapter 24

Pam Haver sat with her hands folded in her lap and stared straight ahead as Singer slid behind the wheel. "Is there anything you need in town, Pam?"

"Could we stop at the funeral home? Apparently there is another piece of paper to sign."

"Sure. Nothing else?"

"No."

"Olivia will be staying in the main house. Don't expect too much from her, or the old A-frame. Alan and Steven lived in it when they first came to Glenphiddie. No one's lived in it for years, but it's made of good stout logs. Olivia and I checked it out. The electricity works and we turned on the water."

In the clearing, beside Olivia's Volkswagen with its missing fender, was a pickup in even worse shape. "Bill's here," Pam said. They were the first words she'd spoken since they left Kilborn. In the bed of the truck were two bags of feed and the crates full of chickens that had come from Cooper's Island with Pam. Out by the barn a man raised his arm in greeting and then went back to work on an enclosure he was constructing along the side of the barn.

Singer parked in front of the small A-frame with pink roses climbing up the front. Pam said, "It's beautiful."

"Don't get your hopes up," she warned, but Pam had already opened the passenger door and slid to the ground.

Singer dragged a garbage bag of Pam's possessions off the back seat and followed her into the tiny structure. The downstairs was one large room with the kitchen at one end and the living area at the other. Overhead, in the peak, was a sleeping loft. On the small table sat a jar filled with wildflowers, an offering from Olivia. Except for the yellow and blue flowers, the space was sparse and uninviting, reeking of dampness and decay.

"We can bring out some furniture from the house."

"No need. I've made do with much less than this," Pam said.

Singer set the garbage bag on the table. "So have I, but I don't want to anymore." The truth of her words surprised her. She tilted her head to the side and considered them. The time on Glenphiddie had changed her in some fundamental way. Making do was no longer enough. It had been a long slow slide to life in a van and she didn't want to fall back there, back to where her main interaction with others was being yelled at and told to move along. She didn't want to just survive one night at a time. Something gelled and hardened in her. No matter what, she was never going to live that way again. "I'll get the rest of your stuff."

When Pam had stowed her few possessions, they checked out the chicken run. The man pounding steel rods into the ground put down the sledgehammer and came to join them. A man of amazing girth, he wore faded overalls and an endless grin. Pam smiled, a rare sight that took years off her face. "This is Bill. He sells me my chicks."

"I'm just about done here." He smelled, not unpleasantly, of dust and sweat. "Damn hard work." He took off his frayed baseball cap. His gray-streaked hair was damp and matted to his head. "Damn hard to drive in these bars," he said and wiped his arm across his forehead. "The ground is all rock. Well, it would be on a mountain, wouldn't it?" He chuckled, pleased with himself. "But I've come up with another way." He waved his hand at the partially completed fence. "I'm alternating the rods with these." He picked up a concrete block and put it in place before he drove a wood post down into the hole in the block. "It's not as permanent but these blocks will work for now."

Olivia joined them. "Maybe Pam can use your old yellow van for a chicken coop, Singer."

Singer glared at her.

Olivia smiled sweetly. "I'll go make coffee."

Singer and Pam trailed behind Bill and watched him nail the last of the wire to the barn, making its wall one side of the pen. "I'm ready to move the hens into their nice new run. Just got to go back and make this wire a little more secure." He started stapling the wire to the wooden posts.

Pam said, "I'll start bringing the chickens over."

"No hurry," Bill bashed in another staple. "Settle yourself. I'll finish this and then the three of us can get the chickens."

"Count me out. I'm not touching any of them." Singer backed away. "I like my chicken fried."

Bill said, "They don't have teeth, you know." An impish grin lit his face and his blue eyes sparkled. "They'd have to peck you to death." His eyes opened wide in shock at what he'd said. The news of the damage to Trina's face had spread quickly around the island. He rubbed his palm across his mouth and lowered his head. He began to furiously slam staples into the fence.

That's the problem with being around someone in such pain, Singer thought. *Every little thing out of your mouth seems to add to it.* "I'll help with the coffee." She turned away.

Olivia didn't look up when the screen door banged. She didn't seem to have made it to the kitchen. She was sitting on the couch in front of the empty fireplace, legs drawn up under her, writing furiously on a yellow legal pad.

Singer went to the kitchen and started the coffee, put mugs on a tray and added an open bag of cookies Olivia had left sitting on the counter. She then went to the window to watch Bill and Pam carry a crate of chickens between them, setting it down inside the run before they closed the gate. When they carried in the last container a bronze hen escaped through the partially open gate.

"They've got a runaway. You want to go out and help catch it?"

When Olivia didn't answer, she turned from the window to say, "I guess you got over your writer's block, huh?"

Olivia wrote on.

When the hens were all safely in their new home, Singer and Olivia took the coffee outside. The four of them stood leaning on the posts and watched the plump brown fowl pick their way through the tall grass, their movements looking almost delicate, a jerk of their head, a lift of a leg, and then a gentle placement of the foot.

Bill lifted his baseball cap and resettled it. "They'll eat this place clean in a week and next year it will be a good place to plant a garden."

Next year. *Where will we all be next year?* Singer knew only too well what next year was going to bring her. "I'll get more coffee."

"Can't stay." Bill began to pack the last of his tools in a long wooden tool box. "I'll be up to do that bit of electric fencing for you and then I'll bring your sheep up. Might take a day or two because I have to fit it in."

"They'll be fine for at least the next week." Moisture filled Pam's eyes. "Thank you, Bill."

Bill turned away. "No problem."

Singer dragged out a third canvas chair, covered in gray mold and looking like it wouldn't hold a babe off the ground, which was just fine because Pam didn't weigh much more than that. In the kitchen she dug out the bottle of Baileys that Wilmot had brought out the night they cooked steaks and slept in front of the fire. She liberally filled the mugs with the creamy booze and then added coffee.

They sat and looked over the meadow while their conversation went round and round. No matter how they tried to talk about other things, it always came back to Trina. Even a conversation of future plans led to thoughts of a young girl's dreams that were now dust.

"She had such hopes for the future," Pam said.

"We all live on dreams and hopes," Singer said.

"It's all that human beings have to fight back the dark," Olivia added.

"Yes," Singer said. "But sometimes, when we hold onto them too long, those dreams can drag us down. I sang because I loved it and I was sure I'd make it to the very top. But stardom is a business for the young and I stayed too long, chasing a dream that was moving farther and farther away from me. My vision of the perfect future has changed. Now I hope one of my songs will make it or, if I'm really lucky, maybe I'll sing backup on a hit."

Olivia stretched out her legs. "My dream came true but it didn't last."

"Dreams aren't supposed to last."

Olivia waved her arm in a grand gesture. "Not only don't they last; they turn into bloody nightmares."

"Boo hoo, life treated you cruelly."

Olivia grinned. "It's true. Success treated me badly. At twenty-five I had a bestselling novel. It shot to the top and disappeared just as suddenly. But still my publisher picked up my next book. It fizzled. Rightly so."

"You can write another novel."

"I did, but not one publisher was interested. At the moment I'm a has-been."

"That's the way of life—good things, bad things, none of it lasts."

Olivia nudged her and said, "I was right. You're a bit of a philosopher."

"That's me, a roving bard dispensing wisdom."

"Or crap," Olivia said, "depending on the day."

For a moment, they'd forgotten Pam. Now she said, "Trina was so sure she wanted to be a writer."

Olivia reached out and placed her hand on Pam's arm. "Trina would have been a great writer."

"You're very kind."

"No," Olivia said. "I'm not being kind." She sighed. "I never am." She lifted her head up to the sky. "She had talent, a gift."

Pam covered Olivia's hand on her forearm. "It doesn't matter now."

And that was the truth of it. It would be a long time, if ever, that anything mattered again for Pam.

Singer poured the last of the Baileys into Pam's mug. Pam stared down at it. "It's not only the grief of losing a daughter, my only child, but I'm tormented by thoughts of Trina's last moments. When I lie down at night, I wonder, did she call out for me? Did she beg to live?"

"Perhaps it was quick," Singer said. "She may not have even been aware it was about to happen. Easiest to believe that, isn't it?"

Pam gave a snort of disgust. "Can you make yourself believe what's easiest?"

"Pretty much," she said. "I have that knack."

Pam closed her eyes, squeezing back tears. "I hate that people who didn't know her will be whispering about her, saying it was her own fault."

"No one will think that," Olivia protested, but Singer wasn't so sure. Most people would suspect that Trina must have done something wrong, been in the wrong place, trusted the wrong person. It was what people did to make themselves feel safe. Telling themselves that if they did everything right, nothing bad would ever happen. They would be smarter than Trina.

The three women sat with no words of comfort to share, deep in their own thoughts. Over the forest the sun was setting. Singer pulled herself awkwardly out of the flimsy chair. "It's time for me to leave." With twilight every curve became more dangerous. "I'd better get down before the deer come out to browse." Deer were everywhere on the island, including the roads. Not a week went by without someone hitting one.

"And me," Pam said. "I need to check on the chickens."

Singer watched Pam walk away. "I'm sorry I landed her on you."

"I don't mind." Olivia watched Pam come out of the barn with a bucket in her hand and enter the chicken pen. "Besides, I doubt I'll see very much of her."

"Do you suppose she has food in those cardboard boxes we carried in?"

"She'll always have eggs." Olivia gave a bark of laughter before her hand shot up to cover her mouth. "That's awful. I shouldn't make jokes."

"Yeah, you should, or grief would never cease."

The late afternoon had grown cold, as it always did up on the mountain. Singer headed for the house, leaving Olivia slouched in her rickety chair. No light was on, and the silent house was still open to the outside. She stepped into the dim interior. Olivia's personality had already stamped the house as her own, leaving Singer feeling displaced.

But there was no time to waste on sentimentality. She hurried upstairs to where she stored her clothes. That's how she thought of the master suite, the place where she hung her things. She didn't think of it as her bedroom really. It was just a place to keep a few possessions. She didn't think of any of it as hers. It was still Stevie's and she was there temporarily.

She threw open the closet. Seeing the clothes Lauren had picked out for her always made her want to clap her hands with delight. They were the belongings of a real person, someone who counted. Tenderly she stroked the sleeve of a beautiful rose-colored sweater. She'd hardly worn it, saving it for something special. Perhaps she should take it with her. Louis would like it. He liked fine things, but she was afraid of spilling something on it, dropping ashes or coffee. She lifted the soft material to her face and ran it along her cheek. Yes, she'd wear it for Louis. Soft and feminine, perhaps that's how she'd seem to him when he touched the cashmere. Besides, if she was leaving soon…she couldn't finish that thought. Saving anything just wasn't part of her plan. She slipped the garment from its padded hanger. She'd take the trousers Lauren had picked out to go with the sweater. Lauren knew about things like fashion, but it was an outfit better suited for the city than the island where women wore either jeans or long skirts. She didn't care about other women. She wanted to be her best.

She gently placed the outfit in her carryall and then added underwear, clean jeans and T-shirts. She zipped it up and hurried downstairs, eager to be away. She set her bag down by her vehicle, and went to say goodbye. Ten feet from the A-frame, she saw the two women through the window. They were sitting at the kitchen table deep in conversation. Was Olivia there offering friendship or digging for details for her story?

She turned away. She'd left it very late to go down the treacherous twisting road. Scary enough in the daytime, when the light faded and long shadows fell across the pavement, hiding wildlife, windfalls and giant potholes, it became teeth-clamping terrifying.

She threw the carryall onto the back seat and took one last look at the fiery sky in the west. The beauty filled her with a sense of loss. The closer the end came, the more precious every second was and she dreaded the changes that were coming. She shook her head in disgust. It was only since she had choices, had something to lose, that she'd become timid and afraid of it all slipping away from her.

She snaked her way out the lane, through the high banks of vegetation, driving at a snail's pace over the board bridge, hearing the clank, clank of the shifting wood, silently praying that it would hold, and felt a strange sense of foreboding.

Chapter 25

Singer sang at the Ferryman until ten and then sat talking to Tom Woods until after eleven. It was fully dark when she walked down the main street, going back to Olivia's apartment. With no streetlights, the only illumination was the light shining from the dim interiors of stores. In the park Christmas lights shone in the apple trees and flowering cherry trees. Here and there, beyond the park, a few tiny pricks of brightness indicated boats. It was a walk through an enchanting world and it was all hers. Not another person was there to share it. Unlike Singer, Kilborn was a town that went to bed early. But she wasn't afraid to be alone in the night. Instead, it gave her a feeling of ownership and specialness.

  She crossed the street, heading to the waterfront, still too pumped by a night where the music came easily and the audience loved her. A lone car went slowly by, but she felt none of the panic she experienced walking empty city streets after a gig. Even Trina's death hadn't taken away the sense of peacefulness the island emanated. She leaned on the railing and lit one last cigarette, smoking it slowly and watching the lights disappear from the houses up on the hill at the north end of town. The sound of a woman's laugh came from one of the boats docked in the slips. A rustle in the grass. She looked down and saw the shining eyes of some small animal staring at her from the tall grass of the bank below. And then it disappeared.

  When she'd finished her cigarette, and ground it out under her toe, she headed for Olivia's apartment. A narrow passage between two buildings led to the alley and the apartment over the health food store. It was even darker here. It gave her pause for a moment. "Don't be silly," she told herself and stepped into the dark tunnel.

When she entered the alley, Singer stopped and cursed her luck. The light at the top of the stairs had gone out. She'd left it shining because she knew she'd be back after dark and would have to climb the long flight of wooden steps. Suddenly uneasy, she looked about her, searching for danger.

Like a feral dog she sniffed the air for anything foreign, all the while telling herself this was no back alley in some skanky industrial town. And yet... Years on the street had given her an extra sense of danger. But what choice did she have? There was no way she was going back up that mountain road. She could either continue up the dark alley to the stairs, climbing them without light, or sleep in her vehicle. A shiver of apprehension tickled the base of her spine.

She shook off her alarm, choosing common sense over visceral feedback, and headed for the stairs. As she approached, her feet slowed. She paused, listened and then sniffed the air again... Nothing, no smell of aftershave or sweat.

She edged forward and was almost on the stairs when she heard something—the scuffle of feet, a stone turning over, some slight sound that didn't come from the natural world. Intent on listening, she froze in place.

But there was no other sound. She eased forward and placed a foot on the first step. That's when she saw the figure separate from the darkness under the stairs. She spun awkwardly to face it, lifting her guitar case up to protect herself and block the attack she knew was coming. Shooting forward, a man grabbed the railing and flung his body around the newel post to trap her against the stairs.

His momentum knocked her backward onto the steps. She crashed down hard, the sharp edge of the step biting into her spine, but the guitar case stayed between them. Pushing on the case and kicking out with both feet, she screamed.

His fist shot out over the guitar case. Knuckles struck her in the mouth. She tasted blood. "Shut up, bitch," he growled. His hand covered her mouth. Singer bit down.

"Shit." He scrambled off her.

She kicked out at him but he'd moved away from her reach. She shouted, "Get away from me, you bastard."

He backed away. She raised the case like a shield, and pushed herself up onto the step behind her, waiting for the next attack. Instead, he ran. The echo of his pounding feet faded quickly. Fear fixed her there, clutching her precious shield, waiting. When several minutes had passed and he didn't come back she got to her feet and ran up the stairs, watching over her shoulder while she fumbled with the key, nearly dropping it before it slid into the lock and turned.

She was trembling so much she misdialed Wilmot's number and had to start over. As she listened to the phone ring, she tried to remember if he was on night duty or if he had switched to days. She should have called the emergency number. She knew at night all calls were transferred to Vancouver Island because there wasn't enough staff to man the detachment's phone lines after the municipal employees went home. How long would it take for help to arrive? Keeping an eye on the door, she stretched the cord of the receiver into the kitchen, reaching out for the butcher knife sitting in a wooden block. She was sure her attacker would come crashing through the door at any moment. And then she remembered the bedroom window on the fire escape. It was locked now but that wouldn't stop him.

If he came through the window, she'd run down the staircase. If he came through the front entrance, she'd try to get down the fire escape. In the meantime, she was tied to the kitchen by the phone cord and the ringing coming down the line.

When she heard him say, "Hello," she managed to choke out, "It's Singer. I'm at Olivia's. Please come."

Within minutes, he called out her name from the stairs and then said, "It's Louis." She flung the door open and leapt into his arms, almost driving him back down the flight of stairs. He grabbed the railing, regaining his balance, and then held her for a moment before he led her inside. "What happened?"

"I was attacked. Outside."

"Christ! Are you all right?"

"Yes." Both of her hands dug deep into her hair. She took a deep breath and let it out slowly. "It just scared the shit out of me."

He tilted her face so he could see the bruise swelling on her face, and then he wrapped her in his arms again. "We need to treat your face. Perhaps you should go to the hospital."

"No," she wailed into his neck. She couldn't bear to be separated from him.

"All right, sit down." He pulled a kitchen chair away from the table and saw the knife. He picked it up, put it back in its wooden block, and then got ice, wrapping it in a kitchen towel before holding it gently to her face. "Tell me."

She put her hand up to hold the ice in place. "I don't know who he was." She told him about her feeble attempt at protecting herself. "I don't know if he was trying to rob me or rape me. He just suddenly pulled away and ran."

"I'm going outside to see if there's any sign of him."

"He's gone like spit on sand."

"He might have left something behind."

"Please, Louis," she held out her trembling hand. "Just stay with me a minute."

When Singer felt safe, Wilmot went down the stairs with his flashlight to see if there was any evidence. As she'd predicted, there was nothing to be seen. At the top of the stairs he tightened the light bulb. It shone brightly. He went back inside to find her sitting on the couch with her knees drawn up to her chest. Arms wrapped around them, she rocked gently back and forth.

A woman who normally radiated confidence, swagger even, he'd never seen her look so frightened and small. He went to her.

As he sat on the couch beside her, she said, "I just figured it out."

Her body was stiff and unyielding when he pulled her into his arms. "What?"

"It wasn't me he wanted, was it?"

"No."

"He was after Olivia."

"Yes."

"He took out the light, but then he couldn't tell in the dark it wasn't Olivia. It was the guitar case, that's when he knew."

"Yes."

She looked up into his face. "You already figured it out."

Instead of answering, he asked, "Did you tell anyone about changing places with Olivia?"

"No. Should I call Olivia?"

"I'll tell her in the morning. Olivia is safe up the mountain as long as no one knows where she is. And you'll be safe at my place."

"But attacking me tells you something, doesn't it?"

"What does it tell me?"

"Well, first it's a man." She was sure it wasn't Hannah who had attacked her, though Hannah's voice was deep. "It was a man. I heard that when he swore."

"Did you recognize his voice?"

"No." She drew the word out. "But I think he was youngish. From his voice and movements, somewhere between twenty and forty." In her mind she ruled out Dr. Glasson, who looked and moved like a man well beyond his forty-some years, but then, she'd never seen him excited or desperate. Would that change how he moved?

"When he ran, he seemed... well, athletic, young." She almost said, "Someone like Cody."

"Was there anything else to identify him?"

She shook her head. There was something she didn't want to ask but needed to know. "If it had been Olivia, would he have killed her?"

"There's nothing to say this was connected to Trina's death."

"Great, a stalker *and* a killer on the island."

"And you're sure you didn't recognize his voice?"

Her brow furrowed. After a few minutes thought she shook her head. "I don't know."

He stood. "Come on, get your things together and we'll go to my place."

At his apartment she watched as he fussed around the bedroom, clearing a shelf for her things and hanging up the clothes she'd brought with her. "I have to go to the station." He looked over his shoulder at her. "But I can be back in minutes. Keep the phone on the bed with you."

Singer nodded and then she said, "Louis, we need to talk before you go."

Wilmot froze with the closet door half closed. "What?" He shoved the bi-fold into place.

"When I went to see Hannah again, I spoke to her mother." She watched her fingers picking at the fuzz on the blanket, unable to look him in the eye. Minutes of silence followed until she blurted out, "Shit, doing the right thing is harder than I ever knew. No wonder I never do it." She took a deep breath, sat up straight and looked into his eyes. "Diane told me that Ward Cutter thinks his daughter killed Trina."

She saw his shoulders relax. What had he been expecting her to say? Did he know about the letter, the one she'd picked up from the post office on Friday, the one buried deep in her bag?

"Why?" He came to sit on the bed beside her. "Why would a young girl like Hannah kill Trina?"

"Apparently she's lashed out at people in the past. Duncan knew about it and mentioned it when she interviewed Hannah. Knowing Duncan, it probably didn't mean anything, but Ward thinks it means that you have evidence against Hannah."

Wilmot stayed silent. His face gave nothing away.

She bit down on her cheek, hating what she was about to say. "Ward Cutter wants to take his daughter away, to protect her."

"He's a fool. The world's become too small to hide."

"He has a friend up in Nanaimo, that's where they're going, but it doesn't matter as long as you know Hannah wasn't involved. I'm sure it wasn't Hannah who attacked me tonight. Can you just ease Ward Cutter's mind, tell him you know it was a man who killed Trina, so he doesn't do something silly? If Hannah realizes her father thinks she's Trina's murderer…" She lifted her shoulders and let them fall.

He leaned over and kissed her. "What makes you so sure Hannah wasn't involved in Trina's death?"

"She has an elastic bandage, a very neat elastic bandage, on her right arm. She's right-handed. She didn't wrap that herself, didn't put in those little metal clips. I saw it Friday morning." She tucked her legs up under her. "I went to see Dr. Glasson. Two things I wanted to know. How did she hurt her arm and who bandaged it?" She paused and then added, "Well, there's a third. Exactly when on Thursday night did she hurt it? That's why I went to see Dr. Glasson."

"What did he tell you?"

"He told me it was none of my business." She frowned in annoyance.

When Wilmot gave a hoot of laughter she delivered a light punch to his arm. "I'm sure Dr. Glasson did bandage it for her. And when I saw her Friday, I'm sure she was suffering from a massive hangover."

"God, what a waste."

"What is?"

"You. You should have been a cop. You're a natural, better than all the fools I've had to work with."

"What about Duncan? She's no fool."

"No, she's not."

She waited for him to say something further, tell her something that would let her know she had nothing to worry about. There was so much she wanted to know about Wilmot and Duncan but could never ask. He smiled at her and smoothed back her tangled curls. "How'd you get so smart?"

"In clubs and bars, the places I've spent my life, everyone is on the make in one way or another. You meet liars and cheats and outright crooks, trying to steal songs, or sex, or even your loose change off the table. Anything you can lay claim to, someone will be there to take it away from you if you're not careful. You learn to watch and size people up pretty quickly, or you die."

"You're describing my two years undercover."

"Hey, maybe part of a cop's training should be to work in dives for a year, existing on tips from waiting tables and eating scraps from the kitchen. It would toughen them up. Smarten them up too."

"We found Trina's backpack. That's why Duncan and I were at the Cutters'."

"Where did you find it?"

"Diane Cutter found it hanging under a jacket on the coat rack in the front hall. Her husband didn't want her to call us. It proves Trina went back there. Hannah may have seen her or maybe Trina just snuck in and left her backpack and then slipped out to meet someone. Either way, Ward Cutter will see the backpack as more evidence of Hannah's guilt."

Or maybe, Singer thought, Trina had bumped into Dr. Glasson. Had she been wrong about him? She'd definitely put both Hannah and Dr. Glasson back in the picture by telling Wilmot about Hannah's bandage. Either one of them could have seen Trina that night.

He searched her face. "Have you told me everything?"

A rush of dread. "About what?"

"Everything you know about Trina's death."

"What makes you think I know anything else?"

"Because I've got you figured."

"God, I sincerely hope not." She smiled and wrapped her arms around his neck. "Maybe I'm just keeping a few things to myself to give you a reason to come back."

"Oh, I think you already did that."

Chapter 26

Singer couldn't sleep. She found herself listening, first for someone creeping up on her, and then for Wilmot returning. She watched the red numbers on the clock, got up and paced for an hour, and then returned to watching the clock. By six she gave up.

She had coffee ready and a warm welcome when he finally returned.

He held her close. "I won't stay long. I have to go up and see Olivia. And I have to talk to Pam Haver."

"Why are you talking to her again?"

"She lied on her statement when she gave Frank an alibi. We have to take a new one."

"So many people are lying."

"That's what people do." His words were matter a fact. "My job is to get the truth out of them."

"Was Trina raped?"

"No, but that isn't for anyone else to know."

"Then why kill her?"

"The usual reasons. Maybe she rejected him, or…" He grimaced. "This also isn't for anyone else to know."

She nodded.

"We have the autopsy report back." What the report had shown most clearly was that although Trina hadn't been raped, the murder had been committed by someone who got off on inflicting terror and pain. "Trina didn't die quickly or easily. The coroner found ligature marks that weren't obvious at the crime scene." He didn't tell her that there was DNA evidence. It would help them get a conviction, but it wouldn't help them find the murderer.

"Was there anything else?"

Wilmot had been about to say he was certain the murderer would kill again. "I've said too much already."

"No. You've only said enough to scare the shit out of me." She rose and went to the kitchen counter to pour a mug of coffee. With the carafe still in her hand she glanced at him and asked, "What kind of monster is out there?"

"And is he still out there?" Wilmot ran his hand back and forth across the nape of his neck. "That's what worries me. If it was a tourist, he could be long gone and we'll never know who killed Trina. If that happens, people will always wonder, will always be willing to believe the worst of their neighbors."

"That's what Peter says too."

"For me it will be a failure. If I don't solve this, I'll never get back to Major Crimes."

"Is staying on Glenphiddie for the rest of your career the worst thing that could happen to you?"

Wilmot smiled. "Here, in the kitchen with you, it doesn't seem that it is."

"As nice as that sounds, you'd better solve it. What time was Trina killed?"

"Why?"

"Curious."

He studied her. He knew there was more to the question, but he was also perfectly aware from past experience that Singer wouldn't tell him anything until she was ready. And even then, she would reveal only what she wanted him to know and no more. She couldn't be bullied. He'd blasted the staff and volunteers for leaking evidence, and he had already told her way too much, but Singer had given him solid information. The horrible sight of Trina's body preserved in photographs ate at him. Finding the killer went beyond his own ambition or even his reputation. He stared at the table top. What he really saw were the stiff limbs of a brutalized corpse. Extremities that were well past the peak of rigor, and beginning to loosen.

She touched his arm. "Louis…"

"Judging by rigor mortis..." His gaze moved to Singer. "And with the stomach contents—the medical report suggests she died sometime around midnight." He knew she'd asked her question for a reason. "Does that fit for you?"

Instead of answering she said, "You need sleep. Why don't you go to bed? Olivia has to know that someone is after her, but you can't just call her. I'll go up the mountain and warn her."

"No you don't. I'm going." He raised his hand to stop her arguments. "The attack on you is a crime and you're a victim. This isn't personal, it's my job. Stay here until I come back. Promise me you won't leave the apartment."

She nodded.

"Say it."

She looked up at him and smiled. "What, are we back in grade school?"

"Say it."

"I promise I won't go back to Olivia's apartment without you."

"That's not what I said. Don't leave this apartment either."

She planted her elbows on the table and rested her chin on her hands. "Actually, it's an easy promise to make. I don't know karate and I don't own a baseball bat. I mean to correct that oversight immediately."

"Just stay here and I'll be your baseball bat."

"Hmmm." She raised an eyebrow and gave him a knowing glance. "You think a lot of yourself, don't you?"

They grinned at each other.

Chapter 27

Now that it was light, Wilmot rechecked the alley. There was nothing to see, no signs of struggle, no evidence left behind. *Not like the movies. The guy didn't accidentally drop a business card.* These wry thoughts didn't console him. It felt like this case was spinning beyond his control.

Driving his own personal car, he headed out of town to see Olivia. He hated taking his Mustang up the twisting lane into Singer's place, but he'd left the squad car at the station. Thoms would be driving it now.

Out Harbor Road, past Blind Man's Cove, white swans rode the waves of the incoming tide, floating close to each other and dipping their heads gently as if acknowledging and bowing to their own grandeur. Wilmot was just admitting to himself that the beauty of the island could pull you in when a deer ran onto the road. He slammed on the brakes, felt a gentle bump, and then his car skewed sideways. The deer didn't stop. It jumped across the ditch and disappeared up the embankment and into the underbrush.

The car settled on the very edge of a twenty-foot drop. Wilmot sat clutching the wheel until his heart stopped hamming against his ribcage, and then he got out and examined the Mustang's fender. A few hairs were stuck in a three-inch break in the shining paintwork, but there was no blood. He tugged the silken threads free. He stood there for some time thinking how easily a life could disappear. The rain, spitting on his face, chased him back into his car.

He went first to talk to Olivia. He hardly recognized her. She was wearing the castoffs of a larger person of indeterminate gender—an old shirt, gray with age and stained with a red sauce, over a ragged blue sweatshirt and track pants rolled up at the waist.

When he'd delivered his news she said, "I told you someone was after me." Instead of being shocked or terrified, Olivia was triumphant. "I told you he would kill me next." Barefoot, she strode back and forth in front of the fireplace, her voice rising. "I told you."

"Yes you did. Sit down and tell me who might want to attack you and why."

She yelled, "If I had any idea who broke into my apartment, don't you think I'd already have told you?" Suddenly, as if her outbursts had drained her of all strength, she flopped down in a leather club chair and flung her legs over the arm. The bottoms of her feet were black with grime. "This is exhausting and it takes me away from my work. I think I have to go away."

"If you leave the island, let me know where you're going."

A snort of disgust. "I'm not going anywhere. I can't afford to leave. I'm staying here until you find the guy."

He looked around. "How is it here? I would never have pictured you living in a place like this."

An easy laugh. "Me neither. But it's good. No distractions. And I feel safer in this place than in town."

"What about Pam Haver?"

"She brought me eggs when I was out for a walk this morning, slipped in and left them in the fridge. It's like living with a ghost. But it's good, comforting to know someone is nearby."

He nodded. "Someone being around is a good thing."

"Ah." She canted her head to one side and considered him. Then she bobbed her head in understanding.

"What?"

"Nothing." She was grinning. "Somebody's gotten under your skin, haven't they?"

He rose. "I'm going to see the rest of the commune."

He'd been surprised at the changes when he'd driven in. The tall grass had been mown and raked and the red tractor now sat beside the barn. He went to have a closer look at the old Ford, a piece of machinery that had always intimidated him. He'd tried to start it, just wanting to take it out and drive it around the meadow, but couldn't raise as much as a cough out of it. In the end, he figured his failure was a good thing. He could see himself taking out the back wall of the barn while he figured out the gears on the ancient piece of machinery.

Pam Haver came out of the barn, wiping her hand on a rag. Wilmot stepped away from the tractor. "Good morning." He waved to the mown pasture. "Is this your work?" There was no way Singer had hired anyone to cut the grass, and it certainly wasn't Olivia who'd done it.

Her eyes followed his hand. "Yes. I had a little trouble getting the equipment operating, but it worked out okay in the end."

He wanted to ask if she'd eaten since he'd last seen her. Bones covered by skin, that's all that was left of her. How could anyone lose weight that fast? "You've done a great job."

"I'm clearing up the outbuildings and getting ready to stack the hay inside. If Singer agrees, I'll put up some temporary fencing for the sheep."

"Sheep?" He felt stupid even as he said it. "You're going to raise sheep here?"

"My ewes and their lambs have to leave Cooper's Island if I'm not there."

Sheep and hens were alien life forms to Wilmot. He nodded and looked out over the field to the small orchard where trees blossomed, some pink, but mostly white. He guessed that different colored blooms were a sign of different types of trees, but felt too foolish to ask.

"Come and see my chickens." She walked away without waiting for him to consent.

He didn't have time for chickens, but it felt cruel to deny her something she seemed to need. At the enclosure, she pointed at two black-and-white striped fowl among the russet brown hens. "Barred rock. They're good for eggs and meat, and they don't mind our cool weather. They like it up here." The thought seemed to please her, as if she'd truly been worried about whether the hens would approve of their new home. "I'm going to get some more. Should have changed over long ago."

He nodded as if he understood. Along the outer wall of the barn someone had installed boxes with sloped and hinged roofs. A fat hen stood on the roof of one of the boxes while the rest of the birds pecked at the ground below.

He wasn't sure what was expected of him. "You've done a lot of work."

"It's the only thing that keeps me sane. If I sit still for a minute..." She couldn't go on. She took a deep breath and reached out to grip the fence as if to keep herself upright. "Have you any news?"

He heard the longing in her voice, an echo of the emotions of every victim's family he'd ever spoken to. Even though the causes might be far different, the unbearable pain of the living was alike, the sameness of grief. "We've made progress but we haven't found the man who killed your daughter."

She swung to face him. "What progress?"

A fly buzzed around his face and he slapped it away. Flies meant swallowing hard to keep from retching, and telling family shocking news. Flies reminded him of bodies, of carrion, and the eggs the flies laid there. Death, that's what flies were to Wilmot.

"At this point it is all about the science of the crime and gathering evidence, none of which is any help for you to understand what happened to Trina."

"I want to know."

"What do you want to know?"

"Everything."

"The details of the investigation won't help you." What good would it do to explain that her daughter's face had been battered to pulp, and then eaten by crabs, before her body was put on a table and dissected? She didn't need to know any of the awfulness of forensics or the crude malice of nature. Better for her to remember her daughter alive and vibrant. "I have nothing to ease your loss."

"Did she die on Ghost Island?"

"Yes."

She turned to face him now. "How can you be certain?"

He didn't want to explain about lividity, about blood pooling after death when the heart stops pumping. Even if a body is moved, the blood stays in the place it was in when death occurred. "I don't understand it all. The medical people can tell if a body has been moved. Trina hadn't been moved."

She nodded, accepting his ignorance. She turned back to watch her hens scratch up a cloud of dust. "Do you think she suffered?" Her voice was calm but he saw her fingers curl cruelly around the top wire of the fence, saw her nails bite into her palms until her knuckles stood out white beneath the skin.

"I don't think she even knew it happened." It was a lie he'd told many times before.

Her shoulders relaxed and her fingers uncoiled. "Good." She stepped away from the fence, brushing a flutter of hair back from her face. "Good," she said again.

"I need to go over the statement you made."

A small nod of agreement. "I didn't tell you the truth. Frank left the island. I don't know what time he came back to the island or if he stayed there or if he went away again."

"If he wasn't on Cooper's Island, do you know where he'd have been?"

"He was probably with a woman." Cool and matter of fact; her husband's infidelity held no interest for her. But then distaste rippled across her face. "I'm sure he went to Kilborn, maybe…" She couldn't speak the unspeakable. "If I knew, believe me, I would tell you."

"Even if it meant your husband's arrest?"

Her body jerked as tight as a drawn bowstring. "I want justice. No, I want revenge for my daughter's death. I'd never protect him." Words spewed out with hate. "And if I find out he killed Celastrina…" She turned her head away, speaking to the chickens now. "I want the person responsible for Celastrina's death to be punished. I'd do it myself if I got the chance, and believe me, my justice would be a lot more ruthless than yours."

Chapter 28

Locked in Wilmot's apartment, Singer felt caged. The television only seemed to make her feel worse, so she turned it off, and in the sudden silence heard an argument going on in the apartment to the right. There was a crash. A door slammed. Footsteps pounded down the concrete corridor outside her door. She went to the window and watched a man run down the stairs. On the street beyond people hurried by, focused on their destination, while she was trapped there in limbo. Was someone out there really waiting to attack her? But that wasn't right. The attacker had thought she was Olivia. She was sure of it. She turned away from the window.

Even knowing she wasn't the focus of the attack, fear kept her from going out to the small balcony for a cigarette. Instead, she opened the bathroom window and turned on the fan, blowing the smoke upward. The phone rang. She dropped the cigarette into the toilet and darted into the bedroom to answer it. She hesitated with her hand on the phone. Would Louis want her to answer his calls? But it might be him. She picked up the phone with a tentative and cautious, "Hello?"

His laughter sang down the line. "You sound like something might jump out from the receiver and bite you."

"I didn't know if you would want me to answer your phone."

"Oh," he said.

She waited.

"Look, I just wanted you to know everything is fine up here, more than fine. I'll tell you about it when I get home."

Home. It was a beautiful word. "Okay," she agreed, and then she added, "Did Olivia know anything that might help?"

"Nope."

"Louis, I've been thinking."

She heard an engine start in the background. "Doing my job again?"

"It has to be someone they both know, Olivia and Trina."

"That could be hundreds of people. Living on this island, we all know the same people."

"I hadn't thought of that."

"I have one stop to make and then I'll be home."

Home. She smiled as she went to the kitchen. She opened the fridge but it was even barer than hers, an inch of milk, no juice, and Wilmot had eaten the last crust with his coffee. She looked at the overcast sky through the window over the sink. She'd promised not to go back to the apartment and she had no intention of going there. A ten-minute walk to the grocery store would be safe. And she wouldn't go anywhere there weren't loads of people. Surely that would be all right. Why would anyone want to hurt her? But then, why would anyone want to kill Trina?

She headed for the door. Standing in the opening, she searched for danger. There was no one about. A fine rain had started. In five minutes the sun would come out again, but still she would be wet by the time she got to the store. She went back to the closet and got Wilmot's yellow slicker.

She couldn't lock the door or she wouldn't be able to get back in. She wouldn't be long. No one would know. No one would be there waiting for her when she came back.

At the entrance to the market she met Peter coming out. Shifting his bag of groceries to his left hand, he held the door open for her and asked, "Have you talked to Olivia?"

She shook her head. "She seems to have gone on a holiday." She pulled out a grocery cart, gave him a small wave and started inside.

He put out a hand to stop her. "I need to patch things up with her. Tell her... Well, tell her I was wrong too. We need to talk."

"I'll tell her if she calls." She had no idea what he was talking about, but she nodded and headed for the produce section, preoccupied by thoughts of the things she wanted to buy. If she was going to be stuck inside for a few days, she was going to have food. Life was all about finding food and a warm place to sleep.

She pushed her cart around a display tower and into the meat section. Frank Haver, a red plastic basket over his arm, looked up from the cold meat case. "You," he said and stepped toward her. Unshaven and wearing the same clothes he'd had on when she last saw him, he moved in a rank cloud of body odor.

She spun the cart to the left, positioning it between them.

"Where's Pam?" he asked.

She shook head. "I don't know."

He jabbed a square finger at her. "She went off with you, twice."

She tried to back away but he gripped the wire cart, keeping it in place.

"I don't know where she is," she said.

"You know." He stared at her and rattled the cart from side to side. "Tell me."

"Ask Wilmot. He took her to a shelter. She didn't want to go back to Cooper's Island."

"That's a lie. Bill came to check on her damn sheep this morning, said he'd come and get them next week. They're going to the same place where he took the chickens." He pointed at her. "That's where she is. You know where that is and so does Bill."

"Then ask him."

She could see it in his eyes, the shift to the side at the idea of facing Bill. He was afraid, a bully who only felt strong when he thought someone else was weaker than him. She jerked the cart out of his hands and then jammed it into him, catching him by surprise, the frame ramming into his leg. His wince of pain brought her pleasure. "I don't know where she is so get the hell out of my way."

Around them all movement stopped. Heads turned as shoppers waited to see what violence was going to grow out of the raised voices. She jabbed the cart at him again and he staggered back, grabbing his shin where she'd struck him. That's when she saw the bandage on his hand, right where she'd bitten her attacker.

"You're the..." She clamped her mouth shut. "Go see Sergeant Wilmot," she said and wheeled the cart around him. She didn't look back, pretending to be unconcerned, but her hands were shaking as she picked up the bacon.

The rain stopped and the sun came out, turning the yellow slicker into a walking sauna. Sweat ran down her spine. She'd bought too much. Her arms were being pulled out of their sockets by the weight. Unnerved by her confrontation with Frank Haver, she walked as quickly as she could manage, panting with exertion and glancing from side to side, half expecting an attack. If he came at her, she'd use the heavy grocery bags as weapons. They were all she had.

She huffed halfway up the stairs and hesitated. *Fool.* Leaving the place unlocked was a reckless invitation to a killer. Footsteps on the stairs behind her. She swirled, ready to fight.

It was the man from the next apartment. He hesitated, brows furrowing, knowing something wasn't quite right. He greeted her guardedly.

Singer forced a smile. "Hi." She hurried up the few remaining steps to the green door with the number seven on it. The man followed, moving close to her. Her throat was so dry she was afraid she wouldn't be able to scream.

He reached past her and turned the doorknob. "You've got your hands full," he said before he went on to the next apartment.

Terror ruled her behavior. "Thank you," she called out, loud enough to be heard down on at the dock and startling her neighbor. She wanted anyone waiting for her in the apartment to know that she was not alone. She took a deep breath and stepped inside.

Only the sound of water dripping in the kitchen sink greeted her. Everything was as she'd left it. She dropped the bags on the table and locked the door.

The groceries were put away and the bacon was frying when she heard a key in the lock. She wrapped her hand around the skillet's handle. The door opened and Wilmot stepped in.

She released her death-grip on the pan. *Insane, I've gone completely insane.*

He raised his nose and sniffed. "You're cooking. Where'd you get it?"

"Not in your fridge. A girl could starve in this place." She raised her hand to stop his words. "I just went to the store, where there were lots of people." She turned on a second pan and cut a slab of butter onto the surface. "How do you like your eggs?"

What he wanted to tell her was to take more care, to say that his heart would break if anything should happen to her. He knew it was useless. She would do exactly what pleased her. Or perhaps, if he was honest with himself, he just didn't want to seem that vulnerable. He said, "The same as I like my women, over and easy."

She smiled at him. "'Over and Easy' would make a great song title." She smiled. "Like in, 'I was easy and now it's over.'"

"Nothing easy about you." He laughed at the truth of it. She wasn't easy to hold onto and she wouldn't be easy to forget.

She joined in his amusement. "Oh, I don't know. I was pretty easy. Didn't try too hard to fight you off."

Her curly black hair, flying out of control, and her dazzling smile made his heart misbehave. He turned his back to her and pulled off his jacket. The smell of coffee and melted butter in the pan—moments like this were suddenly precious. "I thought you told me you couldn't cook."

"Well, I can't, unless you consider this cooking." She cracked the egg and dropped it into the pan. "And opening a can, I'm awfully good at that." She took a second egg out of the carton. He came to her and took it out of her hand. "I've signed up for cooking lessons at the winery."

Her amazement showed in her voice. "Why would you take cooking classes?"

"Because you won't." He kissed her lightly on the nose. "Cooking is like some rite of passage in a relationship, isn't it?"

"I thought it was sharing booze and drugs." She went to the cupboard and took down two blue plates. "I only know how to cook eggs because the one straight gig I ever had was working in a diner back in Taos. I learned a few things, but they all involved a frying pan and about fifteen minutes."

"One day, when this case is over, I'll cook one of my mother's dishes. She was French Canadian. All of her food takes lots of butter and cream and plenty of time."

Time, the one thing they didn't have. "I'll help." She opened the cupboard for coffee mugs. "But nothing that takes talent, just chopping and peeling stuff." It was good to plan for the future, life without terror, good to know that a future was a possibility.

"We could ask Duncan to dinner," he said.

A stab to her heart. She turned away and set the mugs on the table. "Would she come? I thought she didn't like you."

"Well, I must be doing something right. I heard her tell Thoms I'd solve this case. Maybe she's starting to like me."

She dropped bread in the toaster and pushed down the lever. Lately, whenever she saw Wilmot and Duncan together, she hadn't known if it was possessiveness or dread that ate at her. "With Duncan, how can you tell?"

He flipped the eggs. "Because, while she's never been polite, she's become downright rude."

She glanced up at him, trying to see if he was making a joke. She could see he was pleased. She watched the toaster instead of him. A fresh and bitter emotion gnawed at her. "Does she know you want to be a detective again, to leave Glenphiddie?"

"Sure. Duncan wants to leave too." He took the frying pan to the table but he didn't plate the eggs, just stood staring at something she couldn't see. "Maybe I can't go back. Perhaps I've already lost my edge."

"Don't start growing cabbages quite yet." She picked up the bacon from the paper towel and put it on their plates. She licked the grease off her fingers as he slid the eggs down to join the bacon.

"This is perfect," she said, looking at their feast.

He took the skillet back to the stove. "I'm going to get some steaks and make you something my mother used to cook for us, potatoes, carrots, rutabaga, parsnips, any other root vegetables she grew in the garden, all mashed together with cream and butter. It's a lovely golden color. I don't know what it's called, but sometimes that's all we had to eat for dinner. With a slab of her bread, it was enough." He juggled the hot toast and hurried to the table, dropping the toast on her plate. "Oatmeal for breakfast and mash for dinner. We were eight healthy little heathens."

"Eight?"

"Chaos. I think that's why I went into the police—a longing for order. Strange, because now I know policing is all about turmoil, the mess and mistakes of crazy people, anything but order. But it was either the police or the church and, since I had no particular belief, I became a cop." He took the buttered toast she held out to him.

He bit into his toast and then reached into his pocket. "I got this made for you." He put a key on the table between them.

She reached out for it and held it as tenderly as if it were made of crystal. Tears trembled on the edge of her eyes.

"You aren't going to cry, are you?"

She squeezed her lips together and shook her head. "It's just that no one has ever given me a key to their place before."

"Never?"

She laughed and wiped at her eyes. "Not unless I gave him money first and promised to be gone by checkout time the next day."

When they finished eating, Singer told Wilmot about meeting Frank Haver. Wilmot listened without speaking. When her story was finished, he took his jacket from the back of the chair, kissed the top of her head, and said, "See you later."

"Damn," she said, as the door closed behind him. The trouble with telling him things was that it always sent him away.

She sat there staring at the litter of dirty breakfast dishes and decided she needed a little extra protection for when Wilmot wasn't around. She knew just where to get it.

When she'd cleaned up the wreckage of breakfast, she left a note on the table and locked the door. And then she unlocked it again with her new key and stepped inside. She stood for a moment, feeling a real sense of entitlement. With her very own key in her pocket, she could come back any time she wanted to. "Home," that's what Louis had said.

Chapter 29

The gun wasn't under the seat of the yellow van where she'd left it. *Olivia. She must have found it.* She headed for the house.

On either side of the steps to the porch, weathered wine barrels were being used for planters. Someone had started digging the dead plants out of the one on the right. A trowel and a pile of weeds, wilting in the sun, lay discarded on the walkway beside it. Singer stepped over the abandoned gardening project and went inside without knocking, calling, "Olivia."

The living room had become the reverse of Olivia's apartment. Everything was neat and tidy, but a small table pushed in front of a window was littered with papers. More were tacked on the wall around it. Single pages of frantic writing had been taped to the window frame with duct tape. One sheet was nothing but a list of names, some of which had notes for character traits written in beside them. Singer stepped closer to study the sheet of Bristol board that Olivia had pinned to the log wall. It looked like she had started drawing a chart, with the days of the week in a line across the top and events written underneath. Arrows and lines went in all directions. She read a bit, but it made no sense. "Crazy as a loon," Singer said softly.

She heard the bathroom door open upstairs. Olivia leaned over the rail and said, "Hey."

Singer waved her hand at the mess of paper. "So, it's really happening."

"Looks like it." Olivia jogged down the stairs.

Singer pointed at Olivia and said, "I can't believe you actually own a pair of those." The waistband of Olivia's paint-stained gray sweats was rolled over several times, but the legs still pooled around her ankles. Above the sweats she wore a navy top with the arms scissored off to her elbows while the bottom was unevenly cut off over her belly.

Olivia looked down at herself as if she'd only that second become aware that she was wearing clothes. "Peter's," she said and headed for the kitchen. "I'll make tea."

"Tea?"

"Cheaper and quicker. I don't have much time. Why are you here?"

"Well, hello to you too. Have you taken anything out of my old van?"

Olivia's waxed hair stood up from her head like she'd suffered an electrical shock. "Why the hell would I bother with that old rattletrap?" She turned off the tap. "There's probably all kinds of wildlife living in it."

"Are you sure?"

"About what?"

"Being in the van."

The kettle slammed onto the burner. "I haven't been near the van. I still think you should use it for a chicken coop." Olivia went to the cupboard and took down cups. "But Pam said she would fix my flat. The Volks doesn't have a tire iron, never did as far as I can remember. Pam went to look in the van for a tire iron. She didn't find one, so unless the van works, we're stuck up here without transportation." Her hands paused on the fridge handle. "Actually, will you take me downtown to pick up my last paycheck and buy a few groceries?"

"Only if you go dressed just the way you are." Olivia frowned at her. Singer said, "I'll go ask Pam if she needs anything."

Pam was in the barn forking hay into a large crib. Specks of dust and chaff danced in the air where the sun streamed through openings in the roof. The odor of mold and hay was overpowering.

Pam turned when Singer's body blocked the light. She stared at her silently, but with little real interest, as Singer studied the barn. She could see the signs of Pam's labors everywhere.

Pam followed her gaze and said, "Steven Davids left everything you need to have a lovely little farm."

"Whoopee." The smell of the hay tickled her nose. "But what would I do with a farm? It's like tossing a computer to a monkey." She sneezed. "Damn." She squeezed her nose, beating down the urge to sneeze again. While she waited to see if the sneezing fit had passed, she watched Pam work. Loss had turned her into a walking cadaver. "Pam, have you been eating?"

"I cut the meadow," Pam said. "The hay will keep the ewes going when the rain stops coming this summer." She lifted another forkful from the small cart and threw it into the crib in a rhythm as old as time.

"You have to take care of yourself or you won't be able to take care of the sheep."

"They'll eat that field down in no time." Her fork didn't stop for conversation.

"Good," Singer said, not really sure if it was. "You've done so much." The barn no longer seemed derelict. The floor had been swept and things hung up. "Even I can see the improvements." The fact was the barn looked in better shape than Pam. "Maybe you should take it a bit easy now."

"I'm fine."

"You're working yourself into the ground."

"I can't sleep." She leaned on the pitchfork as she explained. "Physical work helps keep me from thinking and I need to be exhausted to fight back the bad thoughts."

"Probably isn't the worst thing you could do." Singer shoved her hands deep into her pockets. "There was a time when my own mind was my enemy, but it wasn't work I resorted to. My ways of dulling the pain were much more destructive."

Pam stacked more hay. Her arms were bare and Singer watched her long sinewy muscles flex with each lift of the fork. For all Pam's thinness, heavy labor had defined and developed her body over many years until it was as strong as a man's.

"We're going down into town. Do you want anything?"

"I do need some things." The fork stopped and she turned to Singer. "Would you mind?"

"Of course not. I'm just glad to know you'll be eating."

"Hate feeds me. It makes me strong and gives me a reason for living." She went to the workbench and jerked open a drawer. She took out a pencil and a pad, yellowed and curled with age, and began to write.

She brought the list to Singer. "I'll get you some money."

"No need. You can pay me when I bring your order back." She looked briefly at the note and saw a small sketch of a guitar in the corner. Stevie's work. She folded the paper and put it in her pocket. Singer looked around the barn. How many guitars had he built here and where were they now? Some of them were in the main building. She'd have to find a home for them. Maybe she should give one to Hannah, the blue one, blue like Trina's tattoo.

"Pam, Olivia says you were in the van."

"I started it. The key was in the ashtray. I thought you might want it in running order." Pam picked up the pitchfork and folded her hands on top of it, waiting.

"Why were you under the driver's seat?" Singer asked.

"I was looking for a tire iron. Olivia's tire is flat. I'll fix it while you shop." She rested her chin on her hands. "Why did you keep a tire iron under the seat and not with the spare tire?"

"Protection. On the road, living in alleys and behind roadhouses has its drawbacks. Why did you take my other piece of security?"

Pam's mouth tightened into a hard thin line and she straightened, but she didn't answer nor did she look away.

"I know all about revenge," Singer said. "It's a really bad idea."

Pam lifted the fork and jabbed it viciously into the hay.

"If you're planning on using my gun on your husband, don't."

Pam pulled loose a forkful of the hay and glanced at Singer. "Oh, I'd never do that." Her smile was sweet, almost angelic, but then her face changed. "Unless he killed Celastrina." She began her rhythmic labor again.

"Pam, listen."

Pam stabbed the fork deep into the hay and swung to face her. "No, you listen. I was a coward. I should have left him. Instead I sent my daughter away. Two years she was here and I only saw her on the weekends, and not every weekend at that. I should have been here with her. Look what he's cost me." She yanked the fork free, swinging it in a wide arc.

Singer backed away.

"Her death is my punishment for being weak." She jabbed the fork savagely into the hay pile, working at a manic pace.

"Pam, please." Her pleading went unanswered. Hate burned through Pam like a firestorm, her need for revenge pushing her beyond normal limitations.

Singer retreated from her rage, but still she wanted to argue with Pam. Singer was frightened by the implications for herself. Would she be guilty of aiding in a crime if her weapon was used? Did that make her an accessory? She didn't know and she couldn't ask Wilmot, couldn't tell him that Pam had her gun. If it all went wrong, she'd just deny everything. The gun was unregistered with no way to trace it to her.

The old van had always been her safe hidey-hole. She'd left the pistol there because she was afraid if she moved it to the Yukon a mechanic might find it. Or Wilmot might come across it if she kept the gun in the house. She knew certain things about Wilmot, lines that he wouldn't cross. The first one was; the law is absolute. He might bend the rules himself but he always kept the laws. One night he'd tried to explain to her what the motto, "*To serve and protect,*" meant. She'd asked, "What about stupid laws? Do you keep them too?" He answered, "Yes, until someone changes them. 'MAINTIENS LE DROIT'— 'defending the law,' that's what it says on our badges. I can't choose what laws I enforce and what ones I don't. That's not my function. People in law enforcement don't have the luxury of thinking for themselves. It's beyond our own life and needs. There are no exceptions, no making it up as we go along. It's black and white. At least it should be, because without laws we return to survival of the fittest."

So the gun had stayed in the van until she might need it. Singer's hand went to the back pocket of her jeans where she had slipped his key. She didn't want to test him in any way, not yet. There was just too much at stake, but what if… It was a question she couldn't answer.

She'd just hope that the police found Frank before Pam did.

Olivia waited in the Yukon. Her frayed jeans, out at the knees and splattered with bleach splotches, and a washed-out T-shirt from a long ago rock concert, were only a small improvement from Peter's remnants. "Even grocery shopping seems like an outing when you've been up here for a day," Olivia said. "Couldn't you get Pam to come? She works from sun up to sun down. But then, there isn't much else to do here."

Singer pulled the safety belt snug. "Do you miss not having television?"

"Nope, but I'm going to stock up on books." Olivia's window slid down. "I think Pam's a little crazy."

"Losing a child would do that to you, and having a husband like Frank would finish the job."

"That Frank is a sorry son of a bitch," Olivia said. "Someone should do something about him."

Chapter 30

As they left Kilborn to head back up the mountain the air was rich with the scent of rain. Ominous low clouds made it seem more like November than a spring day. When they turned off the road onto the lane, Olivia scanned the sky. "I want to get the flowers in before it starts to rain again."

Singer braked for the bridge over the gorge. When they'd rumbled over the wooden trestles and up the other side, she let out the breath she held and said, "I'll put the groceries away if you want to plant your flowers."

"Good. It will only take a minute and then I'll make us something hot to drink." The first drops of rain drummed on the roof.

At the house, Olivia grabbed the flat of blood-red geraniums while Singer took two plastic bags over to the A-frame. She suspected Pam wouldn't approve of the plastic bags.

"Hello." She banged at the screen door with the toe of her shoe and then pulled it open with a finger. Squeezing her shoulder around the edge to hold it open, she stepped inside. The room had lost its musty odor. "Hello," she called again. No answer. There was no one in the A-frame to answer. She put the bag with perishable food in the refrigerator and left the other on the counter.

Outside it was raining in earnest now but Olivia was still at the planter, digging in the last of the flowers. "Where's Pam?" Singer asked, pulling her sweater tight around her.

Olivia didn't look up. "Haven't seen her."

Singer looked to the barn. "Funny. You'd think she'd at least come out when she heard us pull in."

"I told you she's crazy." Olivia pointed with the trowel. "Look, the front door is open. I know I closed it. She must have gone in after me and left it wide open."

Singer reached into the Yukon for Olivia's shopping. "She probably ran out to lock up her chickens." She picked up plastic bags in each hand, and then straightened. She called, "Pam," and waited for a reply. When it didn't come, she set the bags down again. "I hope she hasn't had an accident. I'll check the barn."

The rusty hinges squeaked in protest. "Pam?" The drone of flies was the only answering sound.

It took time for Singer's eyes to adjust to the dim light. It took her brain more time to make sense of what she was seeing. Pam's fingers were still curled into claws as if she'd been scratching her nails into the dirt surface, trying to dig her way to safety.

"Jesus." Singer clapped her hand over her mouth, then slowly lowered it to whisper, "Are you all right?" Stupid question. With the pitchfork pinning Pam's body to the floor and with her brains spilling out onto the blood-soaked ground, how could she be anything but dead?

Singer stepped closer, needing to confirm what she already knew. "Pam," she whispered. Senseless thoughts chased through Singer's brain. Should she take the pitchfork out of Pam's body? Beside the body was a hammer. Blood clogged Pam's hair and a halo of gore and gelatinous brain matter stained the dirt around her head. Someone had beaten in her head as well as stabbed her with the pitchfork.

Gagging at the stench of death, of blood and other body fluids, she fell to her knees beside the body. The odor was overwhelming. "Oh, Jesus." She pinched her nose shut and swallowed the rising bile. The flies had already found the body and were feasting on the blood.

She stretched out her hand to Pam's wrist. There was no pulse, but then she'd known there wouldn't be. She eased back on her heels and looked around. Had Pam been running away and come in here to hide or had she come in looking for something to fight back with? Maybe neither of those things had happened. Maybe someone had come into the barn and taken her by surprise. But who? They hadn't met any cars on their way up Mt. Skeena. So where was the murderer? Was he still here?

Terror, sharp and overpowering. She was on her feet. Her concern was no longer for Pam but for herself. She backed away from the body and bumped into the workbench. The slightly opened drawer triggered a memory. There was something she needed to remember.

A shadow moved across the entrance to the barn, a figure blocking out the light. Panic. She grabbed a basin wrench from the rack above the worktable and twisted around to face the danger, her arm raised to strike. That's when the screams started.

Olivia's face was contorted in horror. She backed away from Singer, her eyes fixed on the wrench. Singer lowered her arm. "I didn't do it. I found her like this."

She wasn't sure that Olivia heard her or believed her. She pointed the wrench at the hammer beside the body. "Look, that's what killed Pam."

"Oh," Olivia said. She stared at Pam, her startled eyes wide. "Oh," she said again.

"Go call an ambulance."

Fixated on the body on the dirt floor, Olivia didn't respond. Singer went to her and shoved Olivia out the door. "We need an ambulance."

Olivia didn't move toward the house. "Where's the car?"

"What car?"

"The one that the killer came in. You said there's no one up at Johnny's mansion since Lauren left."

"What are you saying?"

Olivia sang a high whine of terror as she shuffled backward, away from Singer.

"I didn't do it." Singer dropped the wrench and rushed at Olivia. "Go call 911!"

Olivia was already running.

Singer turned back to the barn. A small burr of an idea had half-formed in her head before Olivia showed up. She pulled her sweater up to cover her nose and stepped cautiously inside. She looked from the hay rick to the work bench, trying desperately to bring back a fleeting thought that had seemed overwhelmingly important, but she couldn't remember what it was. *Think.* It was just before she picked up the wrench. What had it been? Something had jumped out at her, but panic had chased it away.

It no longer mattered. She had to get away from here. She spun around, about to run for the house. A flash of lightening. She was startled into immobility, shaken by the nearness of the bolt. Thunder boomed. She looked up at the sky as Olivia shot off the porch, running for her life. "Someone's been in here," she screamed and ran toward the SUV. She slid on the wet grass, going down on her side like she was sliding into home plate.

Singer moved now. Stumbling to Olivia, she reached out to help her.

Olivia rolled away from the offered hand. "No," she said, "No." She shot to her feet and circled around Singer.

Singer brushed away the rain pouring down her face. "Did you phone the Mounties?" Only one thing was clear to her. They needed help.

"No. Someone's been in there. They've ransacked it. It's a mess." Olivia gulped air, her chest heaving. "What if they're still in there?" She didn't wait to hear from Singer. She ran, scrambling into to the driver's seat and slamming the door shut behind her.

Singer looked from the Yukon to the house. The only phone was in the house. Was Olivia right? Could there be someone in there? She brushed away the rain and sodden strands of her hair. If the murderer hadn't left, he'd be watching them. Her thoughts pinballed around her head. No movement at any of the windows, not a twitch of a curtain. There was no car. He was gone. Was she positive the killer was a man? And it had to be someone who knew where to find Pam. A nasty jolt of suspicion. Olivia could have borrowed a car and come back up Mount Skeena and killed Pam.

Singer swung back to the pale face staring at her through the windshield. She couldn't decide if it was a rational idea or merely a crazy fear. Did it matter? She had to get help. She took two strides toward the house. The engine started. She twisted around, expecting to see Olivia waiting for her, motioning her toward the vehicle, but the Yukon was already moving. She darted forward, throwing her arms out as if she could physically stop it. Olivia drove straight at her. Didn't even pause. She was trying to run her down.

Singer jumped away. Olivia kept going.

Singer ran behind the Yukon. "Wait. Don't leave me here."

The Yukon didn't slow. In fact, Olivia was driving way too fast. She'd never manage the jog before the bridge, and even if she did, trying to maneuver the huge vehicle over the planks at that speed, and with only a four-inch board on each side as a barrier... The bottom of the gully was a drop of at least twenty feet. Singer listened for sounds of a crash. She heard nothing except the cruel chortle of ravens.

She turned slowly around. The rain fell straight down.

Where was safety? She processed the options. She could hide in the forest, but she risked getting lost. Besides, the deep woods had always petrified her. Then there was the barn. That's where Pam had been running to, going for a weapon. But maybe it wasn't a hammer or a wrench that Pam wanted. Maybe she wanted the gun she'd taken from under the driver's seat of the old yellow van. "Of course," Singer told the ravens.

The drawer from which Pam had taken pencil and paper contained the gun. Singer was certain of it. When she bumped into the workbench, her back hit the half open drawer. Pam had been going for the gun to kill Trina's murderer. There was no one else Pam would want to kill.

Singer wiped the rain from her face and studied the entrance to the barn. It didn't take her long to decide. As much as she wanted the security of her firearm, she couldn't go back in there. The house held a phone to bring help, but she was too terrified to go in there. She licked the rain from her lips and spun in a circle, hoping to discover safety while expecting to see a monster coming for her.

She had to make a choice. Beyond the porch the access to her home was a black hole. She tried to convince herself it was safe. Cautiously, she edged forward. By the shocking red flowers, she faltered, unable to force herself any nearer. It was no use. She couldn't go in.

That's when she heard the sound of a vehicle coming fast. Whimpering with fear, she swung to face this new threat as it burst into the clearing, speeding toward her.

It stopped ten feet away from her.

The driver's door swung open.

Chapter 31

Singer slammed the door behind her and locked it as Olivia climbed into the passenger seat. "Why?" Singer asked.

"You... Maybe you..."

Singer put the transmission into drive. "But I'd be covered in blood." She turned to stare at Olivia and saw a flash of an unidentifiable emotion cross her face. "Yes, that's what I thought. That's why I came back."

"But..."

"What?" Olivia asked.

"Nothing." Clothes could be changed. And everything Olivia suspected of Singer could be true of Olivia.

Rain pounded the roof. The curtain of clear wet beads streaming down the windows made it difficult to see. Singer drove cautiously. The soft thunk of the windshield wipers became hypnotic. Beside her, Olivia was shaking with shock. Tears rolled down her face. It was only when the tears pooled on her own lips that Singer realized that she was crying too.

Mist filled the valley and rose up into the trees. The aftershock of violence, heightened by the weather, created a tiny surreal space in which they were imprisoned, each with her own thoughts. Slowly and silently they made their way down Mount Skeena.

When they reached Harbor road Olivia said, "I'm sorry. I panicked."

She didn't reply.

"Singer, please."

"We'll go to the Mountie station."

"And then what?" Olivia said. "What do we do after that?"

"I don't care what you do after that."

"I can't go to my apartment, it isn't safe."

"Book into the Ferryman."

Olivia shook her head. "I'm not staying on this island."

"Go to Victoria."

Olivia turned shocked eyes to her. "Aren't you coming with me?"

"No one's after me."

"No, he's after me. That's why Pam died, he was coming for me. And maybe that's why Trina died, by mistake. Maybe he thought it was me, just like he did when he attacked you."

Singer glanced over at her. "That doesn't make any sense." Even as she said it she wasn't sure her words were true.

"It doesn't matter. I don't care who he's after. Until they arrest someone I'm out of here."

Wilmot laid his cheek on top of her head while she wailed against his chest. After the first wave of emotion passed, she leaned back in his arms and said, "Louis, when we were going down the mountain to Kilborn the first time, I saw Cody turning up that way."

Wilmot nodded and tried to pull her back to him, but she wanted to get it all out. "And then, when I went into Pam's place with her groceries, I saw a sympathy card on the table that wasn't there this morning. I looked at it. It was signed by Cody."

"And?"

"I've been wondering if he's just a decent kid expressing sympathy, or if he's a killer who tried to distract her by giving her the card. Either way, I think he was there today."

"Is there anything else?"

"No. Oh, wait, there is one thing. There's no phone in the A-frame so Pam would have to come..." She swallowed and started over. "She had to come into the house to phone. If she called Cody, that's how he found out where she was…"

"I can get the phone records and see if she called someone." He leaned in and kissed her forehead. "I have to go. Will you be all right on you own for a little bit if I take you to the apartment?"

"Is it safe?"

"I can't be sure, but I think so. Keep everything locked. I'll be back as fast as I can."

"Olivia's going to the Ferryman for the night. She wants me to come with her."

"An even better idea. Thoms will take you there."

What she didn't say was that she no longer trusted Olivia.

Tom Woods looked up from the desk as they entered the lobby. First came surprise and then a quizzical expression spread across his face. His gaze went from Singer to Olivia. "What's wrong?"

Olivia started to cry again.

Without comment, Tom came around the desk, put his arm around her and steered her into the office. Constable Thoms, who'd followed them into the inn, waved a hand and left them.

When he had the whole story out of them, Tom went to the front desk and got a key. Singer took it and got to her feet. "Don't tell anyone we're here, will you, Tom?"

"Nope, and I've given you the room closest to the desk. I'm shorthanded so I'll be on the desk all night. I'll be right here if you need me."

Tom led them down the hall and went inside with them. He went to the window and checked it was locked before he drew the curtains. "I'll bring you some dinner."

"A drink," Olivia said. "I need a drink." She crossed her arms over her sodden shirt. "And a hot bath."

Tom nodded. "A bottle of wine and two glasses. I'll bring it myself. Don't open up for anyone else." He needn't have added that.

Chapter 32

Wilmot and Duncan, dressed in white jumpsuits, stood outside the barn where Pam Haver still lay with the pitchfork in her back. Wilmot said, "The Ident team will be here within two hours. Until the forensic team gets here, the body will have to remain where it is. The helicopter can land in the meadow. For now, we'll secure the area with tape and do a basic search of the grounds."

"Singer's involved. You have to excuse yourself from the investigation."

"When I called Major Crimes, I told them that. They said to carry on because they can't get here for twenty-four hours."

"What?"

"They have too many ongoing active investigations to get a team together with a scene of crime vehicle and get it all on the last ferry from the mainland. It isn't going to happen today, but I've brought them up to speed on everything. They want the coroner's report on Trina and the witness reports. By the time they get here they'll be good to go. In the meantime, we carry on."

"But they're not coming today?"

"Nope."

"I thought they were pushing for you to turn this over."

"They were until that double homicide in Burnaby and a cop shooting up in Courtenay. The world has gone mad."

"Not to mention that the islands always come in second."

No matter what he told her Duncan would always complain. Either Major Crimes was pushing in where they weren't wanted or they were ignoring them. It was just her nature to always see the downside.

He said, "Let's get started and do the basic crime scene investigation."

Duncan kicked at the ground. "We're going to find your fingerprints all over the place, aren't we?"

"Yes. I was here earlier today to interview Pam and Olivia." He wasn't going to explain his life to Duncan. "My fingerprints are on file."

Duncan sighed. "It's going to be another long night. We better get started before we lose the last of the light."

"While you start here, I'll go find Cody." With Singer's statement that she'd seen Cody driving up Mount Skeena, he was now the chief suspect. Wilmot had already put out a call to have him picked up. "If he's responsible, I want to get him before he destroys any evidence. We'll get his clothes and impound his truck. When a forensic team gets here they can go over it and check for blood. Let's hope they find something."

At the Ferryman Inn, in the bed farthest from the window, Olivia snored lightly, but for Singer sleep wouldn't come. It was impossible to turn off her brain. With one hand behind her head, she stared up at the ceiling and tried to find answers to the questions that consumed her. Had Trina made plans to meet her murderer? When Singer had eavesdropped on Cody and Trina's conversation at the bank, Trina had expected to spend the whole night with him. She didn't have plans to see anyone else. So after she left Cody's house she'd met someone. But then, maybe she'd never left Cody's home.

Olivia whimpered. In the dim light from the clock Singer watched Olivia move restlessly. There were things Olivia wasn't saying about her relationship with Trina. Obsession, that's what Peter called it. And Olivia hadn't told Wilmot about her affair with Cody.

Footsteps outside in the corridor. Singer sat up and reached for the empty wine bottle on the night table. Her hand tightened around the neck. She waited. The footsteps moved on and she laid back down.

Olivia called out, "No," her legs thrashing as if she were running.

Singer went back to studying the ceiling. The creep, who was the creep? She'd identified everyone in Trina's diary but him. "He followed me home last night," she'd written. Followed her from where? Where did Trina go at night alone? She must have been alone or she would have said, "He followed us home." Trina was back at the high school one night a week for the writing class. Rehearsals for the high school musical were also in the evening. But rehearsals had been over for weeks. Had she been followed before or after rehearsals ended? Singer rolled onto her side. She would see Hannah in the morning and ask if Trina had said anything about a stalker. Had Trina really used the pronoun "he" when she wrote about the stalker? She wasn't sure. And what had Trina said about Hannah just before that entry?

She turned over to watch Olivia sleeping in the next bed. Tom had been angry with Olivia for leaving early on the night Trina died. Where was she when Trina was killed? Singer had asked her twice and been rebuffed. And then there was her involvement with Cody. *I should have told Louis.* Olivia was her friend but that didn't matter anymore. She rolled over to face the window. The soft glow of passing car lights shone behind the drapes and then disappeared.

Three hours, that was enough time for Olivia to go up the mountain and kill Pam and get back downtown to build an alibi. *I'm letting my imagination take over.* Except for the two dead women—she hadn't imagined them. Olivia had been to the library. She'd been carting a plastic bag of books with her groceries when Singer picked her up. How long would it take to pick a few books off the shelf and check them out, giving her an alibi? Easy enough to borrow a car and pull on coveralls. Cody could deliver both of those things. Perhaps Cody and Olivia were both involved in Pam's death. She could imagine it all.

But Olivia had been afraid. That at least had been genuine. Memory jolted her upright. Olivia was not only a writer and a painter, she had also been a professional actress before moving to the island.

Singer had known Olivia for months, but in the last few days she'd come to doubt that she knew the wily writer at all.

It was after midnight when someone knocked softly at room 102 at the Ferryman Inn. Singer slipped quietly from bed and peeked through the spy hole. Her spirits lifted. She'd been waiting for him.

She rushed out into the hall and into his arms, but their embrace didn't last long. She had a question she was desperate to have answered. "Have you found out who did it?"

He shook his head. "Cody admits he was up at the farm today but not until I told him I had a witness." Any thought of keeping information from Singer was long gone from Wilmot's mind. "He says there was no one there so he only stayed for five minutes. But there's no way of telling if it's true."

"He didn't see Pam?"

"He says not."

"And he didn't go into the barn?"

"Nope."

"Strange. I saw him on his way up. Surely she wasn't dead when he got there. But then, maybe she just stayed in the barn until he went away."

"That makes sense."

"Did he meet any cars on his way down?"

"Only one, but he doesn't remember anything about it except to say he thinks it was a light sedan."

"So if he's telling the truth, it was the killer on his way up Mount Skeena." She thought for a minute. "How did Cody know where to find Pam?"

"He says Bill told him. They serve on the volunteer fire department together."

"I wonder who else Bill told."

"I'm going to ask him that question first thing in the morning." Wilmot leaned back against the wall.

She saw his exhaustion, but she was too sleepless herself to sympathize. "Have you found Frank?"

"Not yet. Duncan went to Cooper's Island but Frank wasn't there and he doesn't seem to be on Glenphiddie. The local police in Ladysmith will check out his sister's place in the morning."

"Olivia is taking the first plane out in the morning."

"She's a witness. We need her to stay here, need to get a formal statement. She can't leave the island until she gives us that." He pushed away from the wall.

"Don't wake her now. Leave it until tomorrow. Besides, she drank three quarters of a bottle of wine. You'll get more sense out of her in the morning."

They stood there in silence, each busy with their own thoughts, until she asked, "You're pretty sure it was Frank, aren't you?"

"Pam thought it was him."

"What if it isn't Frank?" She put her fingers on his lips to stop his words. He pulled her hand away from his mouth, encircling it in his own hand and holding it to his chest, as she went on. "I know you think it was Frank who killed Trina and Pam, something domestic, and that the break-in at Olivia's has nothing to do with the murders, but what if you're wrong? Besides, Olivia said the house was searched. Doesn't that say they were looking for something of Olivia's?"

"Only if someone knew she was there."

"She says she didn't tell anyone." She leaned against him. "If they were searching Olivia's things, wouldn't it mean Olivia was the target? Olivia has said all along that someone was after her. Pam may have been killed by someone looking for Olivia."

"Possible." He made a face as if his next words gave him pain. "It's your house. We can't rule out the possibility that someone was looking for you."

"I've thought of that, but I can't think of any reason for someone to search my stuff. And I haven't been here long enough to make an enemy who'd want to beat my head in—except maybe Duncan. Then again, why would someone want to beat in Trina's or Pam's?"

"Did you tell anyone that Pam and Olivia were at your place?"

"No." Was it true? What if she'd given it away without realizing she had? She frantically went back over the conversations she'd had since Olivia moved up to Mount Skeena. "I'm sure I didn't, but someone could have followed us. Or maybe the person who attacked me reasoned that if I was in Olivia's apartment, she might be at my house."

He scratched along his whiskered jaw. "We have Trina's journal."

"What?"

"Someone dropped it through the book return slot at the library today. It was in a plain envelope with the words 'Give to the Mounties' written on it in block letters. Do you know anything about it?"

"Not a thing."

"But you don't look surprised."

"I'm well past being surprised."

He smiled at her and rubbed the back of his knuckles along her cheek. "You need sleep."

"I'm having a little trouble sleeping without you beside me."

He laid his head on hers. She closed her eyes and drank in the scent of him.

"I'll come as soon as I can tomorrow and take you home," he said.

Home. There was that magic word again. When had such an ordinary word become so astonishing?

Chapter 33

The morning sun filled the room. Singer stretched and felt happy—for a moment. Then she remembered.

She rolled over. Olivia's eyes were open. She smiled weakly.

"You okay?" Singer asked. She'd been awakened twice by Olivia calling out in her sleep.

"Still afraid."

"I know. As soon as you give your statement to the Mounties, you can get away from here."

Oliva pushed back the covers. "I need clothes. I've got enough at the apartment to get by with but I'm not going to go over there alone."

"Okay. While you have your shower I'll call the station and see if we can get an escort." Singer waited until the shower was running. She hadn't remembered to tell Wilmot about Cody and Olivia. Duncan answered. When Singer asked to speak to Wilmot she was told he was unavailable. There was no way Singer was going to talk to Duncan about Olivia and Cody. Too many things she shouldn't know might come out. She'd wait until she saw him. "Olivia is leaving the island and needs clothes."

"You can't go back up Mount Skeena. It's a crime scene."

"I realize that. Olivia says she has enough clothes at her apartment, but neither of us wants to go there." Singer ran her hands through her hair. "Could we get someone to go with us?" It was humiliating to ask a superwoman, a woman who was far too close to Wilmot, for help. Duncan would probably double up with laughter when she hung up.

Duncan said. "I'll come over now if you're ready."

Was the disdain Singer thought she heard real or imagined? "We need half an hour."

"Fine." The line went dead.

Singer and Olivia were barely dressed when the knock came. They froze, staring at the door and then at each other. "Killers don't knock," Singer whispered.

Another knock, impatient and louder and this time accompanied by the words, "It's Corporal Duncan."

Outside the inn, the storm from the day before had stripped most of the cherry blossoms from the trees, leaving a sodden mess on the sidewalk. Duncan opened the back door of the cruiser like she was arresting two criminals. Olivia slid in.

Singer walked away. "Aren't you coming?" Duncan said.

"Nope, I've got someone to see."

Duncan scowled. "I think you should come."

"Why?"

"Sergeant Wilmot won't like you wandering around on your own."

"He'll get over it." She gave a wave and headed to the Cutter home.

Hannah's parents were both at the fish market so it was Hannah who opened the door. She took Singer up to her bedroom, and then Hannah plopped down on the window seat and ignored her. She picked up her guitar and began to play an old Jimi Hendrix riff from *Purple Haze*. She had to concentrate hard to get the fingering right. Singer sat on the bed and studied Hannah. She was different. What was it? She seemed... well, lighter, less plodding, and no longer defeated. That was it. And she'd lost bulk. The oversized baggy clothes were gone. Under them she'd been hiding lush curves.

Hannah felt Singer's eyes on her. She looked up. Her eyes, intense and hard to read behind a fringe of hair, watched Singer. It was difficult to tell if the formidable glare conveyed distress, rage or a warning, but somehow Singer found the stare threatening.

"Did Trina have a calendar in her room?"

Hannah straightened. "Why do you want to know?"

"I'm interested in her routine, where she went, that sort of thing."

"She didn't go anywhere, just to school, drama club and that writing class Monday nights. What else is there to do on the island?"

Singer smiled. "You tell me."

Hannah went back to picking out chords.

"Did Trina go out for walks at night?"

Hannah's head came up. "No." A flicker in her eyes gave her away.

"Did she go out to meet Cody?"

"Sometimes, but most of the time he came here. My mom and dad play duplicate bridge two nights a week. Cody would sneak in on those nights."

"So no calendar?"

"The police took everything." Hannah planted her elbows on the guitar and gnawed at her right thumbnail.

"Including her journals?"

A defiant shrug. "How am I supposed to know what the cops took away?"

Wilmot had already told her that Trina's old journals hadn't been found. He hadn't been unduly worried, saying, "Maybe there aren't any because she'd just started to keep a diary." Singer didn't believe it. Olivia had said writing was a habit and that journal writers were the most devoted. If she wrote one journal, there would be more, perhaps a lifetime of them. Trina's past diaries could be on Cooper's Island.

"If you have her journals, you have to give them to Sergeant Wilmot. They can help him find the person who killed Trina."

Hannah sucked in her lips.

"Could we look for the journals? I bet you know places the Mounties would never find. They wouldn't search anywhere but Trina's room, would they?"

"My mom packed up Trina's things after the police took what they wanted. She's going to give them to Trina's mom. There isn't anything left now." Hannah spoke about Pam in the present tense. She didn't know Pam was dead.

"Those old diaries are all that's left of Trina. Her mother would like them."

Hannah's face was no longer defiant but lost. "She was going away in June. I wouldn't have had anything left either." Singer could see she was fighting to control herself.

Singer waited.

"I knew I would miss her when she went but I didn't know it would be like this. I miss her so much. But..." She sniffed and wiped at her nose with her hand. "It's easier too. Is that awful, to think that life will be simpler without Trina?"

"No, it's just reality—how things are."

"It's the end of... well, lots of things."

"What about Cody? Have you talked to him?"

Hannah's forehead wrinkled in confusion. "Why would I talk to him?"

"But I thought... Oh, I see." She nodded in understanding. "It wasn't Cody you were interested in. It was Trina. I had it all wrong, didn't I? Did Trina know?"

Hannah turned her head away from her and stared out the window. "It was nothing. Just silliness. My mother says it's not important and it will pass. Now that's Trina's gone I'll be all right, normal again. That will be good."

"Trina knew." Singer was sure about that now. "Did she write about it in her journals?"

Hannah didn't look at her when she spoke. "She thought it was funny."

"Hannah…" Singer searched for words. "Trina was young. She didn't understand she was hurting you."

Hannah jumped to her feet, her guitar making an ugly clang as it fell to the floor. "It doesn't matter. Now that's she's dead I won't have those feelings anymore. It will be better." She spun away and crashed into a chair, fell sideways onto it before righting herself and running from the room. The feminine little slipper chair sat at an odd angle to the rest of the furniture.

She straightened the chair and picked up the guitar as she considered what Hannah had said, trying to decide if it made Hannah more or less likely to be the killer. She had the strength and the strong emotions the killer would need. Both girls could handle the Zodiac. It was entirely possible that when she left Cody, Trina had come back to the Cutter home and the girls had decided to go out to Ghost Island together. How would Trina have reacted if Hannah had made a pass at her, touched her in a sexual way, or tried to kiss her?

If Trina had made fun of her, teased or rejected her, was Hannah capable of picking up a rock and bashing in Trina's head? Singer was quite sure the answer was yes. Oh, not because she thought Hannah was evil or any such thing, but because she remembered the uncontrollable emotions of being a teenager, the overpowering hate and the crushing longings. Hannah was a girl confused and ruled by uncomfortable feelings that she didn't understand and couldn't control. Singer left the bedroom, listening at the top of the stairs, trying to hear where Hannah was. The house was quiet and empty. Singer stopped at the foot of the stairs, undecided if she should search for Hannah and offer comfort or if would only make things worse. She decided Hannah's feelings were too raw for simple words of comfort. Best to leave her on her own.

On the way down the hill to the inn, she tried to remember if she'd told Hannah that Trina's mother was coming to live on Mount Skeena. Or maybe Pam had called Hannah and told Hannah that she knew her secret. Was that enough to make Hannah kill Pam? It would be if Hannah had killed Trina. But Hannah didn't know Pam was dead. Or did she?

Almost back at the inn, walking along with her hands in her pockets and her thoughts bouncing off the inside of her head, she was startled when Wilmot called her name.

The passenger door of the cruiser opened. She pulled it wider and bent over to glance in, trying to read his face. It was impossible. "Duncan squealed, didn't she?"

"It's her job to make sure you're safe."

"And I'm sure she enjoyed that task." Singer slid in. The plastic seat was cold.

Wilmot stared straight ahead and said, "Where were you?"

"Are you asking as a cop or a lover?"

"Would the answer be different?"

"Yup, none of your business or to see a friend."

"A friend like Dr. Glasson?"

The question first surprised her and then made her smile. "I barely know him. Besides, there are more important things happening than an affair." She pulled the letter out of her pocket and handed it to him.

"What's this?" he said.

"My future."

Chapter 34

When he finished reading it, he said, "So the government is expropriating your land."

"So it seems. Unless Pam's murder changes their minds. Johnny Vibald's house is excluded, but the Utt place will be torn down and made into a parking lot for hikers. Mine will become a nature interpretive center. The government wants to protect the watershed and keep the lake out of the hands of developers. On the plus side, they are paying me a nice amount and I don't have to pay capital gains."

"It was always a possibility. People have been trying to turn it into a preserve for years." He handed the paper back to her. "So what will you do now?"

"I have no idea. I've got six months. I'll just have to wait and see what comes up."

"How long have you known about this?"

"I just got the letter."

"When?"

"Couple of days ago."

He knew it was all he was going to get. He put the car into drive. "You still haven't told me what you're doing here."

"I went to see Hannah."

"Why?"

"Maybe she needs a friend."

"Well, you made a lousy job of it. I almost hit her when she ran out into the road. What friendly thing did you say that scared the shit out of her?"

"Here's a bit of news for you. Olivia and Cody were having sex." Betrayal was no longer an issue. "And Oliva left work early on Thursday night. You might want to ask her where she went and who she was with."

Wilmot dropped Singer off at his apartment, but he wasn't at all sure she would stay there. He went back to the station where he found Duncan even more annoyed with the world than usual.

"The duty roster has gone to hell and everyone is exhausted. On top of that, Thoms seems to be having some kind of a marital crisis and hasn't come in yet."

He pushed a chair aside and went behind his desk. "Call him and tell him to get his ass in here."

"Already done."

"We're getting help." He laid his palms flat on the desk and leaned toward her. "They'll be here today. There are still a few things we can be doing in the meantime."

"What?"

"First we find Frank, and then we ask him a question or two. Still nothing on Cooper's Island?"

"Nope, no boat and no Frank."

"What did the sister have to say?"

Duncan made a face. "I told you it was a waste of time. The local detachment up there sent a Corporal Jacks to Ladysmith to talk to her. I could have found out just as much on the phone."

"We don't know it's a waste of time until we do it, and it's harder for people to lie when someone is standing in front of them. What did he get?"

She held up a fax. "He went to her house and snooped around but couldn't see any sign of Frank Haver or anyone else. The neighbors said there hadn't been any strangers around. Besides, they know Frank and haven't seen him there since Christmas. Jacks then went to the hospital where the sister works. She swears she hasn't seen her brother, and the feeling Corporal Jacks got was that Frank wouldn't be welcome there."

She tossed the paperwork on his desk. "Like I said, a waste of time."

He sat down and rolled his chair up to the desk. He scanned the report then added it to the brown file open on his desk and logged the new information on the front cover. "What about the ferries?"

"No one remembers seeing him on any of the ferry runs. But then, why would they? It was a long shot."

"It always is."

"He's taken his boat and gone."

"Maybe. It's an awfully small craft to go far."

"No problem to get up to Ladysmith or Nanaimo or anywhere else along the coast."

"Keep checking the ferries and try that sister of his again in a day or two. He might call for money or help to stay hidden."

Duncan held out another paper. "These are the calls made on Singer's phone. One of them is to Cooper's Island. Pam Haver called her husband the day she died."

"So now we know."

"Looks like it."

"What about the rest of the calls?"

"All local."

He pushed the paper back toward Duncan. "Call Olivia and see if she made those local calls or if Pam did."

"Or Singer." Duncan frowned. "Olivia isn't happy with us. You should have heard her when I said she couldn't leave the island until Major Crimes talks to her. She's got a mouth on her."

He grinned. It didn't take much imagination to know what she'd said. "There's another thing she won't be happy about. She won't be happy when she finds out we know she was sleeping with Cody."

"No shit." Her grin was wide. She stood up straighter and suddenly seemed more awake. "So do we pick up Cody?"

"I'll take care of that. You stay on Frank Haver."

"Right, he's still the most likely. What do you think Pam said that made Frank kill her?"

"No idea. Be sure and ask him that question when you find him."

"Maybe she discovered something that proved he killed Trina."

"How? She didn't leave the mountain, didn't have a vehicle as far as we can tell, and it's a hell of a walk down and back."

"There's Singer's old yellow van."

He hadn't thought of that. He made a grimace of disgust at his lapse.

Duncan thought he was dismissing her idea and said, "Alright, if she couldn't get the van going and leave the mountain, Pam knew something or remembered something. She called him. That's why he killed her."

"Don't get ahead of yourself. We need to check and see if the van works. That's a good idea of yours. It means she could have left the mountain and the killer could have followed her back."

He rubbed the bridge of his nose, trying to erase a small headache humming behind his eyes. Even with frustration and failure nipping at his heels, he couldn't keep working double shifts any longer. He was done. More than that, he was no longer efficient and was starting to miss things. He'd assumed Pam had been unable to leave the mountain. But Pam managed to get the tractor going so she may also have got the van running. That opened a whole new line of investigation. Cody had been adamant that there was no one around when he went to the farm.

Maybe it was true. He pushed away from the desk and stood up. "I'm going to talk to Cody again."

Chapter 35

Singer waited for news at Wilmot's apartment. She tried to watch the small TV, turning it off after only a few minutes. The inanity was more annoying than distracting. The few crime novels in the apartment were too close to reality. She threw the last one aside and went to call Dr. Glasson. This time his receptionist didn't argue, but it took him about five minutes to come to the phone.

"Last Thursday night, what time did you bandage Hannah's arm?"

When he didn't answer she said, "Look, if you don't tell me I'll just get Wilmot to ask the question—or Duncan."

"That's blackmail."

"Isn't that a bitch?"

"It was about twelve thirty."

"Can you make sure?"

"I'll check and see what time the helicopter came to transport the patient."

"I know. It came at two."

"Well, I worked on him for about an hour before they came and I'd been back at the hospital sometime before he went into crisis, so twelve thirty is about right."

"Could Hannah fake being drunk?"

"God, no."

"What if she'd been drinking earlier and was exaggerating?"

"Look, I know drunk. Why are you asking?"

"I'm trying to ease my mind about Hannah. She's carrying around her own baggage concerning Trina."

"Aren't we all. But is hers something I should know about?"

"She was sexually attracted to Trina."

He blew out a breath. "I didn't know that, but I'm willing to swear under oath that Hannah was in no condition to hurt anyone but herself."

"Because?"

"She was drunk."

"There's something else I'd like to know."

"You've got all you're getting out of me."

"Peter says he was at the hospital. Will you find out if that's true? It was about twelve thirty, when you were at Hannah's. He spoke to a nurse and she couldn't find you. I want to know if he was there."

It didn't take him long to make up his mind. "I'll call you right back."

Singer paced the floor with the phone in her hand.

Dr. Glasson didn't take long. "He was at the hospital but it was closer to one, maybe a little later. The nurse remembers he was flushed and disheveled. When she asked what he'd been up to he looked startled and then he said, 'That would be telling and she wouldn't like that.' So apparently he was with a woman before he came in."

Singer dropped the phone on the table. Had Peter been with Olivia? Is that why she'd slipped away from the Ferryman before her shift ended on Thursday night? Unlikely. He'd probably been with Beth Thoms.

Singer frowned. Where had Olivia been? When she'd overheard Cody and Trina talking, Cody had said he was busy that night, had plans. He'd tried to brush Trina off. So who did he have plans with? "Olivia," she whispered. His parents were away for the night. He was probably going to spend time with Olivia. What would she do if Cody stood her up? Knowing Olivia, she'd go looking for him. Had she gone to his place and met Trina leaving?

Singer studied the world through a slit in the blinds, listening and waiting for footsteps on the stairs. Still Wilmot didn't come. The phone rang. She ran to answer it, surprised how much she wanted to hear his voice.

"It's Olivia, Singer."

"Hey," she said and sank down onto the leather armchair, disappointment and an unwelcome quarrelsomeness biting at her.

"I'm still here. They won't let me go."

"I know."

"Is there any news about Pam's death?"

"How would I know?"

"Fine," Olivia snapped back. "There's no need to shout at me."

"Sorry. I'm a little jumpy. Being alone with my thoughts is not a good thing."

"Are you afraid?"

"Of course I am, but more than that, I've been thinking about a conversation I had with Pam the day she died. She wanted revenge. It's strange. I thought she might kill her husband, but instead she was killed. The wrong person died."

"That's a very twisted piece of logic."

Singer rubbed her forehead. "Cooped up here, I've had a lot of scary ideas. I'm going a little crazy."

"Come over to the Ferryman."

The shadow of doubt that still hung between them made Singer say, "Louis wants me to stay here."

"And since when did you take orders from him?"

"Look, I shouldn't tie up the line. Louis might be trying to reach me."

"Oh, yeah, he's got you wrapped around his finger."

An urge to hurt seized her. "Where were you the night Trina died? I hope you put that in your statement."

The phone went dead.

Chapter 36

There were no good thoughts. Singer examined every word and every remembered expression, mining them for answers. It was Olivia she came back to each time. Doubt and dread ate at her.

She turned the television on, flicked through the channels, and turned it off, tossing the remote onto the couch in disgust. Next door a telephone rang and was quickly cut off. She went to the window. Nothing stirred. She turned away.

Tension and anxiety grew with each passing minute. She had to get out. She pulled on a jacket and headed for the waterfront, needing not to be alone. She didn't pass a single person in the three block walk and no cars drove down the street. At the Driftwood Café it should have been the busiest time of the day, but none of the tables outside were in use. She didn't stop. She crossed the street to the park where no children played. Deserted and empty, the town felt like the day after Armageddon.

At the marina, the water taxi that had taken Pam to Cooper's Island was in a slip next to

the fishing boats. The small vessel was being washed down by a man with his jeans tucked into bright yellow boots.

Singer went down the steep ramp, thankful for the wire mesh covering it. The boards, still damp after the heavy rain, would be slippery without the netting. The ferryman heard the rattle of footsteps and stopped his work to watch her.

At the bottom, the floating dock bobbed under her feet in the wake from a floatplane. She stopped, waiting for the movement to subside, and lifted her hand in greeting.

The ferryman's weathered face crinkled in a smile. "Good day to you."

She walked along the dock to his boat. "How long does it take to get over to Cooper's Island?"

He wore a frayed baseball cap, once black but now faded to charcoal, with a fish jumping out of a foaming sea on the front of it. He lifted his cap and rubbed his left hand over his bald head. "Depends." He settled his hat and leaned on his broom. "You're that singer." He made it sound like an accusation.

"Guilty as charged."

His lips tightened in an angry line. "I knew Pam and her daughter. We all did. Terrible thing to happen."

She felt as if she should disclaim any responsibility for Pam's murder, but she knew it would carry no weight with him. People here would make up their own minds. "She was my friend."

He studied her dubiously. "Is that why you're asking about Cooper's Island?"

"I'm asking because..." For once the lie wouldn't come. "Well, I guess I was just curious. Pam was staying with me when she died. She talked about the island. I thought I might like to see it."

He rested the broom against the railing of the boat and jumped onto the dock. A large bulky man, he seemed to occupy more room than was necessary. She stepped back from him, edging nearer to the ramp while he started to uncoil a hose, talking to her as he worked.

"It's only about a forty minute trip, but you might have to clear it with the Mounties." His hands stilled and he glanced over his shoulder at her. "I hear that won't be a problem for you." He turned on the nozzle, spraying water over the dock and onto her shoes. "Sorry," he said. Not looking at all sorry, he dragged the hose to his boat and jumped back aboard. "I'll be happy to take you over if you can get permission." He sprayed water over the floor of his boat.

She followed him back to the boat. "What day and time would suit you?"

The man started to reply but was distracted by someone coming up the dock from another slip. Singer turned and saw Cody approaching with a bucket in his hand. He was bareheaded and wore a pale blue cable-knit sweater, grown short at his wrists and waist. The wind caught his black hair and lifted it from his forehead. Easy to see why Olivia had been attracted to him.

He hesitated when he saw Singer.

She smiled at Cody. "Is this the day everyone washes their boats?"

A brief answering smile teased his lips. "If you work for my father, you do it every day, but I missed yesterday."

He advanced tentatively and waited for the hose to be free. He glanced at her and shifted from side to side, uncomfortable being near her.

His agitation infected Singer and she eased away. She guessed that he was another person who knew about her connection to Wilmot. It was true, there were few secrets on an island.

"Turn it off for me, will you, Cody?" the boatman called.

Cody reached down to turn off the valve and then took the hose from the boatman.

That's when she saw the marks his runners left on the dock, a honeycomb pattern, the very pattern she'd drawn on the edge of her newspaper and given to Wilmot.

A harsh voice from behind her demanded, "What are you doing here?"

Her body jerked away. Her foot hit the raised board used as a cleat to tie boats to the dock. For a second she overbalanced and would have gone into the ocean if Wilmot hadn't grabbed her arm.

"Careful." He pulled her away from the edge and asked again, "What are you doing here?"

Instead of answering, she whispered, "I found the running shoes." She pointed to Cody, dragging the hose down the dock, and then she pointed to the prints already fading on the weather-beaten boards. "His runners have the same pattern as the footprint in Olivia's apartment."

Wilmot let go of her arm and headed for the *Oystercatcher*. "Cody, I want to talk to you."

Singer, with an instinctive desire to put room between herself and trouble, was already walking backward to the ramp, keeping her eye on Cody who reluctantly headed back up the dock toward Wilmot. Head down, Cody appeared totally defeated and harmless.

"Let's see the bottom of your shoes, Cody." Wilmot was already gazing down, expecting Cody to comply, but instead Cody charged Wilmot, driving him down onto the deck. And then he ran. His left arm shot forward to deflect attackers, while his right was tucked in as if carrying a ball.

"Hey," the ferryman shouted and reached out from his boat to grab at Cody as he went by. Cody, the star quarterback of the high school football team, easily evaded the grasping hand.

Singer jumped aside when she saw him running up the dock. But instead of moving out of Cody's path, when he dodged the ferryman's hand, she was right in front of him. The outstretched arm drove her back over the edge of the dock. Her hands reached out for safety but they found nothing.

Chapter 37

Strange what she noticed in the short time it took to fall from solid footing into the sea. On the boardwalk far above the dock, a woman wearing a flowing scarf reached out to Singer as if she could save her. Beyond the woman were clouds and circling gulls. Close by on one of the boats, someone was smoking a cigar. The odor registered just as her head hit the fiberglass side of a boat and the frigid water enveloped her.

She had no thought to hold her breath. Gulping huge amounts of seawater, her momentum carried her down along the hull. The rocking vessels closed over the space she'd fallen through, blocking out the light. Panic at the darkness. Her hands scratched against the slimy underside of a boat, fighting to find a way back up, but the swaying intimacy of the boats left no space to surface.

Within seconds the frigid sea seeped through her clothes, painful and piercingly deep, going to her very core like nothing she'd ever experienced before. Burning cold on her exposed skin. Why hadn't anyone told her that cold could feel like fire? And the fire was in her lungs. They were exploding. Was this what it felt like to die?

Focus on where the light should be. Wait for an opening. She tried to suppress the cough but it was no use. She sucked in more water, up her nose and down her throat. The boats parted, the world above her grew brighter. She kicked hard for the light.

Suddenly Wilmot was there beside her, grabbing the front of her jacket and lifting her so her head came out of the sea. Coughing and spewing out water, she clutched at him. Her head was on fire from saltwater still flooding her sinuses. "Hold on," he gasped and dragged her toward a piling.

As if she needed telling, as if she were stupid, she wanted to say, but there was no room for the sudden anger she felt. She grabbed the tarred buttress. A splinter from the rough wood jabbed into her hand, but it couldn't stop her from wrapping her arms and legs around the support and hanging on for her very existence while she spewed out salt water. Wilmot pressed her against the rough timber with a stream of reassuring words, his breath warm on her face.

A metal ladder was hooked over the dock and driven into the water beside them. Still he didn't let go of her, holding her with one arm while reaching for the ladder and drawing it to them. Singer couldn't wait for his cautious progress toward safety. She reached out for a rung, moving too quickly and making the ladder shoot away from her.

"Careful," Wilmot warned.

Again the flash of resentment, but her annoyance gave her strength. She got a firm hold on the aluminum and dragged herself erect. Water rushed off her.

The first exhilarating step was easy but then the weight of her clothes and exhaustion took over. She clung to the ladder and coughed, spewing out water and unable to move. Slowly she dragged her right leg to the next rung and pushed forward, hauling herself upward.

Hands reached down from above to pull her up, until she was being lifted more than she was climbing. "Easy does it," the ferryman said as they hauled her onto the dock.

She lay on her belly on the planks, coughing and choking, a confusion of legs all around her.

Someone said, "Call an ambulance."

She wiped a hand down her face, dragging away a piece of seaweed, and tried to protest, but a fit of choking made it impossible for her to get any words out. Water ran from her nose and mouth. She drew her knees up in a great spasm of retching and gagging.

A large hand beat on her back and she moved to her side to escape it. She looked up at the ring of alarmed faces staring down at her and a mad thought came to her. *You know you are in trouble if you're lying down and everyone around you is standing up. Deep trouble.* Her amusement brought more coughing.

And then Wilmot knelt beside her and lifted her into an embrace against the sodden roughness of his jacket, nearly smothering her. Singer's fists beat on his shoulder, fighting for air and space.

Slowly the coughing eased. They sat silently on the dock, arms wrapped around each other, until the ambulance arrived.

When she saw it pull up at the boardwalk above her she said, "I don't need to go to the hospital, Louis."

"Might as well." Two emergency workers hurried toward them with a stretcher between them. He pushed himself to his feet and reached out a hand to her and dragged her up. "It's here now."

Her legs barely held her. Her head swam and a sharp pain made her close her eyes. For a moment she thought she was going to vomit. She sat down again and her hand went to her head. She felt the sticky blood on her fingers. She pulled her hand away and looked at the blood in amazement.

"They'll make sure you don't have a concussion," Wilmot said.

In the small hospital only one fulltime doctor worked the emergency room, so each doctor on the island worked a day shift plus one night every third week. Dr. Glasson was on the emergency ward that afternoon. Calm and professional, it was as if she'd never seen another side of him. He had her head x-rayed and he listened to her chest. No dire pronouncements, but he said she should stay "just a little longer."

When they left her alone she thought about what she had lost, not what she had nearly lost. Most of all she was upset that she'd lost her key to Wilmot's apartment, gone with her bag when she hit the water. A silly thing to worry about, but it was a small symbol of hope, hope that her future would be different from her past. She was fighting back tears when Dr. Glasson returned.

"May I leave now?" a request made in a weak and childish voice.

"Just a while longer. You were still coughing when you got to the hospital. Are you having any trouble breathing, any chest pain?"

What he was asking suddenly hit Singer. "You're worried about dry drowning, aren't you?"

"What do you know about that?"

She couldn't meet his eyes. Her hand smoothed the blue coverlet. "I know it's what happens when someone tries to drown you."

His hands froze over the chart. He stared at her. "My god, you have had a rough time of it, haven't you?" He didn't wait for her to answer, but just gave her the facts. "When someone is unprepared to go into the water and they inhale liquid into their lungs, it can cause larynx spasms. It obstructs the inflow of oxygen into the lungs and causes hypoxia. There is a danger of a respiratory disaster up until twenty-four hours after the event. That's why I'd like you to stay just a little longer. And you shouldn't be alone for the next twenty-four hours."

Wilmot would be working. This was no time to ask him to play nursemaid. Singer slid further down into the bed. "I'll stay. I've lost my key. I can't get in and there's no one there anyway." She turned her face to the wall.

He lifted the blue coverlet, pulling it up to her shoulders, and tucked it around her. "Wait until I get off and then you can come home with me."

She turned her head to gaze up at him. "Why?"

"Remember what you said? Sinners like us have to stick together." He smiled. "I'll take care of you."

It was the wrong thing to say if he wanted to stop her trembling lip. She raised her hand to shield her face from him and gave into a wave of emotions, gratitude, shock and an intense feeling of brittleness. "Sorry," she gasped. "I'm not really like this."

He pulled a tissue from a box and handed it to her. "I think I'm probably the last person in the world you ever have to apologize to for anything. My name's Grant, by the way."

Before she could answer, the sound of a siren filled the room. He raised his head and listened. "That's for me."

He started to leave and then he came back. He leaned on the bed over her and whispered, "You haven't told Wilmot or Duncan about me, have you?"

She wiped her cheek with the sodden tissue. Her voice broke as she said, "Told them what?"

He grinned and reached for more tissues. "I've been waiting for them to turn up at my door. This morning, while I was in the shower, the truth hit me. If they find out, it won't be because you told them." He handed her fresh tissues and threw the crumpled one in the wastebasket. "I'll be back as soon as I can, then we'll go to my place. I'll watch out for you." He patted her shoulder and went off to another patient.

Friendship, that's what was being offered with the tissue. Or was it? She was the only person who knew about his crime. If she died from suffocation in the night, the coroner would think it was from drowning. She groaned in disgust. The problem with a suspicious mind, she decided, is that there are no kind acts.

It was nearly an hour before anyone but the nurse came to talk to her. Then Wilmot entered the emergency examination area. He'd changed his clothes and looked as fresh and renewed as if he'd just come on duty.

"Life is unfair," she told him. "We both went in, but you look like nothing happened."

Not in the mood for banter, he sat beside her on the bed and asked how she was and what the doctor had said.

Singer brushed his questions aside. "Did you get Cody?"

He grimaced. "That siren you heard was him arriving in the ambulance. The young fool tried to get away, driving too fast, and missed a curve."

"Does running mean he killed Pam and Trina?"

"I'll ask him when he regains consciousness."

Her hand went up to the bandage on her head. "So maybe it's over."

"Maybe."

"Where was he going?"

"To the north of the island, up where his aunt lives."

She nodded and said, "Oh, of course. I should have thought of that."

"What do you mean?"

"They probably have a boat. You and I would get in our cars and rush for a ferry, but a fisherman's son would try to get away by water. Quite sensible, really, when you know there are..." She stopped and said, "How many islands out there?"

"A few hundred."

"And not many people, so a good place to hide. He could live off the land or break into empty cottages for food. So many of those cabins are only used on weekends or for holidays."

"Yes, and if Cody thought so I'm betting the same idea occurred to Frank Haver." He sighed. "Duncan told me she hadn't found his boat. It's called the *Runaway*. How's that for irony? I've had her talking to the ferry workers to see if anyone saw him leave the island on foot or by car. I should have paid more attention to what she was saying. Stupid of me, but she was on it. She's been searching for his boat and sending out bulletins about it."

"But does Frank know you want to talk to him?"

"If he knows Pam's dead, he knows we'll need to speak to him. He's keeping his head down."

Singer sighed. "Maybe that's what Cody planned on doing, staying gone until you found the killer." The image of him shyly standing on the dock, a breeze ruffling his hair, was clear in her mind. "Why were you on the dock anyway?"

"We talked to him last night. I was there to bring him in for more questions."

"Maybe he just panicked. He's only a kid."

"All things we'll find out if he recovers."

"If?" Jerking upright in surprise added to her headache. She put her hand over the bandage as though to push the pain back down. "You mean there's some doubt?"

The sound of a helicopter filled the room. They both looked up. "Before I came in here to see you I was hanging around outside the operating room. I was hoping Cody would wake up so I could get a statement. I heard Dr. Glasson calling for an air ambulance. It looks like Cody isn't going to regain consciousness any time soon. Thoms will go to Victoria with him and take his statement when he wakes up."

She moved her legs restlessly. "Why were you waiting to take his statement? You'd think you were the only cop on the island. Doesn't anyone else work here?"

"Duncan chased him down Harbor Road. She's filling in the accident report now." He got to his feet. "If it turns out that he's innocent..." He went to the window and stared at the gray wall of the Continuing Care unit across the small courtyard.

"But Cody ran," she said. "Surely it's his fault he had an accident."

"Nobody's going to remember that, only that he was pursued by an officer and chased into an accident. Cody's case is going to be examined to hell and back and Duncan will be tied up for days. One more reason for Major Crimes to get here. They'll be here by tonight, probably on the first ferry now."

Singer picked at the fluff clinging to the blanket and studied his back. More dreams shattered. Wilmot was losing his chance to leave the island. Worse, if there was another demotion, what would that do to him?

"You'll be working late tonight." It was a statement, not an inquiry. "I'll be staying here for a bit and then Dr. Glasson offered me a bed for the night."

He looked sharply at her.

She said, "Seems I need to be looked after until morning. There could be some lung complications."

"From the smoking, likely. Maybe this will convince you to quit."

She didn't argue.

Chapter 38

Kilborn Hospital had six emergency beds. Jammed together in a small space, they were separated only by curtains. A cardiac patient occupied the first bed, closest to the nurses' station and the entrance. That's where the nurses hovered, checking occasionally on Singer.

Hannah walked past the closed drapes of the first bed, looking shy and embarrassed. In her hand was a brown paper bag, leaking grease near the bottom. She pointed her finger at the closed curtains encircling the cardiac patient. "Dr. Glasson said I could come in." She hung there uncertainly, as if she might be asked to leave, and if so, she wanted to do it quickly.

"It's good to see you, Hannah. How did you know I was here?"

"My dad was down at the harbor. He helped pull you out. How are you?"

Singer sat forward, leaning her arms on her knees. "I'm going to be fine, but I'm glad you're here. It's pretty lonely just hanging out on my own."

Hannah risked coming a few steps closer. "But you're going to be okay, aren't you?" Those simple words had feeling behind them.

"Sure. I think they're only keeping me because I live alone and someone needs to be there for me in case anything changes."

Hannah frowned and tilted her head toward her left shoulder and considered Singer for a minute. Then she came closer to Singer's bed. "I can stay with you if you want."

"Thank you, Hannah." Singer's eyes teared up and she caught the corner of the sheet and dabbed at them. "I'm not really crying. It's just all the water I swallowed keeps leaking out."

Hannah nodded and held out the bag. "I brought you a cranberry scone." She stared dubiously at the bag in her hand. "I buttered it."

"Great." Singer pulled the hospital table across the bed.

They only talked about music. It was as if they'd made a pact to avoid the awfulness that surrounded them. When the last crumbs disappeared Hannah said, "So who's your favorite song writer?"

She thought a little while and then said, "I like songs I can sing, so Kris Kristofferson, Willy Nelson of course, Leonard Cohen, and anything by the Eagles. They've got some great material."

"Yeah, my mom's got all their albums." Hannah smashed down the remaining crumbs with her finger and then rolled them into a little ball. "And your favorite singer?"

"Annie Lennox, great voice, and she can really deliver a song."

Hannah worried the inside of her cheek with her teeth. "Trina and I wrote a song."

"Really? I need to hear that."

Hannah grinned and gave a little lift of her shoulders. "Don't expect too much. We're still working on it." Pain clouded her eyes. "I mean we were."

"Soooo..." Singer watched her carefully. "If it's all right with you, maybe you and I can polish it."

Joy lit Hannah's face. She nodded and then turned away as Peter and Olivia appeared from around the curtained bed. Peter came toward them, but Olivia hung back. Something was wrong. The normally brash Olivia walked into a room as if she owned it. Now her drawn face was pale. She looked ill. And she'd been crying.

Peter had also changed over the last few days. His boyishness was gone. Haggard. That was the word for it, like he'd gone from youth to middle age in three days.

Singer realized she must look about the same. Fear and shock had taken a toll on all of them.

After expressing the briefest concern for her well-being, Peter said, "I'd like your version of events for the paper." He pulled a notebook and pencil out of his coat pocket. "Just tell me in your own words what happened. Have they arrested Cody?"

Singer wrapped her arms around her knees. "You'll have to ask the police that question."

He nodded. "So how did you end up falling into the harbor?" He didn't look particularly interested in her answer.

"I was standing too close to the edge. I fell in. Stupid of me."

His eyes came up from the page and locked on hers. "Cody didn't push you in? That's what the witnesses said."

"Well, he may have accidently bumped me, but it was my own fault. That's what comes of letting singers on docks." She gave him a small smile. "They like to make a big splash. Anything for attention."

Olivia came forward. "Peter came to the Ferryman. He told me about Cody." She rubbed at her nose.

Singer said, "He'll be all right." She had no idea if it was true. Why did someone else's unhappiness always make her say stupid things?

Olivia nodded. "I wanted to see you so I tagged along. I..." Olivia screwed up her face, trying hard not to cry. She lifted a shoulder in a shrug and gulped out, "Sorry."

Singer nodded. "Yeah, me too." Things had changed between them up on the mountain. Trust was gone. But there was still the bonding of two outsiders who shared a common view of the world. And Singer realized that Olivia had come because Singer was the only one who would understand her distress at Cody's accident. It was something she had to hide from everyone else.

Peter glanced around, saw a visitor's chair by the wall and dragged it to the edge of the bed. "Do you really think claiming Cody didn't push you in will help him? He's accused of murder."

"Who says he is?"

"He ran away with the Mounties chasing him. He did it, all right. Two murders. You could have been one more."

"But I'm not. I'm sitting here eating treats with Hannah."

There were loud voices, a shout and curses before a small knot of men pushed into view. Constable Anderson and Wilmot held Frank Haver firmly by the arms. Blood covered his face and his hands were cuffed behind his back, but still he fought to get away. Throwing his weight forward, he dragged the officers down almost to Singer's bed before they got him under control again.

Dr. Glasson followed them in and pointed to the hospital bed next to Singer's. "Put him here. I'll dress his wounds and then you can take him away."

Between them, Anderson and Wilmot hoisted Frank onto the bed, but he wasn't having any of it. He rolled away from them toward Singer's bed, kicking and thrashing about. His bed knocked against the bedside table. The water jug fell over, rolling onto the floor, and water gurgled out.

Shouts and curses ensued. Peter's chair overturned as he scrambled to get out of the way of Haver's flailing legs.

When the Mounties finally had Haver handcuffed to the bed, Singer looked down at the water on the floor. That's when she saw the hexagon pattern.

"Oh," she said. "Oh." And then she called frantically, "Louis, Louis." She slid off the bed, scrabbling for him.

Wilmot, face red from exertion and still holding Frank Haver shoulders down on the mattress, turned his head to face her. "What?"

She pointed at the footprint on the floor. "Cody wasn't the only one at the Ferryman that day. He was there too." Now she pointed at Peter Kuchert.

Peter backed away from them. "What in hell are you talking about?"

"And at the break-in at Olivia's apartment. You were there too, and you left a print."

Peter tapped his forehead. "I think the bump on the head did some damage." His voice was too loud, as if by shouting he could beat down Singer's accusations. He walked toward the exit, distancing himself from his accuser.

Singer started to shake her head in denial but a sharp pain stopped her. "You were right, Olivia. You said that the break-in and the murders were connected."

The room had gone silent. Even Frank Haver had stopped yelling.

Peter snapped his notebook shut and put it in his pocket. "Don't be ridiculous."

"No, it isn't ridiculous. You killed Trina and you broke into Olivia's apartment. You also attacked me."

"Why would I do any of those things?" He looked at the others as if someone might help him understand. "She's mental."

"You wanted your story back but you couldn't find it." Singer was working her way through it, figuring it out even as she spoke. "That's what's been driving you wild. Every time I've seen you over the last three days you've looked more and more desperate. Now I know why. There's something in that story that points to you as the killer. Were you carrying out a fantasy, Peter? Stupid to write about it."

"What in hell has she been smoking?" Peter tried to laugh.

"And then there's Pam. Pam wanted revenge. She told me that. My guess is she figured out who killed Trina and was going to exact retribution. She called the killer, told him she knew he'd killed Trina."

"Cody killed her," Peter said. "That's why he ran."

"No he didn't. He was with Olivia when Trina was killed." Singer turned to Olivia. "That's true, isn't it, Olivia?"

Olivia was crying openly now. She couldn't answer, but she nodded her head in agreement.

"The two of you could have alibied each other."

"Cody..." It was all Olivia could choke out.

"He didn't want anyone to know about your affair, did he?"

Olivia shook her head.

"Hannah told me his folks were really religious."

"They'd freak out," Hannah said.

"So his aunt gave him an alibi instead."

Singer turned back to Peter who was still staring at Olivia. "That leaves you, Peter." She smiled when he swung to face her. "Do you want to know where those essays are, Peter?"

He couldn't help himself. His face gave him away.

"They're in Olivia's car. In the Volkswagen."

"No..." He stopped.

"You may have looked in the Volks but you didn't open the trunk because Olivia had wired it shut. I saw the essays when we were moving. She undid the wire and opened the trunk to put in boxes. I'd forgotten that the trunk of those old Volks are up front."

Olivia wiped her face with her fingers and said, "I have to keep it wired shut because otherwise it flies open and I can't see where I'm going." She sniffed back tears. "It's true, Peter, that's where they are."

Peter closed his eyes as if in pain.

Singer said, "So simple. You could have had them at any time. So easy, and then you would have been safe. And Pam would still be alive."

"I don't care about that stupid story anymore." He licked his lips. "It was just something between Olivia and me."

"Really? I don't think so."

His eyes darted wildly from one of them to another. "This is just one of her stories." He was no longer shouting. In fact, it sounded like he was begging them to believe him.

Wilmot said, "The DNA will tell. Did you know you left DNA?"

Peter bolted for the entrance.

Wilmot started after him, but it was Hannah who stopped Peter. The water jug had come to rest by her feet during the melee and she'd automatically picked it up before moving to safety. Now she smashed the jug into the side of Peter's head, driving him to his knees, before Wilmot slammed him to the floor.

With a knee in Peter's back, Wilmot pulled out his handcuffs and began cautioning him.

Chapter 39

Singer and Wilmot drove up the mountain for one last night in front of the fire. The next day Bill and his mates would come to move the furnishings into storage, but she wanted to take Steven David's six remaining guitars herself. She collected them all and lined them up against the wall, saying, "I think I'll give the blue one to Hannah. She'll like that."

"They're worth thousands of dollars," Wilmot protested. "You can sell them."

She shrugged. "Hannah needs it. She's had a hard time and there's more to come. Her silly mother, telling Hannah that her feelings will change. Besides, she has real talent. She'll make beautiful music on it. Stevie would like that."

He smiled at her. "You're a soft-hearted woman. You know that, don't you?"

"Soft-hearted or soft-headed, soft either way."

They'd lit the fire, but the day was really too warm and the heat drove them outside. All but one of the canvas chairs had disappeared. She sat in the grass, leaning back against Wilmot's legs. The meadow had grown long again and the air was full of the scent of ripe grass and wood smoke.

She said, "Tell me about Peter's story. Was I right about why he killed Pam?"

"As near as I can tell, you were absolutely right. When Pam took the spare tire out of the Volks, she found the essays. She was looking for Trina's but she came across Peter's. Pam read it and guessed that he killed Trina. It was titled, *The Mind of a Killer*. He was writing his fantasy. Finding Trina alone and vulnerable that night, he took her out to Ghost Island and acted it out. I don't think he planned it. He just acted on impulse."

She stripped a grass head, rubbing the seeds between her palms and watching the roughage fly in the wind. "How often have you heard someone say 'I didn't mean to do it, it just happened?' He was jealous of Trina. That was clear. If she rejected him, his anger might have been uncontrollable. That would add to his bloodlust. But I'll never believe he wasn't intending to kill her when he took her to Ghost Island."

He grunted in response and then said, "Well, Pam intended to kill him. She wrote out a confession on the top page of his story, and left it there in the trunk with the others. She found the gun in the barn where Steven left it."

Singer felt a stab of gratitude. She drew her knees up to her chest and wrapped her arms around them.

His hands went to her shoulders, idly rubbing them as he went on with his explanation. "She called Peter and told him she had something to tell him, told him to come up right away while she was alone. Said if he didn't come the police would. He's a smart bastard. He guessed that she knew. He told her he couldn't get there until later. He went up the mountain to Lauren's old home and then walked down past the lake. She didn't think of that. She expected him to drive in, knew she'd hear him coming. She was feeding her chickens, thinking she had time to get the gun." His hands stopped. "Maybe she left it there because she didn't want you and Olivia to see it if you got back before he came. Or maybe she was going to take him into the barn and kill him. Either way, Peter told us that when she saw him come out of the woods she ran for the barn. She was going for the gun, of course, but he was too fast for her. She never got to it."

She sighed and got to her feet. "I better check on that dinner. Olivia said it was an easy casserole but I'm not sure about her instructions. God, I hope she's a better chef than she is a housekeeper."

He reached out and grabbed her hand as she walked past him. "It's not really food I'm interested in."

Hours later Singer went outside while Wilmot did the dishes. It was her time to say goodbye to the place she'd once thought would be her forever home. A raucous and accusing raven squawked from the top of a fir tree. She looked up and said, "Shut up. This is still my land." With the words came the memory of Pam talking to her chickens. It was a strangely comforting thing.

She sat in the wobbly director's chair and stretched her legs out in front of her, considering the mountains beyond the meadow. Beautiful as this place was, it had never really been home for her. She would keep the memory of it with her forever, but it was time to move on.

A small blue butterfly settled on her ankle.

"Hello, Celastrina," she said, and smiled.

Visit *www.phyllismallman.com* to read excerpts from her Singer Brown and Sherri Travis books.

If you enjoyed this book, please consider writing a review on your favorite review site. It doesn't have to be much more than, "I liked this book." Reviews get a reader's attention and help authors sell books.

For my Valhalla family.

Acknowledgements

I used to think a book was written only by the person whose name was on the cover. I now know differently. Thank you to Brock Clayards for supplying the details of RCMP homicide procedure. Any mistakes are mine. I also would like to thank Elle Wild for her story editing skills and Jayne Barnard for being a first and careful reader, and of course, Lee. You all made this a much better book.

Editors
Lenore Hietkamp
Linda Pearce

Made in the USA
Columbia, SC
20 December 2017